Loss

The
InkerMen

InkerMen Press
2009

Loss
by
The InkerMen

This edition copyright © InkerMen Press 2009

Cover image: 'Dead Bee' © Rose Sanderson 2009
www.rosesanderson.com

InkerMen Press
Ashby-de-la-Zouch
info@inkermenpress.co.uk
www.inkermenpress.co.uk

978-0-9556259-9-2

First Edition
Published 2009

British Library Cataloguing in Publication Data

Loss.
1. Loss (Psychology)--Fiction. 2. Bereavement--Fiction.
3. Short stories, English.
823'.0108092-dc22

ISBN-13: 9780955625992

Loss

The
InkerMen

List of Illustrations

Cover image 'Dead Bee' © Rose Sanderson 2009
www.rosesanderson.com

Page 26
Rejection. Illustration
Copyright © Kathryn Siveyer 2009

Page 63
Grim Reaper. Illustration
Copyright © Katharine Orton 2009

Page 67
The Lake. Illustration
Copyright © Louisa Currier 2009
louisacurrier@hotmail.com

Page 78
No Direction Home. Illustration
Copyright © Luci Gorrell Barnes 2009
www.lucigorellbarnes.co.uk

Pages 120, 131, 133
In the Confidence of the Night. 3 Model Photographs
Copyright © Hannah Taggart 2009
hannahmation@hotmail.co.uk

Page 161
Cell. Illustration
Copyright © Amanda Mazonowicz 2009
amandel@hotmail.com

Page 244
Untitled. Illustration
Copyright © Rebecca Edelmann 2009

Contents

For all the lost boys and lost girls

The Ditch

Antony Pickthall

1. Awake

I'm missing. And I don't think I'll ever find myself. Which I guess is OK. Who was I? I know who I am. Probably not that far from what I am now. A slightly balding, slightly overweight man, existing in rented accommodation in a small village. I work at the local pub, the *Square and Compass*. I serve frothy beer and clear plates and glasses because I just don't remember what else I might have done.

How do I know I'm missing? Because I just don't remember anything before I found myself lying in a ditch. Was I a drunk? A drug addict? I started to examine my arms and legs. There were scratches. There were bruises. My belly tight—except for a girth of fat. What did I eat? Who did I eat with? I borrowed an old cassette recorder from Alice and taped myself reading from a newspaper. Don't like my voice. A nasal whine. Not from here. Christ! I'd have kicked myself out. Was that the story? I fantasize about 'my family'. Are they missing me? Hiring a detective to track me down. Bring me back. My hands are not calloused. I think I worked in an office. I'm not sure though. I'm from the South. Though, the bloody postie thinks he can find a trace of Manchester in me. They all know here. They all take it seriously.

And before you ask. I didn't have a mobile phone on me. Did I own one? That would have been so easy. Search for 'home', press dial and just say, 'It's me. I'm lost. Who am I? Can you come and pick me up? Please.'

'You need to be regressed', she said, when I told her on our third date. She's not from here. She lives in Narberth. I go on the bus. We have been to the cinema, three times. I can't think of anything else to do. This time it was *Mama Mia*. I knew I would hate it. She was not much better, but she seemed to sing-a-long.

I'd managed to resist details. Part of my skill-base now. Resisting the natural urge to tell-all. Well, for me at least. Trouble is there's not much to tell.

Where were you born? What family have you got? Or did I lie? They all died in a plane crash. Lockerbie. All gone. But you can't burden people with the truth of it, if it is likely to shock them. So you skirt.

Angela was interested in me, up to a point. She had a son who was now away at Uni. Bath. She had been there twice. Her ex was a plumber. He was good at all the little jobs. I was in a pub. I told her I travelled about the country. Pub to pub. No ties.

What had we seen before *Mama Mia*? *Mission Impossible*. She liked Tom Cruise. First date was a rather stupid comedy, totally unsuitable, about Siamese twins in America. We left after an hour and had a very nice drink.

Angela was anxious now. I could tell. Her eyes were burning.

'You never tell me anything about your past.' That was it. What could I say? Make it up a voice whispered. But I didn't want to. Why should I? We didn't leave on good terms. I said goodbye—well actually, it was see ya. That could be a clue. 'See ya.'

But I know strange things, There's a group of men who come into the pub during the week. Wednesdays and Thursdays. Just for a chat. Derek, Bob and Ioan. They keep me company from 11am. They introduce glimpses of a world. Derek has retired here. He bought a house and some land and hates it. His wife walked out. He can't sell. Doesn't want to know. He can bear misery 6 days a week. Ioan asserts his local connections. Which means he is a pompous arse at times. What do I know? I'm an incomer. Bob, good old Bob, is a painter and decorator. They were talking about gardens. I don't know why but I had to join in. Normally, I'm a sports or nothing man. But the sun was shining and I had had a dream about digging. They call me Steve. Have I mentioned that? I am indifferent to it. Am I Steve? Who is Steve?

I was in an open space; I think it was an allotment. I had a conversation with a woman in a tight woolly hat. Our breath was visible. The spade broke and I fell on to the newly turned soil. No matter. Their constant bickering about seeding potatoes got to me. I told them about timing and crop rotation and I had authority. Which pissed Ioan off. He quickly changed the subject. Local elections. I went back to my pot washing. My hands red and puffy in the water and detergent.

Today is a Monday. I don't make friends easily. Hence dating through the local paper. The landlords at the Square and Compass like me well enough. Occasionally I baby-sit their children Alice and Jac. I like seeing the different ways they order their lives—the children that is. Jac is the youngest. He puts all his toys—animals, plastic, wood or soft fabric into one bin, all his military hardware into another. Alice goes more for building tight mounds. Or she will select one and isolate it. A doll or a teddy. Spend weeks with it.

They trust me, Simon and Janice. Janice knew me from the ditch via a friend of hers, Sally. PD, post ditch. Where it all started. All I knew. The ditch. I woke, that much I know. I was cold. So cold my teeth could not chatter. My trousers were soaked. All the way from ankle to bum. There was a beetle for a while. When I came to, I don't remember how I felt. I just knew

I could not speak. My mouth hurt. My left ear was ringing. Sounds beyond the ditch were muffled. The water was still moving, off the fields. A clump of trees was just visible to my left. Sally has a dog, 'Stinger'; out walking they found me curled up. Feral is how Sally described me. Berry splattered mouth, constantly asleep from exhaustion. Like I didn't want to stop. Eventually I had to.

'So you weren't dumped?', Bob the painter asked again. Clearly striving for the point of it all.

How do I know?

The pub gets noisy on the weekend. At first I was slow with everything. The till is auto. You don't have to think. I don't drink myself. I don't want to. Janice was quick to watch me around the bottles. She relaxed once she realized I just wasn't a drinker. Sally had clearly told her I didn't smell of alcohol. I did have a brandy a month ago—to be sociable. Bob was 50. He made me chase it down. I was meant to drink a pint straight after. But I was scared to. Simon and Janice wouldn't approve. I don't like what the alcohol made me feel.

I live with this guy now who has a job as a chef. Except he's hardly ever there. My room is at the back, upstairs, under the eaves. He had another lodger. But she left to work in Shrewsbury. She had a degree in Biochemistry and worked for the Rural Development Agency.

I feel old. Don't know how old. I look like Bob's age. But he has such a warped and out of touch outlook that I just don't think I am. Last week I heard an organ sound coming from the church. I felt a curious and familiar longing for its mournful notes. I might go and have a look at it. Why not?

I first noticed I was quite good at things when I started to help Alice with her homework. Even she sat up and took notice, as I explained some aspect of British constitutional history or French. I can speak French!

I started to learn Welsh. I did it to rile Ioan.

I knew what I had to do. If it meant lying in the ditch for 12 hours, a day, a week, a month, a year—forever. It had to be done. I would smell my way out. I pestered Sally for information about how she had found me. How my arms and legs looked. What if I could will myself to remember, somehow? It had to be worth it. Just in case I was a cop killer or a rapist or simply a terrible old fool who was lost. Indefinitely.

I was walking in the village one lunchtime. I had had the morning off and instead of staying in my room I had decided to go for a walk. The walk had taken me a few miles, almost to the coast. For some strange reason, as I walked, I stuck out my thumb. It didn't take long. A van stopped. The driver was from Cardiff and he took me to Fishguard. A port. The streets felt familiar. It was early afternoon. The sun was starting to drop a little. It would be dark soon. I didn't know what I was doing. What I would do. I needed to be back for six. There might be a bus, but I didn't feel like going back. I wanted to stay out. The *Square & Compass* was not the world. It wasn't even my world. It was a temporary stop. It was all I had wanted to know for months. Now I was rebelling. I had stayed because it was where I had been found. In the ditch. I had stayed close because I didn't know what else to do. Would someone come looking for me? Would there be some clue as to who I was, where I was from?

Nothing had changed. The one thing I knew was that I had to do something else. I had played at trying to find a way of life.

Three months of dating and I had not had so much as a sniff of underwear. I hadn't really wanted it. There had to be something else. I could have done something about it. I could have looked more desperate. I could have made more of an effort. You see when I meet people; I'm not sure what I want to do with or about them. We meet. I observe. I listen. I ask myself, is this the person I was with? I know it is not. I know it can't be.

I clearly wanted something to happen. Now it had occurred to me that I had to make it happen. Make it. For me. My future. My life.

I had been mulling all this over as I sat in a rather damp café near the harbour. I could get a boat. I could get the train. I could go anywhere. I had to be back by 6pm tonight. I didn't have to be back.

Then I noticed a familiar handbag slung over a shoulder. It was Sally.

'Didn't expect to see you here. Mind if I join you?'. I shuffled over along the bench feeling the roughness of the wood through lightweight jeans. She looked surprised, then smiled and sat down.

'What are you doing?'

'Killing time.' I must have looked really miserable. She put her hand on top of mine.

'Well, I know how that feels. What shall we do?'

'I've got to be back by 6pm.'

'Me too. I know, let's got to some of the little galleries.'

There was something in her voice that suggested we were colluding. Sharing in the gathering of a basic need. We were bored and looking for input. Creative or otherwise. I suddenly felt as if I was a fish being gutted and then boned. I could feel the sharp slash and swish of an experienced hand.

Sally dragged me round a cluster of little shops that sold pictures and photographs by local artists. A piss-poor selection they were too. I could smell defeat in all of them. Why did these people do it? Surely they could see—or had friends of family who could see for them—that they were not good enough? The artists I hated most seemed to appeal to Sally. She was clearly itching to spend money. Then the dreaded question.

'Who should I buy?'

'What are you asking me for? Me? I don't know anything about art.'

'Nor do I. That's what I'm asking you for.'

'None of them', I said bluntly. 'I could do better.'

'Could you?'.

'I reckon. I reckon I could. Why not?'

'Didn't notice you were an artist.'

What was I saying? But I bloody well could. I knew it.

'Buy me something to paint on and something to paint with. I'll show you.'

I was late back to the pub. Sally rang through for me. They weren't too bothered. Suggested I could stay out until 9pm. I didn't want to. I wanted to be back behind the bar, washing glasses. Dreaming I knew who I was.

On the way home Sally asked me if I had any plans to find out who I was. It struck me as strange. She didn't trust me. I could have lied. But the truth is, I wanted to phone a friend. Any of you, out there?

2. Disturbance

I had a dream. In my dream there was a woman, Maggie and a little girl, Rachel. They were fuzzy.

Maggie was arguing with her eldest daughter. Rachel, aged about five. She had a badge that said 'I am 5!'. Arguing. But I could not hear what they were arguing about. It did not make sense. I then started to make it up, in MY dream Rachel said it must be two years ago. Maggie said it was two months. She said it again and again. Two fucking months. Two months.

'But it seems a long, long, long, long…'—was all that Rachel could say. She had no face to speak of only a voice that seemed shrill and awkward and scared.

Maggie grabbed Rachel's hand, perhaps a little too tight, and they crossed the busy rat-run, Maggie keeping a sharpened eye out for cyclists or big fat clunky cowcatchers.

They are late.

Rachel runs ahead along the pavement, then turns sharply, startling a woman in a black burka. Maggie says sorry. Rachel carries on until she reaches a mess of bells by the front door to an imposing house. A house converted into flats. Rachel stabs a finger at the bottom left bell next to the legend, 'Prime Time'.

An abrupt voice buzzes them in. A woman's voice.

'Is she your friend?' says Rachel.

Maggie almost drags Rachel up three flights of stairs. Rachel could almost bounce step to step.

Maggie pauses at the top of the stairs before knocking. Rachel swings low on her Mother's hand and stretched out towards the passing curl of a cat's tail. The cat, black-brown and scruffy, sucks its tail back down and shot away to a nearby door. The cat flap swings as the black-brown fur disappears into the flat.

Maggie pushes the front door open as another buzzer sounded and the two of them find themselves in a small corridor with a couple of chairs. Maggie sits on one. Rachel thinks about sitting on the other, then spots a low table onto which is scattered hundreds of brightly coloured glass beads. She quickly pounces on the surface using her left hand to sweep the beads onto the wooden floor.

Maggie tries to grab her hand but is too late, it is almost as if she is trying to help Rachel sweep the beads off the table even more. Rachel laughs, loudly. Her laughter convulses into giggles. Then they both stare at the door. The door looks immoveable. The door seems to get bigger and bigger. I lose Rachel in the grain of the door and Maggie, Maggie slides underneath where what seemed a tiny gap is now a chasm between door and floor, alive with air and fluff and the stuff that threatens to overwhelm me.

3. Pot

I am asleep. I am breathing. I do not want to open my eyes. Beside me I feel the comforting throb of my mobile on 'vibrate'. I go to answer it. But as I try to grip the phone between my fingers, in the palm of my hand, it seems to skip away from me. My fingers chase the phone down my leg. Then I lose it.

I am shaking. I stare out of the window in my attic room. I am on anti-depressants. The medical profession's contemporary catch-all. I stare back at the cluster of pills I was due to take about three hours ago. I am not going to take them. I am not.

4. Kettle

I am awake. I have no phone. I seem to have been dreaming. It is early in the morning. I hear coughing. I am coughing. I am not awake. I am asleep. I am coughing in my sleep. This is not good.

5. Black

I meet up with Sally again today. Sally has a secret. We drive to our café in Fishguard. Over strong coffee She tells me her secret then I show her my first painting. She tells me she has wanted to tell me ever since she first found me. I show her my waves.

She has been holding on to my mobile phone. There was one message on it. Only one.

I am stunned. I want the phone.

'I threw it away', she says, casually. She gets up and starts to walk away from the table. Out into the street. Down the street, towards the harbour. I am running, but I cannot compete with her walk. The harder I concentrate on running, the faster her walk seems to be. I am not letting her go like this. I summon the energy to compete, to fight for her, to catch her—I want her.

I catch her. Pull her to me. Feel her body close to mine. I bury my face in her hair. I smell her hair. I am not thinking in the past any more. I hear the shriek of gulls.

'Why?' I ask.

'Because the moment I found you in the ditch, I knew my life could change. I knew I wanted to be with you?' she said.

I take it in. I am her foundling. She has played a long game.

6. Next Year

I am never sleeping again. I don't want to miss a beat. But now I have to climb in—one last time—to climb out.

I stand over the ditch. I stare into the ditch. I start to kick at soil and grass. I look around. See no one.

There is a bird overhead. It is gliding on a thermal. It is assured. It is strong.

I climb in. I want to lie down.

I lie down. I pull the soil and grass about me, like a quilt. I pull flattened cardboard under my head. It begins to rain. The droplets thud onto the flap of cardboard sticking out from behind my head. It stops raining as I doze.

Somewhere. Ahead of me. Above me. I can hear bird song.

Blackbird.

Music.

Life.

Hope.

I am awake; I have found a coat I did not know I had. It was in the ditch. In the pocket is a receipt. The receipt was for a list of groceries. The receipt is from a shop in Bath.

I have told everyone in the pub. Sally has promised to drive me to Bath. I have decided to go to the shop.

I will start at the shop.

It is Sally who asks if I have tried the coat on. Of course not, who else would lose a coat in a ditch?

7. The Year After

I have not been to the shop. The coat sleeves came as far as my forearm. Not even *my* ditch.

I fucked Sally three months ago. Well, she fucked me really. She lied about taking me to Fishguard and drove me to a holiday let she owns in Tenby. She has long hair and she let me hold it whilst I took her from behind. It all sounds so mechanical when I explain it like this. But it was not. It was beautiful. Last week I painted her. Not nude. In her jeans. In her sweater. Her smell is floral. I think her children are OK. I am afraid for them. Her husband, Mark, is not OK. He told Simon and Janice that he thought I was 'having it off' with Sally. His wife. Where was my own family? Why did I have to take someone else's? I am the baddie. Sorry.

Sally asked me to go to the Doctor, I agreed, we went together. I told him what had happened and he sent me for tests. I have been to the hospital in Swansea three times now. Each time I think I am going to find my past. But I don't, they just don't know. There are no clues. I am like a man who took all his clothes off, burnt all his possessions. She wants me to keep on looking. I am not looking. It was a habit. A bad habit and the kind of bad habit that I can lose. But I will always be that lost man, inside. May be I am a robot.

I apply for my name. Steven. Steven *Mathry*.

I am painting. I am quite good. Good enough to sell to tourists. I like the sea. I paint waves. Not big waves. Not little waves. My waves are like the opposite of a ditch.

All day long, I paint the waves. Do they wonder where they come from, or do they live for where they roll next? Before they disappear. Before they re-emerge.

8. The Year After the Year After.

I have an exhibition. Sally is driving me to the Arts Centre in Aberystwyth. There will be people to meet and an opportunity to meet other artists. Her hand reaches for mine as we walk through the door into the gallery.

I am assured. I am strong.

Last

Kayleigh Moore

My tutor for life drawing insisted that we *find the life* in our subjects—make them pulse with breath and blood in our sketches. Three years of an art degree and I still couldn't get on with the idea. Most of the time, none of us are even aware of the life in people, so I had no idea how to draw it. People move by as flesh and shadow: some wrinkled, some dark, some hidden behind veils. Nothing special. The way I saw it, the invisible but continued presence of life only draws attention when it's gone. Or is about to go. There was a time when the only family photographs taken were when a member had died. Families were documented, grainy and dim, gathered about a corpse. Generations marked out by deaths.

Now I sketch people who are poised on the brink, copying over to canvas afterwards in thick oils laid with pallet knives. The paintings sell well out of space I rent in the back of an art gallery a few blocks from my apartment. People say there's something about the people in my paintings—something alive in their serene but loaded expressions, framed by hair and cloth always being whipped in a breeze. I usually get two or three new studies a month, but during the holiday seasons more come up. Stock market dips don't bring out as many as I'd expected.

Just off the middle of the bridge seems to be the best place to sit and wait, right between two blue signs asking people not to take the plunge and to call the special suicide number instead. Free of charge. After my first month spending my mornings here, the suicide patrols ignored me. They must know what I'm doing by now, though.

It's two men watching today, nodding to anyone who stands at the railings on their own for a long time without a camera. They'll wander over with the famous San Francisco smile and ask if they're 'alright.' If they need directions—that don't include 'straight down.' It's only if the hapless subject laughs it off that the patrol really leaves them alone. Any other reaction and they go off a little way to watch, ready to throw the flare in after them and radio the recovery team if they can't run back to the railing in time.

It's usually in the morning that it happens, I've found. It used to happen at night the most, but then the bridge was closed to pedestrians, which stopped it. Everyone walks too. No one cycles or drives to take the four-second dive into the black water. Don't want to hold up traffic and cause a fuss, I suppose. There's never a jump in rush hour.

I've got a feel for them now. I can usually pick out who's going to do it before they get to their spot. They look normal enough. Men in old festival t-shirts that will shred if they don't come off completely. Women with their hair and makeup done for work or lunch, both going to be ruined by the tearing water. It's how they move that gives them away: with their shoulders up and eyes down like they're worried they'll get caught. There's a kind of steadiness in their walk, that kind of security that comes with not having to worry about anything but a step out into space. They think it'll be peaceful. It's not. When they get pulled out of the water by the recovery people in orange jumpsuits, they look like they've hit concrete. I've only seen one survive, and he screamed until the recovery boat was out of range. I didn't paint him, just held on to the sketch. Just in case.

Today, my subject has long blonde hair, the kind that dries curly but doesn't frizz. It's swept back from his eyes with a blue and white bandana, the triangle flap at the back flipping in the breeze. His long leather coat chases about his ankles as he walks, thick boots moving in long certain strides on the far side of the bridge from me. Surf Rocker. I get out a stick of charcoal and a white conté crayon, making quick notes on how his hair and coat move at the top of the page for later. My binoculars are at hand, but I won't need them today. He stops eight suspension lines to the left across from me, and I see his face in flickers between the traffic.

I'd expected more of them to cry up here, or to look out of the ordinary in some way. Nearly all of them are calm, casual even, not treating it like a ceremony. A few of the younger ones will stand on the railing first, spread their arms wide and tip their heads up to the sky so that the horizon rises up to them as they topple over. An MTV penchant for the dramatic. The older men tend to sit on the railing for a minute first, swinging their legs. Some take their expensive watches off to put them in their jacket pockets, like they do when they need to fiddle with something in an engine or are about to play ball with their kid. Women rub and pull at something whilst they think. Hair, sleeves or jewellery. Who knows how many diamonds are on the riverbed.

Surf Rocker leans his elbows back on the red rail and picks his nails, squinting up at the sky and taking quick glances back over his shoulder at the bay. He's got small eyes beneath his wide eyebrows, set back in shadows made darker by the high points of his cheeks. I guess him to be about twenty-six, his body young and lean. I watch sparkles of light come off his hands as he takes his rings off and puts them in his back pocket.

Their names become the titles of their portraits. Yankees Fan. Jamaican Jogger. Captain Greybeard. What they chose to wear on their last day fascinates me as much as the time or whether or not they take their jewellery off. I wonder if it's orchestrated so there are no clues for anyone who saw them leave their house or apartment. Of if they didn't know that today was the day until they got to the bridge, and their wardrobe was caught unprepared.

They wear good but not exceptional suits, the bad ones obvious from a long way off because the shoulders shone synthetically. Polyester jogging clothes seem to be popular in Spring. Literally running to death, but sitting down to catch their breath before they jump. A few collage kids. The girls tend to take their bags with them. The men put their satchels and briefcases down carefully against the railings as if they were going to pick them up again later. That last moment of pointless familiarity endears me to them. I love them all—the life in them demonstrated in the smallest details. I get them down fast with charcoal and a fistful of coloured pencils. Not many of them linger long enough for a full study, and I can't hang around afterwards to finish as the cops show up almost immediately.

It looks like Surf Rocker is going to be a quick one, gripping the bar and flexing back and forth. I have two rough sketches down when he turns and gets his leg over the railing, the chain from his hip to the wallet in his back pocket clanking silently against the metal. No one's noticed. His coat and hair pull to the left in long, slow ripples, undulating like the dirty river below and beyond. I scratch out the angle of the light, the point on the horizon that his gaze settles on.

His long body pulls straight as if he is taking a slow breath, and I imagine his hands tipping to play with the wind, like children who flow their arms out of car windows. His body tipping forwards starts subtly, and then, suddenly, gone. No one seems to notice at first, then the space of an inhale before someone screams and there's a rush for the edge. The patrol comes back and the red flare spins end over end as it falls. The recovery boat sets off.

Sometimes I wonder if the cops will ever recognise a jumper in my paintings at the gallery. I doubt it though. Everyone looks straight ahead on the bridge, or just glances out at Alcatraz before they get back to the road. Even the cyclists don't take in the world they're apparently saving. Just push on. Like the jumpers. No marching band; no screaming; no heaving, tearful phone calls. Without ceremony, they take a minute to compose themselves, choose feet or head first, and just go.

The sketch of Surf Rocker is perfect, a privilege, and I date and name the page. Strangers as they all are, I feel their last portrait shows them at their best before death. An honest snapshot, so real and nakedly alive that I couldn't paint anything else now. I'm sure that on their way down, runway models don't look as good as they do.

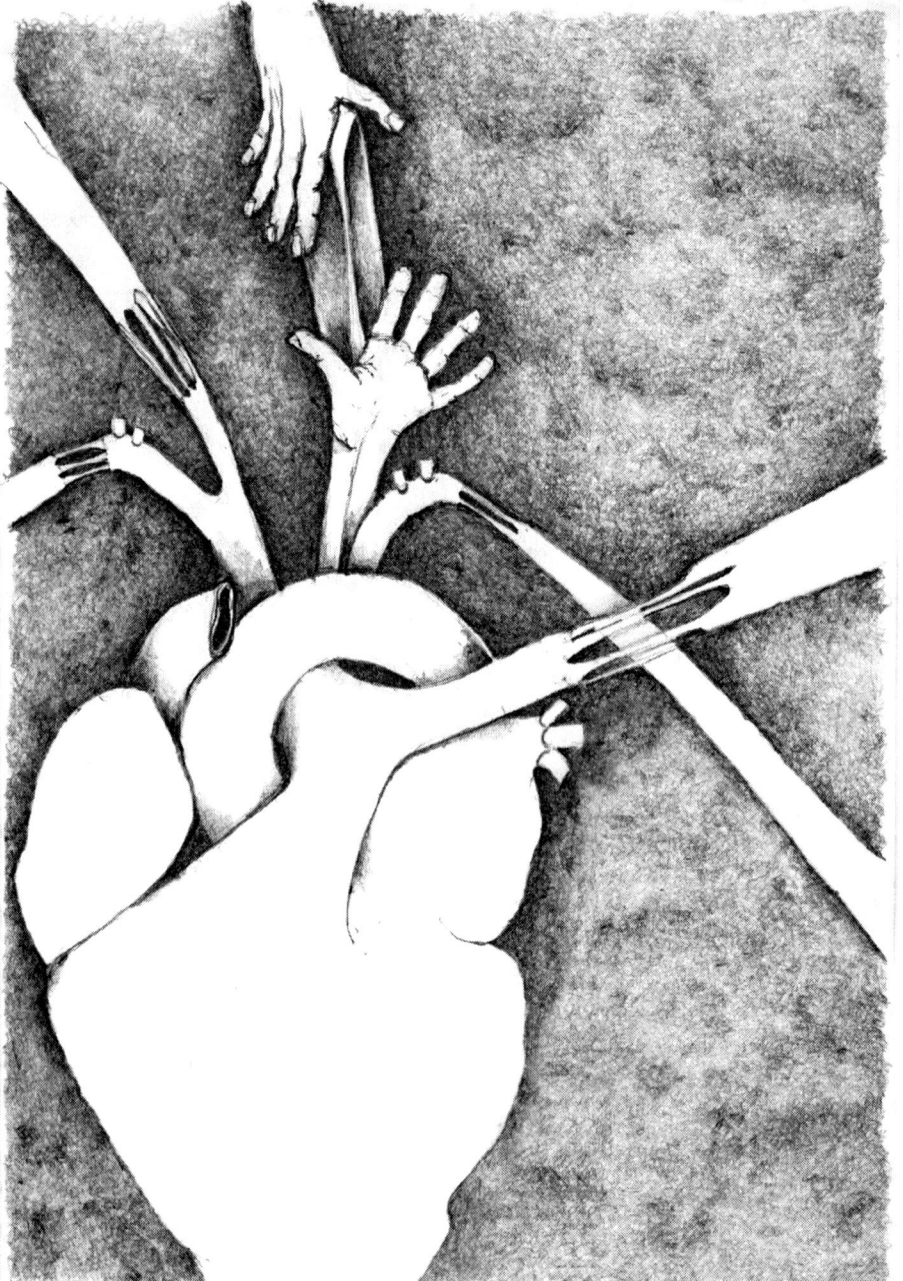

Gain

Brooke Biaz

Takes hold now of the snow shovel from the front step where he's found it, propped. Lifts it up in front of them both, lengthwise, like a tribal offering.

'I swear, Wanda,' says Alex, 'it looks exactly, *exactly,* like the one I loaned Phil.'

Only, isn't that ten, twelve, fourteen, who knows how many, years ago? No need for it now, they've long bought a replacement.

∞

Around these parts there's a fair spattering of the semi-famous: club-singers, motivational speakers, restaurateurs, the earnest Heads of High Schools and the like. Suited men fill the street in the mornings. Women in sports cars leave and arrive.

Folks who live here live quietly (but for the occasional seasonal gathering). They treat each other with respect. Drive courteously. Spend their winters away. Employ gardeners. Drink wines. Always school their children. Care annually for the disadvantaged. I think you could say this is a lucky street. The proximity of the beach, yonder, is one thing. But also, life goes on. Lights glow in homes at night. Lawns do not suffer from the heat of the summer: no browned edges, I mean. And no flower beds where dahlias limp low and heavy as pendulums in the mid-afternoon and the steady spread of midge grass intruding on the deep dark of soil. There are no cracks in the long white pavements. No propped up caravans. When things go wrong somewhere you would swear this is not the place.

∞

3.00 pm. A van pulls up. Alex has gone to the office. So it is without prior warning that the delivery takes place.

Wanda, in her bathrobe, fresh from the pool. The delivery guy is pleasant, in that kind of aching, larval way of delivery guys. He and his workmate bring the delivery in from the van and Wanda watches from the hall as they manoeuvre it carefully, professionally, into the front room, centred and large. It's covered in plastic, slightly opaque; and she signs for delivery with the vague sense that something, somehow, is out of kilter.

The guy smiles, achingly. And she wonders, distantly, if she should tip him. But his mate has started the van and before the moment concludes another has overtaken it, and the van pulls away.

She stands, slightly damp, in the archway of the room. When, finally, she gains the momentum to tug at the plastic, she uncovers too much.

∞

'Well, if it isn't *the* one,' Wanda says, loudly, 'then it is *very* much like it.'

Alex, on the other end of the phone. He tells her not to do anything. Wait. It must be some kind of . . .

Clerical mistake?

But she sounds to him as if something might break, some unearthed spark of a thought she is having that might ignite an entire room, or the house, or the entire neighbourhood. He knows her well enough to recognise that.

He says: 'I'm on my way.'

∞

They stare now at the lounge chair. Uncovered. Now with an opaque plastic skirt. He can recognise it too, though he had not seen it often. A low, wide heavily bolstered black chair. It always reminded him of men; men that were not him, other men. If this isn't the one, she is right, it is certainly very close: that chair that once sat in her apartment, before they moved in together. The chair beside her window, back to the balcony, the breakfast bar to the right, the TV to the left, a round sun-coloured rug in front of it; a two-seater in the same black faux leather, further left; a book case; a glass stereo cabinet; the door to the bedroom.

'Well, yes,' he says, 'point taken.'

But the delivery company isn't answering the phone.

∞

Evening comes. The neighbourhood glows. Yet downstairs, in their house, something is not right. At the back door, those rear French sliding glass doors, out on the dark slate paving, a stray dog is pacing, happily. They stand and watch it; as does their new dog, Trig, her spaniel temperament curious but unsure. She's young and curious and eager.

Back and forth the other dog goes, steady, not urgent or clawing. No rush. No concern. Rough dusty white and skinny, it looks up now and then at them, its tongue out, the long thin lipped jaw giving the expression of a smile, the kind of smile a kid might like in a dog, if he'd never had a dog before and his father bought one home, picked up from the pound or from some guy he worked with.

'Benny?' Alex asks.

But the dog can't hear him through the glass.

What would he know anyway, even if the dog could hear? How could he be sure it was answering to him? It paces as if it has nowhere else to go, not sadly just with determination; and its unmistakable (or so he's beginning to think) mouth, and the clicking of its claws on the dark paving, and the shake of its wiry coat.

'Ben?'

Surely it is.

∞

At breakfast, or what constitutes as breakfast—neither of them has slept, though both feel strangely restedthe snow shovel in the garage, the chair now half-uncovered behind them, and 'Benny' curled against the back door glass, Wanda says:

'I feel . . .'

Standing there in the kitchen she takes Alex's face in her hands.

His cheeks are now slightly unshaven. She kisses him out of that room and past the living room, and on. They make love in the hallway, on the floor, beside the stairs, maybe seen, maybe not, beneath the sidelights that face out toward other homes, and the day already warm, and the sound of someone mowing the lawn, somewhere, distant, or close, and the pool filter starting and the beach beyond, a sand plough preparing it, and somewhere upstairs, now, a sound.

∞

Outside, suited men fill the morning. Women in sports cars. It's a regular tableau. Folks are treating each other with respect, driving courteously. Gardeners are arriving to start their days. There's the chink of wine bottles going into the recycler. The burble of neighbours discussing their holiday plans. Next winter: Morocco, the Maldives, a month in Crete . . .

∞

Up in their guest room, clothes have been arranged on the bed, though neither of them has arranged them. Somehow the room still appears empty. Yet, obviously, it isn't. There's a pair of beige trousers, a long chocolate tie, a checked white-brown shirt, a navy suit jacket. On the floor: brogues, tan, highly polished, worn to both sides so that they sit off-centre.

And now Alex and Wanda reach the door.

2

Two hours ago, Wanda's father appeared in their guest room. Back, as it happens, from the dead.

You would think this would have been too great a shock to bear, but perhaps because it still feels like he's gone it takes the edge off. And it came at the right time, Wanda and Alex had made love for the first time in six months. The light rain now on the skylights, which have taken on the green, cracked appearance of those in the old beach house Alex's parents once owned up the coast. The sound of The Eagles singing *Hotel California* on a crackling radio downstairs. Out in the drive, seen through the stair windows, Alex's elder brother Gavin, who moved to the North West some years ago, after which they lost touch, has turned up and is under the rear of his Kombi van, revving its engine, as once he did. The whole picture of him shimmers out there their on the late Winter drive.

∞

Wanda's father, whose silver hair seems remarkably dark and luxuriant in his newfound life, yet still silvery somehow (both!), has taken to hanging out on the porch. He's found a glass of Pernod in what appears to be a new teak drink's cabinet that's appeared by the wall in what Alex has begun referring to, unexpectedly, as his 'den'. Or in more current form: 'the spare room'. All for the best, however, because Wanda's mother has also turned up; in fact, both of them have: her natural mother, whose fateful death at the age of 93 (she continues to avoid the stairs) seems long behind her as she hops on the 'bounce-o-net' she's brought from her visit to her friend Nancy's to see her 'super new sewing machine' (sic), and her adopted mother, who seems to have taken to her predecessor with unprecedented enthusiasm and equal distrust, as they call 'Benny' toward them. He nips and yaps around.

Comradely, warily, they head out the door, in the direction of the beach, or somewhere, crying out:

'What's buzzin', cuzzin?' And:

'Come on. Lay a patch!' And:

'I really need to check my email!'

∞

What thoughts Alex is having seem to be growing ever more confused. While he works as a litigator in the offices of Earnshaw & Mable, and has done these past twenty-four years, he's suddenly considering becoming a pro-windsurfer or one of those guys who runs an ice-cream box down on the beach, or maybe he'll join what he refers to as 'The Hounddog's Expedition to Hawaii.' What?

This confuses things considerably. Though he's only twenty, or maybe forty-four, he wonders: 'What next?' On the phone is Tim Earnshaw, the practice's principle, who's called to find out when Alex will be 'finished the Montrose brief?'

'Soon,' says Alex, meaning, actually: 'Do I know?'

There's a chance, he figures, that if he works some more hours down at the Beach Hut around the (Newly? Long standing? Built up? In the process of being built?) beach at Lantern Bay, he might be offered some kind of permanent thing. Windsurf in the morning and work the Hut in the afternoons. Then, of course, he and Vikki can maybe take off to Indonesia in their gap year.

∞

'*Who* is *Vikki*?' Wanda is wondering, and not too happily, it has to be said.

'What do you mean, 'gap' year?' she asks, dressing all the while for her forthcoming recital.

Arms akimbo in her bright floral frock, right there in the bathroom. She's hardly one to talk. Young Kirk Thomson and

Mike Abelman are in the back room playing pool on the table that's appeared there, along with the room itself, which 24 hours ago did not exist, at least not both as a room and as their swimming pool, drinking from their beer cans, their shirts off, hung over the colourful king-sized bean chairs in the corner with no sense of all that they, each as tanned as a rock, have been one following the other, in an order that shifts—one is, and one isn't—Wanda's current boyfriend. Or, indeed, any knowledge of Alex, who wonders what they are doing here; but simultaneously welcomes them in. He has his own issues.

3

Hard to convince the authorities that such a rapid amassing and also removal of funds, in bank accounts both current and supposedly closed, is not the result of criminal activity. What makes it worse is that even those direct creditors—whose financing of this home and their previous apartment, eight cars (of various colours and brands; one for each of them, at a time), several holidays, trekking, skiing, cruising off the coast of Greece, the installation of a pool, the purchase of a pair of rare Australian blue lorikeets (both of which have now returned to their perch in the abandoned garden aviary, which Alex has been using, usefully, as a shed), the funding of 'unnamed' surgery by Dr Pierce Wilferlieft, of the renowned *New Classic Clinics*—even though those direct creditors have returned their funds they do not wish the return of their goods and services. The house is growing full with things, and the knocks on the door, and the garbage that now begins to amass at the door, only to appear also inside, in its original packaging, its boxes and bottles, is matched only by the need to buy more, and pay less, and deal with its purchasing and deal with its removal and deal and deal...

∞

If he and Wanda could indeed re-visit chronology, and sit each thing, each response to the world, which arrives one over the other at present so that nothing ends and nothing begins, then maybe this accumulation would make sense. But time now has become short, even if it actually *seems* long. Wanda is working both at the Weight Loss Centre, where she has worked for some years, and back at the Peacock Club, where she once worked. Her singing and her weight, as if to challenge all logic, both rise and fall hourly, oppositionally, as does Alex's, in fact—as if they are two strangely animated balloons. It is impossible, Alex thinks, to tell exactly who Wanda is because, to make things difficult, her hair, the depth of her tan, her eyebrows, the presence (or lack) of glasses, her want of new clothes, her wearing old clothes, her nails, her shoes, eyeliner, the sharpness (or otherwise) of her features, change each moment.

The audience there at the Club seems to know nothing of her studying at the University, of her ambition to sing Angelina in Rossini's *La Cenerentola*. The university is where Alex keeps seeing her, when he does not see her at home (of course). And, in those meetings, which take place fleetingly, he thinks of her as remarkably exotic, as she makes her way across campus toward the Music studios, and home at the same time, him spouting some new knowledge, which comes to him day and night, at work, now at the university, in the playground at School, out in the street, all of which he visits simultaneously, with an equal share of joy and pain that this brings. At any one moment there seems be so much knowledge, old and new and new and old, that they can barely learn one thing before another interprets, can barely form opinions before those opinions are challenged, can barely believe in something before something else overwhelms it.

Alex feels himself younger, but wiser, and the clash between these two things would be worse, if not that the return of his parents and grandparents brings new challenges, while also recovering old ones. He feels the drift away from the office. The gardener seems unsure how to address him. Suited men, out in the street, watch him cautiously as he leaves and enters his home. He wants, desperately, to return the things, the aspects, the lives, that he has re-required. But no matter how he thinks of it he cannot imagine a scenario that would lose one thing without gaining another. Downstairs, Wanda stares at the ever accumulating store of furniture which follows her from one room to another, the deliveries now daily and her sense that her own shape, while at the core is some recognisable thing, has no real substance. This thought haunts her late into the evening.

She drifts between her parents, her boyfriends, the teachers from her junior school, who visit her as if it was just yesterday she won the School Singing Medal, and asks them all what they are doing here, but in each conversation another is waiting, another moment.

Only Trig seems truly happy. She, as it has turned out, is pregnant. Her and 'Benny' bounce around the back garden, lost in the moment: the old and the new. No idea of the simplicity their news represents; the sheer, clear totality of it. The Spring is ahead. So, maybe, who knows, there'll be women in sports cars? Gardeners. Wine. The proximity of the beach, yonder. A glow in the homes at night. Green lawns. Dahlias tall and big and bright in the mid-afternoons. Long white pavements.

Desire Lines

David Gaffney

Geoffrey discovered his nemesis in a pool of rusty water on the edge of the building site. A stem of weed twitched, and a crest like the hump of a miniature nessie flicked the surface. Dozens appeared, corkscrewing in the water, flashing tell-tale orange spotted bellies and purple frilled combs. Clumps of grey jelly floated on the surface with black pinpricks of new life inside.

Great crested newts.

The Poppyfield project was dead when the environment agency found out. The spawn would have to be allowed to hatch, the newts moved to a safe site, taking the project into autumn and beyond and then waiting, waiting, waiting.

Hopelessness pounced. This moonscape was supposed to become a gorgeous enclosure of air and light, fizzing with footsteps, laughter and dreams, a building to reach up and touch the hand of god. All these dreams would be lost, millions of pounds too. But that wasn't the point. The point was Geoffrey's father, who was invited to the topping off, possibly the only opportunity for him to see one of Geoffrey's buildings. Something inside Geofrey swelled as he imagined his father reading *Geoffrey Lange, Lead Architect* etched on a plaque. That's if he would even understand who Geoffrey was; the progress of his disease was horrifying, whole sections of his brain, of his life, of his personality, seemed to have been eaten away, like there was some evil Pacman bleeping through his head munching cell after cell after cell.

Since his father went into the hospice Geoffrey had experienced an urgent desire to create. There hadn't been a lot for his father to be proud of till now. Geoffrey ditched had university, there was the drugs, then the gambling, then the depression, then the affair. Then Sharon and the kids had left, and who could blame them? But he was putting things right. The Poppyfields development would put things right. He had a new love, Althea, he was in contact with the kids, and he'd picked up his architecture where he'd left off and graduated with a first. If anything, his period of dissolution nourished his new, successful self, offering a fresh angle on everything. Buildings require spontaneity, spaces where things no-one had thought of could happen, spaces for paths others would make, so-called desire lines, imaginary gossamer threads that marked the routes real people would eventually tread. The architect's job was to make these desire lines real.

Normally when this happened you rang the newt wrangler—yes, there is such a thing, Geoffrey knew him—a pleasant round-spectacled fellah called Norman who supported Carlisle United. But Geoffrey couldn't ring Norman. What he did instead was drive to B and Q where he bought fishing nets, buckets, gloves, and a giant tub of fish food.

It was hard work, rounding up the newts. They wriggled and slithered, they really didn't want to leave their pond. But if just one of these rare creatures was discovered, work would stop. He'd seen it with bats, voles, owls, rare flowers. Why was it so important to preserve crested newts? No-one saw them, they added nothing to the pleasure of life, yet were universally loved. He thought about all the squat, ugly creatures in the world, crawling about unseen, and the time we spent protecting them, as he tossed the last newts into his buckets, shovelling the spawn in on top.

Where to take them? He couldn't take them home (although the kids, when they visited on Sunday, would love to see them) because Althea hated anything creepy-crawly. Neither could he take them to another pond, because Norman the newt wrangler had told him newts had homing instincts and would travel miles to the ponds where they were born.

So he took them to his father's house, which lay empty since his dad went into care.

The bath tap belched out gobbets of rust and he waited until a clear stream flowed then inserted the plug and tipped the creatures in. But the newts didn't like it in there. They panicked, swum franticly, feet slithering against the porcelain, and seemed generally bothered and unhappy in this sterile and antiseptic tub. They would be missing their bubbling, burping, pond, and also, he thought, weren't newts amphibians? Couldn't they drown? To be on the safe side, and to make it all the more homely, he gathered soil, stones and branches from the garden and spread this debris over the floor, then blocked off the overflow and filled the bath to the rim so they could climb out.

He watched them for a time, as flakes of food brought them swarming to the surface, gulping and gobbling. One seemed to make eye contact and Geoffrey touched its nose with his fingertip, and sighed deeply

∞

Geoffrey was watching the first foundation post go in when he got the call. His father had gone walkabout. The last time he was found in Woolworths in his dressing-gown; the time before, asleep in a phone box, naked. But this time was different. The care assistant had a call to say that he'd been seen entering his old house. He still had keys, and he'd walked five miles in his slippers. She wondered if Geoffrey could fetch him back. She was worried. The old man was confused. Anything could happen.

∞

Newts had escaped and were all over the stairs. His dad was upstairs in the bathroom, sitting on the toilet, holding a newt on his lap, stroking it as though it were a kitten.

'Hi Son,' he said. 'Did you get me these?'

'Yes,' said Geoffrey.

His father had tears in his eyes. 'You don't know how much this means. I always wanted some, ever since I was a boy.'

Geoffrey sat down on the floor, amidst the soil, the stones, the branches, the dozens of squirming newts, and took his dad's hand.

'Are you okay dad? Do you want to go back yet?'

'Yes,' he said. 'I'm ready to go back. Just give me a few more minutes with these little fellahs. They are very rare—protected, you know. Wait till I tell Archie'

Archie had been Dad's best friend from school.

'Archie never had newts, only frogs.'

Geoffrey looked at his father's grey head, his skinny, wizened body, his spotless tartan dressing gown, his shiny slippers, his thin, bare ankles like a little boy's, his liver-spotted fingers, caressing the newt.

The sky grew dark, his dad fell asleep, Geoffrey called the care home, and an ambulance arrived. His father forgot about the newts, forgot he'd been home, forgot about Geoffrey.

Geoffrey cleaned up. He wondered if newts had a concept of fathers. He believed he could discern in the newts' faces a tenderness, an intelligence that spoke of social ties stronger and deeper than he could imagine. He wondered if his own son would ever get something like this for him, a fabulous present, something he'd always wanted. This was something to look forward to.

Song Without Words

Pauline Masurel

Nellie set her head against the piano and felt the reverberations of the music waltz through her skull. She did not know who the man was, nor why he was here in her front room, but she loved to hear him play the piano. He played from frayed sheet music which he found in her piano stool and she wished he would come more often.

When the final cadence died away she asked him, 'What did you say your name was?'

'Oh mumsie,' he replied wearily, 'don't you recognise your own son?' He watched the mask of confusion cover her face and then disappear.

'Would you like some tea, Nigel? You've come such a long way to see me. You must be thirsty.'

As they drank the tea he scrutinised her, wondering just how much she really did remember. Where were the memories which should have been laid down over the last twenty years?

'About those little repairs, mumsie. I'll be needing something for the materials. I don't like to ask you for money but I'm between jobs at the moment.'

As she poured the tea and proffered a quaking plate of shortbread biscuits she became quite animated. Nellie was entertaining, just as she had done all her life.

'My son Nigel's in the army. He's stationed out in Ireland. Did you ever meet him?'

'Fifty pounds should cover it. Shall I take it from your purse?'

'Pardon?'

'The money.'

'How much do you want?' She pulled the purse from her bag and began to lay coins one by one on the table. 'That's my son's pocket money. I'm keeping it by.' Then she extracted some notes and looked at them, as if puzzled by the shapes and colours.

The man took the bundle from her and peeled off seven brown notes, handing back the remainder. Then he swung across the room and began playing from a collection of Mendelssohn's Songs Without Words which was already open on the piano. The old woman listened and began to warble the tune. Her voice was light and it cracked through the trills and ornaments.

This was the type of behaviour, together with the teapot rituals, which made his work difficult. He could stomach manifestations of distress. He got that all the time; bolshie oldsters, have-a-go doddery gents who would try to get funny about paying him. He was immune to that. You had to be or you got out of the business. Never mind how much intelligence you did or did not have, however much low-down cunning you possessed, if you once started to think of *them* as people then it was over.

Nellie had known for some time that the man was not her son. It had taken a while to realise. He looked rather like Nigel but when had she last seen him; perhaps fifteen years ago? It had been nice, for a time, to believe but even though it was a disappointment the truth had begun to worm its way in to her consciousness with increasing frequency.

Nigel had never learnt. She had been keen to encourage him when he was younger but he had never shown any interest. If Nigel could not play the piano then who was this man whom she allowed in to her home?

In Nellie's front room the clock beat time with the music, its sonorous voice pacing along with the notes from the piano. Time expanded in that rarely used space, flared out and became a wide river rather than the fast running rapids of life outside. The man felt, some days, as though he were wading upstream against the task of making a living. At other times it was relaxing to float in the old woman's obvious joy at his company.

It was playing a part that he loved most. As a lad he had always wanted to do something theatrical. The other boys called him 'sissy' for his studying, reciting and interminable piano practice. In Nellie he had found the perfect audience of one for his dramatic and musical talents.

Some days the acting came easy because he could believe, in a curious way, that the role was reality. He willed her to believe and when he could see in her watery blue eyes that she was failing him he almost began to shoulder the burden of believing the lie for himself. She belonged to him. He owned this one and yet, with her marble cake and scones, she kept slipping from beneath his heel and winning back her own freedom. Quavering uncertainly in the darkness, there was always a spark of her consciousness which remained to madden him.

He knew he was wrong to have let Nellie soften him up like this. She had begun to remind him of his own granny. He tried to convince himself that he was simply maximising profits. If he kept her sweet he could return time and again to milk the same cash cow. But the longer it continued without violence, the harder he found the job of extracting his earnings. He resolved to realise his investment and move on.

At first, when the man stopped calling, Nellie did not notice. Later she began to count the days. In order to be sure she marked a circle on the calendar each morning. If he came she would colour the circle to mark his visit. After a month, scurrying to the calendar each time she heard the date on the radio, Nellie concluded that the man would not return. She could not remember if he had ever stayed away for so long before. She could not be sure how often he had been in the habit of visiting but she became certain that she would never see him again.

She hated this confusion. She had mislaid him, mislaid him as she seemed to have foolishly mislaid much of the ugly and pointless porcelain which had cluttered her house and been a magnet for dust during her years of cleaning and polishing.

Nellie called the police to report him missing. They wanted to know the man's name. She could not quite remember.

'Perhaps it was Nigel. No, how silly, that was my son's name.'

The constable was patient with Nellie, he was a local man. He remembered only too well the night in 1979 when he had been asked to call to tell her about the death of her son. In his opinion she had never been quite right since then—but the old girl could still make a marvellous spot of gingerbread.

Nellie explained how the visitor had come to play the piano and sometimes done odd jobs for her. She heard the policeman say wearily 'Another "bogus" crime.' But it was not bogus. To Nellie the crime seemed remarkably real. The man had gone away and her piano had ceased to make music.

They did not seem to realise. She had formed an understanding with the man and he had broken their unspoken contract. All he wanted was money. That was little enough to her. What she really craved was time, her own and that of others. Time and company. Time and the sound of the black and white keys dancing as her own fingers could no longer make them. After the phone call Nellie sat with her head against the piano frame and felt the silence seep inside her, wrapping itself around her fragile bones.

Between the Pillow and the Pen

Sean Gregson

A sweaty palmed expression seeps over Justin's face; when you want something it's gone, when it's there these moments you forget. When gone, when gone, oh when all is gone, it's the firing line or firing blank eyes over a table top that, through a trick of light, hides your belongings. The object you require now. A pen. A writing implement. Scour, scour, until you reach the back of the sofa, Justin. Holding a hand that yearns and pulses, Justin fingers the clear plastic of a long lost biro. Teases. Teasing. One more millimetre and you can ease it up with the ridges of your fingerprint. Teasing. Teases. Wrist skin stretched, it slips further back in to the depths of the seating. And, Christ...

Something has to be done. This can't go unsaid any longer.

Dear Anne,

Justin holds his finger out like a sparkler.

Dear Anne, I've been meaning to write this for such a long time now.

Justin's finger is a sparkler.

I couldn't say it. Last time we met, when you asked if everything was alright, I couldn't say it.

Justin's finger dances through the air. He runs out of ink and stares hard into the sun to refill. Another sentence or so and it's gone again. Justin's finger is just a finger. This is ridiculous. That's what Justin thinks, as he rams his hand back down the hidden gape between vertical and horizontal cushions. Then he, Justin, remembers, and drags the memory out from the hole:

In 1987, my dad got two tickets for David Bowie's Glass Spider Tour, and I was twelve. My dad got the tickets and put them somewhere safe. Safely hidden away. I was twelve and this was going to be the happiest day of my life, beyond that year and the years after, this would be the happiest day even then. I was twelve and my dad was thirty-eight. He said there was no way that Bowie would play Rebel Rebel, he had a new album to promote, but I knew he would play Rebel Rebel, and I was twelve. The thirty-eight year old man lost the tickets. Bowie played Rebel Rebel, and the twelve year old was left at home with his thirty-eight-year old dad still saying never mind, he won't be playing his old stuff anyway.

Justin's fingers flit against one of the six sides of the biro barrel. Fumbling in the cavity, he continues:

In 1993, my family moved house, and there, in the inlay of The Man Who Sold the World, were two tickets to see David Bowie. No longer valid; a 1987 use by date. I was eighteen, but in those moments I was twelve again. Looking at those two tickets, their subs still unperforated, six years of supposed growth were exposed as nothing but hair and hormones.

Now hair-and-hormones has his hand down the back of the upholstery, flicking wildly at alien objects. Why not get your hand out of there, Justin, and buy another pen? But no, this pen is part of the bigger picture. The bigger picture which cannot be airbrushed with a finger on to an imaginary canvas. No. Justin has spent his whole life building up to giving up. To pull out now would be another defeat. This must be written, with this pen. You can't walk into any old church, just because your own is out of reach. You can't pray to any god, just because yours doesn't reply at all. This is the pen. This is the pen that will write the words that are in Justin's head.

> Dear Anne, I'm writing this in my head. It's a rough draft that I'll transpose later. Dear Anne, I know and yet...

Gone, gone forever, Justin pushes the biro from arm, hand, and finger's length. And Justin thinks, rather childishly: 'I suppose, I'll find that six years too late too'. When he's lost the ability to write, or lost anyone with whom to communicate, Justin may well stumble upon this self same pen. He contemplates ripping the cushions from the settee; a few smashes and the thing would be in shreds. But this is a flat and Justin only owns those things that can be moved easily by one person.

Justin, his arm slightly tingling, his breath in need of a paper bag, tries again to write his letter on the air. At first, he thinks he's lost his train of thought. A train gone missing. Justin would check himself but... But it's not the thought train that's gone, it's the word train. It's the concept train, it's the theory train. The bloody language, mouth, finger writing, spoken word, train which has derailed. Gone. Poof.

Frozen, Justin wonders what there is to wonder about. What are these things and why are they, also. Nothing is mysterious to a man who isn't aware of mystery. Justin, for a moment, forgets he is human, forgets there was any gain to be lost, and forgets about Dear Anne. Yes, forgets he is human, for what is a human but an animal who has been told to pay attention. Bliss is perhaps made up of detachment and disengagement. The sun is just a thing that appears bright and warm. It is not burning or looming, it is out of reach only to those who imagine they can touch it. Never mind a pen. What is a pen to a man who has lost his signifiers and all they signified? Justin rubs his arm, which is not an arm, it is simply that bit of him he is rubbing. After several rubs, Justin remembers the word 'pain' and feels what it signifies.

> Dear Anne, I think I've just had a heart attack. I felt it all the way down from my shoulder to my writing finger. I think I'm okay now. I'm going to have a lie down.

Justin drops onto the sofa. Lay, connections become unconnected. The pen stops being a metaphor for religion. Two lost tickets to a David Bowie concert at Maine Road stop representing every missed opportunity and disappointment in Justin's life. And Dear Anne, Dear Anne is released from the shackles of embodying every mistake made and hurt inflicted. And Justin thinks:

> Dear Anne, If I had that pen now, I wouldn't write a letter to you. No, in fact, I would draw two parallel lines about an inch apart on each of my wrists, and then spend the rest of the night colouring the bit in the middle. Dear Anne, if I had that pen right now, I wouldn't express myself in words. I'd pick out all those faces that appear in the artexed ceiling and highlight their features. The whole of the roof would be covered in cloud-like faces by the time I was done. Each more grotesque than the last, that's what I'd do if I had that pen right this second. Those are the dots that I would connect if I had the chance to draw them. Not the me and you connections, Dear Anne, no.

Justin keeps on repeating phrases in his head to see if they make sense after his brief disattachment with English, and any other language for that matter. Justin repeats 'rough draft', 'transpose', 'Rebel Rebel'. None of them fit. Justin considers words as he would a new item of clothing. Only, Justin's capacity to use metaphors has gone, so he doesn't really think like that at all. Justin holds words up to the light. He writes words with his finger. He writes 'I was Twelve'.

After some time, Justin has written every word he can think of, and only certain ones fit. 'Pen' does its job. But then, Justin remembers, pen is also a pen, a holding bay, a trap. Also, you pen things that are written, even if they were not written by a pen. Justin gets the dictionary.

At this point, the dictionary is like some holy, unfathomable text to Justin. Pen—an instrument for writing or drawing. Pen— a device used with a writing surface to enter commands into a computer. Pen—an enclosure, a covered dock. Pen—a female swan.

> Dear Anne, Did you know that a female swan is called a pen? Did you, because I didn't and, after what just happened and what is happening, I am very confused by this. This room is a pen, if there were water in here and a boat, it would be another sort of pen, and a pen is a female swan. Remember when we went to that place with the lake and we saw the swanlings, or whatever baby swans are called? A pen. Is this making any sense to you? That day, when we saw the pen with her children, I was happy then. I was thirty-seven and you were thirty-six and I was happy. We sat and watched that pen, I didn't know she was a pen then, but I do now. We watched her for almost an hour. I remember feeling old and redundant. It's funny, that number, thirty-seven, doesn't mean anything to me now, yet it meant so much then. Now, today now, I'm thirty-eight and that number doesn't mean a thing either. It's a figure, all curves and no straight edges. My finger curls round itself when I write it out. When my dad was thirty-eight he mislaid a pair of David Bowie tickets and I was thinking, earlier, that there was an irony there, or some kind of awful coincidence. But now I realise that there is no connection. I've lost you, Dear Anne, and it's got nothing to do with me being twelve, or Rebel Rebel, or that pen I should be writing all this down with. Trap the words, pen them in and pen them down. A female swan.

Justin thinks about things and writes them out like some mime variation of Tourette's. Words flow through his finger and send dust particles whirling on the wind. This man, once a man of letters and now a man of *letters*, is connecting, writing joined up, joining up writing. It's coming out of him in a flowing moment that looks like it won't ever stop. Justin walks to the window and breaths heavily. He repeats this action until the outside world is nothing but fog. On the condensation, Justin writes:

> Dear Anne, When you come to collect the last of your belongings, I hope you come to take one last look at our view and let out a sigh over where we find ourselves. I hope you see the first bit of this and breathe again, breathe until every one of these words is exposed. Instead of 'clean me', you'll see this, you'll see the point that I've been trying to get to all this time. Dear Anne, I no longer sleep in the bed we used to share. I sleep on the couch. That day, when you left, I went into our room. I couldn't stop myself, it's a mess. There's still smashed glass on the floor, and slivers of wood broken away from your chest of draws. But most of all our room, our old room, is covered in the contents of the pillows I tore apart. White feathers, like the feathers of a swan. A female swan. A pen. Forgive me.

Missed

Katharine Orton

This is the end. Right here and now. That final, dreadful full-stop is hovering above the last line, waiting for its moment to punctuate. A pin, poised to prick the taught red skin of that greatest and brightest of balloons. The Big Anti-Bang has arrived.

Here it comes. Any moment now. The last act is so close you can almost see the curtains; feel it approaching as fast as a freight train—rushing up to meet each one of us like concrete at the end of a long and lucid fall. It was fun while it lasted.

Soon it'll be here. Very soon. Humankind's untimely appointment with a most inhuman and unkindly end. Where precious memories and profound thoughts transcend into thin air and habits, both bad and good, go side by side into the void.

For last night, a prophecy of the end crept into the closed eyes of a young girl: one who had dreamed the future many times. Images came to her from outer space in the form of fiery comets crash-landing in her brain, lighting up her grey cells like fizzing roman candles. Projected onto those inner eyelids of hers she saw today's hazy dawn—and knew it would be the last.

In this chaotic sleep, light and noise formed only snippets of scenes, smells and sounds that faded quickly as consciousness muscled in. There was the misty grey morning sky and the tinkling sounds of smashing glass. She remembered that. A coolness seeping around her feet. A ringing bell, distant, behind her. A strange, loping black creature rolling lopsidedly down a dingy side-street, pointed flashes of white fire rising from it—like a dog from hell.

There was the red glow of the setting sun as it tumbled away into space.

Before those youthful, prophetic eyes, everything began happening at once. The world started smashing itself into rocks. Sodden earth was turning, falling. Blackness spread across the distant sun in a flurry of dark ripples. Branches closed in, over and around as the world turned itself upside down and inside out. Above it all was the thunderous roaring of the cracking sky.

And then, the unmistakable visage of Death Himself, stretching out those dreaded bony fingers—to offer the firmest of all handshakes. She had lurched awake to the tinny rattle of her radio: outside was the same hazy grey dawn. There could be no doubt about that.

So take a good look at this blue-green world with its sweeping desert plains and rigorous peaks and crags. Its forests like row upon row of pine cones: broccoli florets packed tightly on the supermarket shelf. See it explode in one big, hard cloud of mangled metal and rock, clogging up space like so much useless junk.

For the end is finally nigh.

Fay settled down for a long and tiresome wait on the warm, dry earth. Idly, she popped wheat from its sheaves, and ran her fingers up long, stiff wild-grass stems, scattering the useless dead seeds. She'd thought of this place all day: a high hilltop, surrounded by knotted woods; her own grassy altar catching the very last sunlight. Perfect for witnessing the end of the world.

Fay's town huddled below. A place that always seemed so grey to her was, tonight, tinted with oranges and pinks. Rainbow light crept over the rooftops: it reflected from the windows of the little semi-detached house where her parents had prepared for another working day. It glanced off the crumbling bricks of the church where, earlier, she'd exchanged words with God's representative (or so he'd claimed).

Light lingered on the spire of the school where she'd taken her morning's lessons with a surprising yet misguided sense of duty. Somehow, then, the husk of routine had been a comfort. Lingering rays could just pick out a flapping silver wind sock tied tightly to the school spire—year 5's geography experiment from several terms ago. Abandoned now. Flaccid and forgotten.

Children would soon be returning to their lessons after lunch. Only Fay would not be. After forty minutes of trying to identify mean numbers, her sense of duty to school had dissolved: routine became bitter, worthless ash. And given the circumstances, she wasn't in the mood for P.E.

She did not intend to die in her gym kit.

Go back to where it all began and you'll see baby Fay, her eyes bright as stars: each dilated pupil a refraction of the universe within. Dragged into her first day by doctors, she'd kicked and screamed like a tiny mule. This exceptional newborn had already lingered too long in the womb as if, knowing what lay outside, she craved to stay in a dream.

Her first vision had been of Uncle Mike. At the age of four, Fay laid her pigtailed head down to rest and saw him sitting on the kitchen floor, pink foam tumbling from his mouth like candyfloss. His stare was glassy—immovable. It was a wonderful game and she cheerfully told her parents the next morning all about the dream, and even how he'd tried to distract her from the 'stare out' by blowing bubbles. Uncle Mike was always joking, laughing and playing.

No one spoke of it again. Fay could only vaguely remember her mother's eyes as she took the call about Mike—the heavy burning gaze that accused and was afraid and numb, all at the same time. And that, for one day, all the adults moped and were boring—and Uncle Mike wasn't there.

If the overdose *was* ever mentioned, she was too young to understand.

At the age of seven, Fay dreamed the boy next door had an accident. 'I saw Billy bleeding from his mouth,' she'd told Billy's mum the next day, earnest and furtive as only seven year-olds can be. 'And, there was something wrong with his face. It looked just like a smashed-up mirror.' Billy's mum had said little, withdrawing from the girl as though magnetically repulsed.

This time, Fay remembered the aftermath. There was a tremendous banging on the door that teatime that made the room shudder. It was Billy's mum, with a furious pink face and raving, spinning eyes. Her own mother pushed Fay away protectively, behind the kitchen door.

From there, she'd overheard the argument. Billy had been playing by the bridge with the bigger boys when he'd tripped and fallen six feet onto the concrete below. He'd knocked his front teeth out, needed stitches in his cheek and surgery under his eye. She thought she heard the word 'witch' shouted. Several times. And shortly afterwards, they moved away.

She hadn't seen Billy again.

As she grew, she understood more about the collective madness of adults. She saw them dumb down to fit in. Small talk seemed to taint them like an infection of the brain. The rising price of potatoes was discussed as though it were a matter of life and death. They picked at the weaknesses of their friends and neighbours—as though Frank's cancer made him a failure, or Sally's fat daughter was a personal affront. Nothing seemed sadder than watching them hunched and peering out from behind net curtains when they thought themselves unobserved.

That's how she learned that 'different' was ugly—and dangerous. Yet every adult she met seemed rife with the fear that, one day, they would be uncovered as a fraud... that someone insightful enough might spot the outsider lurking in each and every one, and crucify them for it.

Fay watched the world around her rush into cars every morning, where moments spewed into nothingness; grumbling at a voice on the radio that could not—and did not—reply. She saw them ridicule, pick, persecute and destroy. And, one by one, she began to dream them dead.

Some people Fay could focus on just as sleep came, and see their future roll out to the very end. But only some. And, just as with Billy, it wasn't always death she saw. Nicki, the school bully, she previewed lifted aloft by the large and long-suffering Natasha who, in a fit of unbridled, empowered rage, smashed Nicki's head through the glass of the second floor science lab window, while the teacher, his assistant and several students tried for minutes to release her grip from around the girl's pulsing throat. When Nicki returned from hospital she found herself friendless, never raising a loud word or a sly snicker at anybody's expense again.

Once Fay understood her gift, she tested it. She tried to change the events she foresaw—sometimes with success. Other times, without. She pushed and strained her mind to see further and more clearly into the future, but sometimes her visions hit a brick wall. It seemed there was a place—or rather a time—she couldn't penetrate: a blankness that drew ever nearer. A time that had finally arrived.

'Fay love, could you bring the milk in?' Her mother hadn't even looked up from the briefcase resting on the sofa that she stuffed with papers and folders, as Fay trod blearily downstairs on the last morning ever. She blinked wearily. Sleep seemed within her still, making everything surreal.

Padding out onto the front step, an overwhelming waft of freshness stunned her senses. The front lawn was heavy and wet with dew, as if the earth itself had been weeping in the night. And there hung the blanched sun—inside that terrible grey sky.

Alarmed and distracted, the milk bottle slipped almost instantly from her clammy fingers and smashed on the stone below. Shards of glass tinkled on the steps around her, and the opaque liquid seeped through her socks. Just as, once it had happened, she'd always known it would.

She thought of the nothingness that rode ever-closer, and a world full of missed opportunities and last chances.

'No breakfast for you then!' chided her mother on the doorstep, who'd heard the smash and come marching to the door. Then she saw her daughter's face: a heavy, daunted expression that made something inside her shudder. 'Are you hurt? Watch where you step. In fact—don't move. I'll get the dustpan.' Fay was left surrounded and with nowhere safe to tread.

Fay's mother came back with a newspaper and a dustpan and brush. Methodically, she picked out the big pieces of glass with the tips of her fingers and dropped them in the centre of the newspaper. She scrunched the newspaper up around it and put it in the bin. Then she used the dustpan and brush to sweep the space where glass could have fallen—the shards all but invisible as they hit the back of the dustpan with an icy chime.

'Here,' she said, reaching out. She leaned over from her safe position on the doorstep and tried to lift Fay across the gap. They ended in an outrageous tangle of twisted bodies and laughter against the door frame.

'Mum,' said Fay, when the two had untangled themselves from each other, 'if everything was to just... disappear, and somehow you were left in a kind of endless void, what would you miss?'

'What kind of question is that first thing on a Tuesday morning?'

'What would you miss most?' Fay's mother thought carefully for a moment. She was used to these odd conversations with her daughter. 'I tell you what I wouldn't miss,' she said with conviction, 'and that's the traffic jams. Cold calls from recorded voices that you can't even shout at. And bleeding junk mail, good god, I wouldn't miss all that rubbish!' She caught a flicker of disappointment in Fay's eye and, as she turned to go back inside, said: 'you, of course. You're my special girl.' She paused, and her eyes were slightly misty when she continued. 'Uncle Mike used to say you were too good to be true. He was terrified you'd grow up and lose what he called your 'spark'. Everyone loses it in the end, he always said. Life beats it out of you. Poor Michael.'

'What's this?' asked Fay's dad as he trundled down the stairs.

'Fay wants to know what you'd miss most if everything disappeared.'

'Nothing, because I would've disappeared too.'

'Good answer. But I meant if everything *except* you disappeared.' corrected Fay. Almost immediately he replied: 'Well that wouldn't happen, would it? No one would know any better if everything ceased to exist—as long as you believe the human consciousness can't survive death, which I do. *If* that's what we're talking about. If some disaster wiped out existence as we *know* it—society, the way we interact, for example—well that's another question altogether. Things don't just disappear, love. Where's the newspaper?'

'If you lost everything—you mean like going bankrupt?' Her older brother was standing in front of the mirror in his sharp pin-striped suit, slapping on aftershave so pungent it could knock out small creatures within a five mile radius and would announce his arrival in the office a good seven minutes before he even got there. Fay was convinced he surreptitiously used fake tan, but could never find the evidence.

'You'll never know, small fry.' he said, straightening his tie, 'You won't make enough dough to lose.'

'I don't care.'

'And that's exactly why. Me, I'm on to a winner with this job. I get my commission today, and then whoop, whoop! I'm going to put a deposit down on that slick new beemer Gary's got in the garage. You just wait and see. Tomorrow, you won't even recognise me in that sweet ride.' John carried on preening before he spotted Fay, still standing in his doorway. 'What do you want, freak?' he asked nonchalantly. 'I'll never understand what you think is important, John. But if that's the thing that'll make you happy, that you want above all things, then you should go for it—today.'

'That's not what I want most. I want to cop a feel of Josie's —' Fay slammed the door. 'Twat!' she called down the hall. 'Psycho!' came her brother's distant reply.

Fay enjoyed the hot shower that morning: needles of water pummelling and massaging her muscles; stimulating her scalp; filling her lungs with fragrant steam. Minutes passed, and she curled up on the floor beneath the full weight of the falling water as though trying to wash every last thought from her mind.

As she left the house she gave both her parents a long hug—pulling away at the first sign of them stiffening with concern. She smiled broadly and openly to pacify them, and left. She didn't dare say anything sentimental or unusual that might raise their suspicion, even though she wanted to. The thought of them anxious on this final day was more than she could bear.

Instead of marching briskly to school with her eyes fixed on the pavement, she strolled, slowly. These moments alone were best: where she could truly savour time alone. Alone, especially.

'Sit still and shut up!' hollered Miss Tripe, Form 8JT's Tutor. 'How do you expect to become good, honest, independent members of society when you can't even obey orders? And take off that hoodie, Brett. It makes you look like a filthy criminal.'

'An item of clothing makes him a criminal, does it?' Piped up a small yet cutting voice. Something in the tone was dangerous. It was Fay. 'Well excuse me. All the youths and hooligans in this area are wearing them. Don't you watch the news, little Miss Attitude?' The classroom hummed with the challenge. 'Why do you listen to the news when all it does is tell you what idiotic new thing to be frightened of?' Fay countered. She'd taken a whole six months of Miss Tripe's crap, and today of all days she was not willing to take any more.

'Why? Let me tell you something Fay Smith. You don't come to school to learn *why*. You come to school to learn how to be an upstanding member of the community.' The bell rang, and children began warily to stand up. 'Nobody move—I haven't told anyone they can leave! You come to school, Fay,' Miss Tripe chided, 'to do as you're told.'

'To fit in?' Fay snapped. Her best friend Angela caught onto her arm as though it would make the words stop. 'Exactly. And with your attitude I have serious doubts about *your* future. Well, what are you all waiting for? Get out!'

As the hushed children bottle-necked at the door, Fay lunged in for a final go. Miss Tripe shrivelled from her as though afraid she might be stabbed. 'Miss Tripe, if everything in the world was to disappear and you were left with nothing— absolutely nothing—what one thing would you miss above all else?'

'You, of course.' Miss Tripe snarled back in sarcasm. 'How could I ever do without *you*.'

'Well at least that's one less thing you'll have to worry about.' Before she could respond, Fay had turned her back, and was gone.

'What did you mean with Miss Tripe?' asked Angela as they settled down in their seats for Geography. 'Are you going to bunk off?'

'No. I don't know what I meant. I'm just sick of her rubbish.' The girls laughed. 'What would you miss, Angela? If there was nothing left?'

'I'd miss Philip. I'd be gutted if everything ended and I'd never even asked him out. And I'd miss ogling Mr Warner!' Amanda nodded towards the Geography teacher in his stripy knitted vest and tight-fitting grey trousers. 'I think you should ask Philip out. Today,' said Fay. 'Seriously, you should do it today. And I think you should go up there right now and... and grab Mr Warner's arse!' They exploded into giggles.

Angela talked about boys, and about herself, until Geography was over. Fay wondered in dismay what the point was. Everyone around her was engrossed in their own shallow, fickle thoughts. The clever ones who filled their heads with facts and figures had their own special, overcrowded form of vacuous ness. And the 'popular' kids had blandness down to a finely crafted art.

Before she left Geography, as the room was near empty, Fay collared Mr Warner and asked him the question. Mr Warner shifted in immense discomfort as he always did under the gaze of girls. 'Er,' he said finally, 'I'd miss... the way that tectonic plates and, er, volcanoes –'

'Sir.'

'Yes, Fay?'

'It doesn't have to be Geography-related Sir. I mean, you can pick anything. Your family? Your job? Your wife?' She prompted encouragingly, but Mr Warner was blank and a little sad-looking. Then he brightened, and with complete conviction, said: 'My electric tin opener.'

'Your what?'

'I hate those fiddly manual things. And I have to cook for myself. With this, all you do is pop it onto the magnet at the top, press the button and away you go. My mother bought if for me.' He smiled proudly. Fay thought a while. 'Well, I'm pleased you like it so much. Maybe you should call your mother and thank her.'

'My mother died. Now, er, can I go please Fay? I'll be late for my next class.'

'Fine,' she sighed. 'Off you go.'

'Reading.' The voice came from the end of the corridor, and Fay wasn't surprised when she turned to see her English teacher striding towards her. 'It doesn't have to be English-related Sir. How did you... ?'

'Ah, the joys of the Staff room. And I know it doesn't have to be English-related.' Mr Baker had a fine grey moustache and blue eyes that twinkled. 'If you were to read one book a week for the rest of your life—70 years let's say—that's still only...well I'm no mathematician, but it's barely one set of shelves out of a whole library's worth. Don't you think that's sad?'

'Um. Yes?'

'Think of all those unique voices you'll never hear, telling stories you'll never be a part of. Everyone has a right to be heard, after all. So to sum up,' he explained, 'I'd say it's not about what I'd lose. It's about what I'd never have. Knowledge, experiences and so on. And the person I'll never become without them.' Fay didn't know what to say. 'See you in my lesson tomorrow, little Fay.' He said, turning with a light bounce and a skip down the corridor. 'Thanks, Sir. See you tomorrow.' She said, softly.

It was during Maths that she finally broke. All the weight of time pressed down on her and condensed into solid mass in that tiny stuffy room. The scratching of pencils and compasses, the seconds filing out into space like row upon row of dominoes set at unbearably equal distances.

She had a final resting place in mind as she tore through the streets, the school lunch bell pealing behind her. There it was: her hill with all its tangled trees and hidden drops, wild creatures and wild flowers, glowing in the sunshine.

The enormity of it all and her small part in it was finally clear. After all, if she were to explain what she knew, who would listen? And what could they do? What was there, even, to tell? Her dad was right. There'd be nothing left when the time came. And perhaps that was no bad thing.

A dark mass of muscle and fur writhed into view and she nearly tripped over in shock, stopping herself from falling with a lurch. The three-legged fox looked up for a few seconds, blinking, before it hobbled expertly across her path and disappeared behind a fence. It had been entirely black but for the white wisps on the tips of its ears and tail: the strange, pulsing black creature with the pointed flashes of white fire—the dog from hell.

Now she'd stopped, she looked around and found herself beside a church. And, deciding it might be fitting to pay a visit on the day of the apocalypse, snuck inside guiltily—feeling like a heathen. The church was completely empty: echoing bricks, marble and mortar. When she came back out she was accosted by a tramp.

'Do you know what time it is, love?' He had a gold-plated wristwatch with a smashed face in his hand, which he studied, shook and listened to intently. 'It's, er, a quarter to one.' Fay replied. 'Not that, not that. Don't you know who I am?' he snapped, 'I'm Lloyd. I'm God's representative. Now what time is it, love?' Lloyd reeked of whiskey and stale dirty clothes. He was obviously a complete crackpot. Fay warmed to him instantly. 'If you're God's representative,' she tested, 'shouldn't you already know the time?'

'Ah,' said Lloyd. 'I *do* know the time. I just wanted to see if *you* did.'

'Right.' Nodded Fay. 'Well time's running out, Lloyd. And I'd better get going.'

'Oh, if you have to, love, but I wish you wouldn't go.' Fay was already making her way down the alley, but stopped and turned back for a second. 'Lloyd, if the whole world was to disappear leaving only you—what would you miss most?' Lloyd looked confused and slightly insulted. 'Are you insane?' he asked, and Fay couldn't help but laugh. 'Whiskey.' Announced Lloyd, and then his eyes grew sad. 'And Jezebel. My sweet little cat, Jezebel.'

'Where is Jezebel?'

'Long dead, love, long dead. Are you mad?' Sensing the conversation was going nowhere, Fay backed away again, waving goodbye. Calling out behind her, she could hear Lloyd growing ever fainter: 'Do you know where my whiskey's gone, love? If you find it, can you bring it back? And if you see Jezebel, you give her a good old fuss from me. You do it. You do it, damn you! Don't you know who I am?'

The sky was now a deep, glowing red that poured down over the town, lapped at the hillside, and flowed over her body like a warm red sea, gently lulling her in the cooling grass. The final heat from the sun was like the warmth from the last embers of a fire. She imagined it, out there in space, flaring and smouldering, and wondered what would become of it in less than an hour. Would the blackness come from its core or from some plotting, outer force?

With a crown of flowers in her long hair, she danced barefoot and joyfully in circles, thinking of the newborns in cot after cot, row upon row, in hospital after hospital. She thought of the shortness of their lives, and was unmoved. So much suffering, altogether, all at once, was incomprehensible.

And yet people suffered everywhere, she knew, every day. Society itself is built on it. People are tortured and murdered for nothing more than a plot of land or an inconvenient philosophy. Animals are reared and culled in misery like so many sheaves of corn. The earth itself groans with waste and disease. But it'll all be over soon. There will be peace, at last.

She danced madly—whirling with the freedom of living without a future. Free to be herself, right now, for the first time. Tomorrow's shackles were broken. The past was already dead. Torn petals cascaded from her hair in soft spinning circles.

And suddenly she realised it was this new feeling she would miss most.

As for the end, there was no telling how it would happen. No instructions, like those that come with flat packed DIY shelves or bottles of hair dye. No signposts to look out for or health risk warnings. No recommended daily allowances. Only the abstract images from a dream; images that came from god knows where, and went the same way. Would it even happen at all?

And then, just like that, the sky clouded.

A light, cool misty rain that she had not foreseen began to fall. No, she definitely had not seen this. Something was different—something had changed. Was the vision broken? Droplets of moisture drifted onto her hot skin and clung there, cooling and quenching her hungry pores.

She felt almost feverish, as though suddenly torn from a vivid hallucination. Her stomach turned over, and she realised life would continue regardless—on and on, endlessly and tirelessly, limping ever-onwards like a lame and dirty flea-ridden beast. And for her, it was time to go home.

In a trancelike state, she tied her shoes back on. They felt claggy and uncomfortable. And with a final look at the drizzling clouds, she made her way down the hill: a normal girl with normal dreams, and a normal day tomorrow.

As her path began to peter out she realised it was not the way she'd climbed earlier. This way was overgrown. Other feet had not dented the long damp grass that flopped and slithered like slippery pond weeds, nor the tightly-wound vines that scrambled across the ground. As she clambered on regardless, she was barely aware the rain had stopped—hardly even noticed the red light warming her back as the clouds parted.

All was in a state of flux. The earth under her feet gave way and she fell, plummeting down into the loosely covered hole that had been concealed by vines. Fay fell away from the red sun, that she now noticed had emerged—too late. All around, black earth and rocks crumbled, turned and dropped away. On hearing the crashing, creaking rumbling, roosting ravens flew out in alarm, momentarily obliterating the sun with their dark flapping wings, which seemed in those moments as though its red flame were snuffed out completely.

And then there was stillness. Peace. As the life drained out of her, a gentle spattering of soil and flowers drifted down gently to rest on the body below. Fay was all alone, with no one to bear witness to the end of her world—but for the sad, setting sun, and the eternal earth that bore her.

Weakly, at the bottom of the pit into which she'd fallen, Fay smiled. Now she knew the truth, she felt so tired. So weary of the world. And perhaps it was in those final moments of life that she looked up eagerly into the eyes of Death, and took his cold bony fingers firmly in her own.

The Lake

S. J. Davies

The lake felt the dislodge of water as her body tumbled in hard with a splash that smacked over the edges. What the lake saw, as only lakes can see at night, was the diffusing of darkness as the blood washed away from her head, and the floating of hair across her face.

At first the still lake could not glimpse her expression through the tangle, some of which stuck to her head. It took a while to work free. Some of the torn strands came away and floated out towards the third island. Finally, the hair was carried by a soft current to one side, thanks to the passing feet of a Canada goose.

It was an agonising sight and she was damaged. The lake looked away from the smudged black eyeliner that now made a parody of her face. Both her eyes were closed over with swelling. She had swallowed two of her teeth with the twenty-second blow.

The light caught on something near her hands. She wore silver rings, but only on her left side and several on one painted finger. A chain hung down straight like a plumb line, caught up in the middle of her bra, having broken in the fight. A telltale welt mark was swelling around her neck.

Hidden fish moved just beneath the lake's surface skin. The lake looked and watched as the mallards moved around her, not certain of this unfamiliar hulk. If the woman had still been living she would have been fascinated by the sprat-like perch that swam underneath her dangling limbs. The smallest ones had been put there by the coarse-fisherman just a few weeks before. The moon came out again, and the fish avoided the woman's shadow, recognising only a predator's shape.

The lake looked upwards, from the bottom of its basin. In the intervals between clouds, it admired the paleness of her skin under the moonlight, particularly the parts that were naked. Her thighs appeared very large from below, and her stomach, which was the only part of her that had hardly changed. The most frightening thing was when the blood stopped and all the ink coming out of her was gone. She just floated in the quietness, suspended in space.

So it did the only thing a lake could do, having already absorbed her blood into its ebb. It held her there and gently supported her head, as her mother would have done the first time she had put her in the bath. It kept her in its secret womb that night, and used its arts of concealment to keep her safe. It bounced the high screech of owl and bat off its surface to keep prying eyes away. Vibrations from the black well carried the slightest stirrings for almost a mile. Humans will never know just how much darkness and cold even a shallow lake can hold, for the night keeps people out with their fear of themselves.

What the neighbourhood didn't know was that the trees would tell each other secrets. The ill-spaced row of 'pavement' trees was the eyes and ears of the street, ascending to the off-licence at the top of the hill. The last tree was on the busy junction, opposite the main entrance to the park, the bravest being in the neighbourhood. There he stood, his roots heaving out of the pavement, as if he was the one in control, breaking out of the boxed urban environment of prescribed angled surfaces. And with his underground root system he would listen and take it all in.

This tree would stand early in the morning, drawing up gallons of water every day, breathing in air and letting out gases. More than five thousand cars would pass by his territory in the morning rush hour, as they hurtled down, barely stopping for the pedestrians, at the bottom of Victoria Park. And it was this very tree that would pass its secrets across the road to the distinct corridor of London planes inside the entrance on the other side. The planes would pass them back.

'Something's starting,' the tree had announced thirty years before.

'I heard the men taking the gates off their hinges.' The pavement trees quivered with disapproval. Later, they noticed the water fountain had been broken up and taken away. Then days later the bravest tree delivered the worst news of all.

'They've come with their machines,' he said, 'the yellow ones that dig from the bottom with teeth.'

'What are they doing?' asked the pavement trees.

'The planes don't know what they're looking for,' the bravest tree replied, 'but they've come to hurt our roots.'

And so the underpass was gouged underneath the park, where the rear gate had been. Within a year it was completed and the women soon followed.

The pavement trees would get to know the girls who stood, sometimes in twos, on opposite corners, but usually alone. They saw the girl who shivered in the cold of a winter's night, before swaggering in her leather boots towards approaching headlights. They watched another pulling her parka around her after an hour's wait. The trees understood the lone girls and their nocturnal comings and goings.

By nightfall the householders were usually tucked up under blankets or in front of their televisions behind lighted curtains, cooking dinners with boyfriends over a glass of wine. Some lay awake contemplating their futures, whilst the other women stood on corners in the early hours, waiting.

Five hours before the woman's body went into the lake, the last pair of adolescents were slinking home to their parents through the park. They steered round the lakeside, hoodies pulled forward, as dark tunnels started opening up beneath the trees. The bats were performing a figure of eight swooping at dusk, as if being swung on a string like a weighted stone. Their crazed flutter came closer than the hooded teenagers knew, skimming dark against a duck egg sky, vanishing against a silhouette of tree. The water started cooling and soon the people-noises faded altogether and gave way to the sound of motorway traffic hurtling through the dark.

About that time the humans started their own flurry. The pavement trees had the best vantage-point of the cars with the blacked out windows coming up the hill, from the rougher approach to the neighbourhood. The sign between traffic islands read 'Police warning', in an authoritative blue rectangle, 'kerb crawlers will be arrested'. Sometimes a lone man was visible in the driving seat, but it was hard to see post dusk. The route was always the same. They would drive up and turn around at the mini-roundabout half a mile beyond the park gate and drive back down the hill again several times before they disappeared. You could know these cars from the way they cruised at a 'certain speed', unlike the newly licensed testosterones whose thumping cars pulled away from the cash point with intent.

The householders passed fix-driven women on their way to the bus stop by mid-afternoon. They knew them by the usual corners on which they stood, their clothes, and sometimes their gestures: the woman who pulsated against a folded umbrella spiked down on the pavement, like a cabaret show without the rain; the most regular day time girl who lolloped along in jeans stretched by an ample rear that moved lazily from side to side. She flicked her hair from the underside over her shoulder, glancing behind her towards the approaching traffic. The show of brown curls stood out from her pockmarked face. Her pale skin could have been in its late twenties, or thirties, it was hard to tell. Women steered their boyfriends around these women as they loitered along pavements. They didn't stare, unless it was to look backwards with furtive glances from the bus shelter, or to peer unseen from a moving bus or car window.

The women in the dark appeared more vulnerable, perhaps because some of them were younger—surprisingly good looking women, with beautiful eyes. The householders would walk past them to the corner shop to buy wine for waiting girlfriends, milk for children's breakfasts. They couldn't help but catch a fleeting glance. These women said nothing and did nothing, blinkered to the pavements, seeing only the road ahead. There was no 'hello' of recognition; there was just recognition of the silent kind.

Women of the neighbourhood occasionally saw the signs of nocturnal happenings on their doorsteps; the telltale separation of figures in the shadows as they squeezed their cars down the back entrance to the road late at night; a condom, full of yellowing liquid in the morning light, dangling artistically from a bramble by the garages. No one wanted to move it, so it perished there for weeks. Only the pear tree saw how it got there, keeping watch all night between branches of fruit, their lovely shape hanging there, bottom heavy, as if about to drop.

The biggest irritation was the cars. It never paid to hang about.

'So you're coming to the dinner. Shall I pick you up outside your house?' the well-meaning work colleague would say to a woman in the flats.

'That's not such a good idea. I'll wait outside the shop.'

They sometimes wondered whether the men could tell women apart at all. When going out for milk or bread after dark, it always paid to wear your tracksuit bottoms and hold your shopping in full view. The police took little notice of what went on along the kerbs or down the back alleys for that matter. During the night, and, indeed, most of the day, the trees were more observant than the police.

Two hours before the woman's body went into the lake, the leaves smelt perfume coming down the back steps through their pores. The trees heard the sound of heels which followed.

'Alright Tam?'

'Yeah, alright. You alright?'

'Yer, was out last night, and the night before. Paid 'im that money today.'

'Yeah? Anyone much about?'

'Young lad, quiet, just 'got out.' Don't think he'll be back again. 'aven't seen 'weird' Jim this week either, but I saw John.'

'John?'

'Yeah you know, brown hair, beer gut, about 40; car smells of lavender. Blue Audi isn't it?'

'Yeah, that's right. John is it? He told me it was Dave!'

The women laughed.

Tam touched the other's shoulder and went down the road.

∞

One hour before the woman's body went into the lake, the trees saw the car slow down and the automatic window moving. Tam leaned through the window.

'You lost and in need of direction?'

'Maybe.'

'It might cost you. Want me to get in?' she said, trying the handle.

'And what if I don't?'

The pavement trees watched as the woman got into the car. Her bare arm pulled the car door shut, just beginning to goose-pimple with the autumn nip. She turned towards him

'Then it could be your loss,' she said, 'but, then again, unless you find out, you'll never know.'

∞

The bravest of the pavement trees had a lower trunk made bald in patches from where small children had swung past him on their way home from school. One of his row was normally stained in patches where graffiti artists tested out spray paint on the way to some wall and admired their jumping red against a muted barky surface. The trees were often pasted up with fly posters, though sometimes taped or crucified with tacks instead. The bravest tree watched her go, but there was nothing he could do to stop her.

'What's your name?' she said to break the silence.

'I'm Jean,' she continued, looking at his clean shaven chin.

'Bet you are,' he said. 'I wasn't born yesterday.'

'You certainly weren't,' she said with a cheeky smile.

'But I've had older.'

The woman looked at her hands in her lap, remembering the pages she'd turned with one hand that night, fanning her wet nails on the other. 'Don't say 'the wolf', Mummy,' her child had said. 'It scares me. I want you to say 'that thing with the sharp teeth' instead.'

The tree saw where they were heading and did the only thing it knew to do. It whispered secrets over into the walled park. With a flutter of leaves it sent them over the corner entrance with its wrought iron gates, which were rarely free of their padlock and chain.

Inside the park, two large avenues of ashes, horse chestnuts and London planes followed the road at right angles on either side of the main gate. But the bravest tree sent its message down the middle, along the taller row of shivver trees that ran diagonally, across the middle of the park, towards the hidden lake.

∞

He braked sharp at the roundabout.

'Mind your driving,' she said. 'I don't want to go flying by the seat of my pants!'

He pulled over and turned off the engine.

'See that tree?' said the man who had just given her thirty-five pounds. His grip pinched the bruise on her inner thigh. She knew where he was nodding.

'Get out and wait up there' he said.

'Give me three minutes,' said his stale breath.

He winked at her as she closed the car door. She looked back and saw him talking to someone on his phone.

She walked around the pile of ice shards glistening on the ground from the smashed phone box and up the path. She waited in the shadows, leaning backwards against the high-ridged bark.

'Beware the oak it draws a stroke' said the chalk rhyme in a child's hand at the base of the tree.

'Beware the ash it courts a flash'; the writing spiralled around the tarmac.

'Creep under the thorn it will keep you from harm', the circle joined back round to the 'B'. But there was never a thorn when you needed one. It wasn't the dark that bothered her.

The avenue of shorter trees had been warned he was coming. This one was unusually quiet and he didn't laugh. They watched as he bent her backwards, like a branch giving in the wind as he bit her neck.

'Something tells me you've been here before,' she said.

He steered her towards the black oak at the crest of the hill.

'What are you, the late night fisherman?' she said, trying to turn him back.

'No one can see us up here,' she said.

They reached the water long after the tree shadows had inked into lake and the darting bats had stilled. He tripped on a tree root as he pulled her arm. The only light on the bottle sheen surface was two silver streaks that followed in the moorhen's wake. The mallards, beaks tucked into their tails, sleeping, launched from the edge as they approached. The woman watched the shape of a tree on the far side of the lake, like a drunk falling, as she pulled up her skirt. She saw the man through this monochrome world and caught a sneer on his face. She recognised a wolf when she saw one.

∞

The willow tree saw a face like it had never seen before. The man gone completely white, his skin the texture of clammy white clay. He curled his lip, like a dog baring its black under-lip to expose a sharp row of bottom teeth. He dropped his head, covering the base of his throat and growled.

The lake heard a slap then shouting and then a skull-crack like a cricket ball resounding on a bat then a screaming. The cracks went on until they were taken over by a noise like a wounded animal beyond recovery. The trees saw her as she held her hands over her head and her knees bent. She became like a gnarled oak in winter, with sawn off limbs. He struck her again.

It was her feet that kept getting caught in the brambles as he dragged her. A branch flicked grit in his eyes and mouth. His spit landed on some blackberries as he paused. It was the first time her head had rested upon his stomach. A tie-dye shaped stain spread outwards from the middle of his shirt. He backed through the undergrowth in the dark, snapping the branch of a hawthorn on the way. The thorn kept its word, though the harm was already done. It made sure to rip a few strands of his hair on the way through, scratching his bare skin with its thorns. She had been dead almost a minute by the time he dropped her in.

And this is how it began, that she arrived with a splash louder that any bird. The man watched whilst she was consumed into black glass, like a dream. He wiped his hands on her skirt and threw it in behind her. The motorway traffic was suddenly louder, as if it might come into the park right towards him. He heard a helicopter hovering above, as if it knew his crime. He waited until it passed over. The lake watched him disappear.

What he hadn't reckoned on was that a lake not only hears but also sees. The watchful lid had seen more than thirty-five thousand night skies, never closing. It saw him this night as he walked away, pulling twigs out of his trousers and buckling his belt.

The lake decided to keep her, for it was entranced by the feeling of human warmth, like a steady patch of sunlight on its surface at the highest point in the midday sun. The lake was fascinated by her smell. Her perfume, though slightly masked by the smell of lake-mud and the iron of fresh blood, was still strong. The lake found her intoxicating.

In more than thirty-five thousand night times she was the first woman who had ever spent a night in these waters. It was as if they belonged together. The lake would keep her like a windfall dropped down.

It savoured the intimacy of the next hour, holding a proper human being, as if taking her back into the womb. It let its water wash gently her every part, as if to make her whole again and distance her from the battle-gore. It examined even the finest hair on her arms. It wanted the woman as the lady of its lake and dreamed it could mend her.

The lake trusted itself. For it could be sure to treasure her more than the world from which she had fallen. It would hide her under its watery skin, away from prying eyes. It would hide her indignity as she floated, mostly stripped, like a young branch, bark ripped down, with its sap leaking. The lake would give her translucent robes that would never cause the discomfort of an itchy label or straining zip, robes that had the power to split light into rainbows during daytime, and the ability to transport her into a bottomless night time world in the dark. The lake was confident it could protect her. Inside its waters, she was away from the badgers' teeth that might puncture cold flesh in the early hours of the morning, away from hungry foxes and the raven's beak.

What the lake could not have known was that, aged five, Tam had been fascinated by fish in the dentist's waiting room. She'd squashed a stubby fingertip against the glass, touching their bright blues and oranges in safety. Tonight her fingers hung down, brushed only by the barbels of a muddied carp in search of food. This one had been caught and thrown back more times than the lake cared to remember. Not that it was small, but just that there were some that got thrown back so many times their lips were missing. For only game fish were ever eaten. The coarse old carp moved on and felt along the bottom in its usual place.

An hour later it was no good, for her trace of warmth had cooled to nothing and a blueness had appeared. The changes had started in her fingertips that went into waxy furrows, like something waiting to be scraped off. Each confirmed that the woman was merely mortal, she would not survive it, this world of extremes. As sure as daybreak, she would swell up like one of those pieces of bread thrown to the ducks if the lake were to keep her. The lake waited until blackness turned back once again into midnight blue.

∞

It was hard giving her up to the indignity of the day. A standoff between Canada geese broke out on the lake surface. The aggressor honked his 'horn' like a football hooligan, churning the waters with his big black feet. A fish wife screech of gull broke in. Its cry gave way to the comic gabbling of duck.

It was a fisherman that found her in the early hours of the morning the following day. Or rather, it was the lake that found him. It was shortly after he cast his rod that he saw some hair, floating. The water hid her until the drama that came. The lake could hear the sirens across the park over the motorway traffic that morning. The white-faced fisherman was taken to one side as plastic ribbon went up on poles. More than an hour passed before she was pulled, almost as naked as his bait, from the water.

Two police officers stood to the left of the main gates, blocking the side entrance.

'The Park is closed. Please use the pavement and go round Sir,' they said.

From this angle, the avenue of trees stood tall in their prime. They took their indignity well, towering over the jailed bunker of a toilet-block which was also often locked, though it still made people hold breath until they had gone past.

Two hours later forensics combed and probed the lakeside bushes. The hawthorn cheerfully presented some skin peelings and snatchings of male hair. The body was bagged and sent to the Home Office pathologist for a different kind of probing.

From these moments onwards, tenants in badly converted Victorian flats cared less about their neighbour's strewn rubbish tempting the rats. The post office keeper, so vocal on the discovery of human faeces in his alleyway the week before, was strangely silenced.

The park reopened. Blackberry pickers no longer bothered eating mush with large pips that got stuck between your teeth. The fruit had been spoiled by Satan's breath. Fishermen were absent from the lakeside. Some said the fish would abandon water where blood lost in anger had been shed, though the coarse fisherman knew they'd stocked it well this season. For others, the white belly of a floundering fish didn't look the same. Few could quite rest easy pulling a fish from a watery grave, even if they weren't going to eat it. Besides, the idea of 'hooking' an unusual catch haunted several who would never admit it. Those that did come out preferred to retrace the riverside path, settling further up stream on the sunny banks of the disused canal.

People would stare out of the top window of the number 34 and 35 bus as it pulled in at the bottom of the park. Not that they could see the lake from the bus stop, but the powers of imagination would draw their gaze along the avenue of ashes to what lay behind the frieze of trees beyond.

Weekenders watched the snake-edge of the water basin and for a few seconds imagined a woman floating in the dark before survival clicked the mind back to something else and their legs kept walking. Mothers and fathers chose their words carefully, holding the hands of small children around pushchairs whilst feeding the ducks. For a collective amnesia was sometimes necessary. The grey lake-eye looked back.

He was an outsider the newspapers said when they caught him. The neighbours, now certain that the motorway traffic had taken residence in the bowels of Victoria Park, were unnerved. You never knew what that road might 'blow in' next.

Women lost their short cut from work, and kept to the pavement at dusk instead. The women that belonged to the dark stood shivering at the street corner, knicker-lines showing through their shabby white dresses. They knew there would be no breadcrumbs to lead them out of the woods or park as they waited, with cold blotchy skin, craving their next fix. They knew you could never predict the swing of the woodman's axe. Some of them were too beyond it to even care.

The lake knew that passers-by looked at her with recrimination. She was no longer the Victorian boating pond of escorted ladies with parasol-shaded faces. Gone was the rosy image of white-clad women, holding their hats against the breeze. Gone was the idea of gentlemen supporting a gloved hand into a wooden boat, the wearer careful to keep her skirts beneath the knee. But the lake had no regrets.

Two years later, the story became shortened as a more cautionary warning for newcomers and students. 'A woman once was killed in the park . . . don't go in there after dusk.' People nodded slightly and didn't ask questions. The phrase covered a multitude of before and afters, but the message was still the same.

Late one night, a woman was dragged screaming by her hair into the boarded up alleyway and beaten. Then the neighbours talked.

'I forget what they call it . . . what do you call it, their 'manager' or something?'

'You mean pimp?' the younger one replied.

'Yeah that's the one,' the older continued.

'Dragged her into the alleyway by her hair he was, slashing at her face . . . hair in clumps on the floor it was and she was covered in blood, screaming,' the younger nodded, knowingly.

'And I gave him a look,' said the older.

'I thought 'you mucky so and so',' she said, with toothless determination.

The wisest women would say, 'The faces change, but the stories always remain the same.'

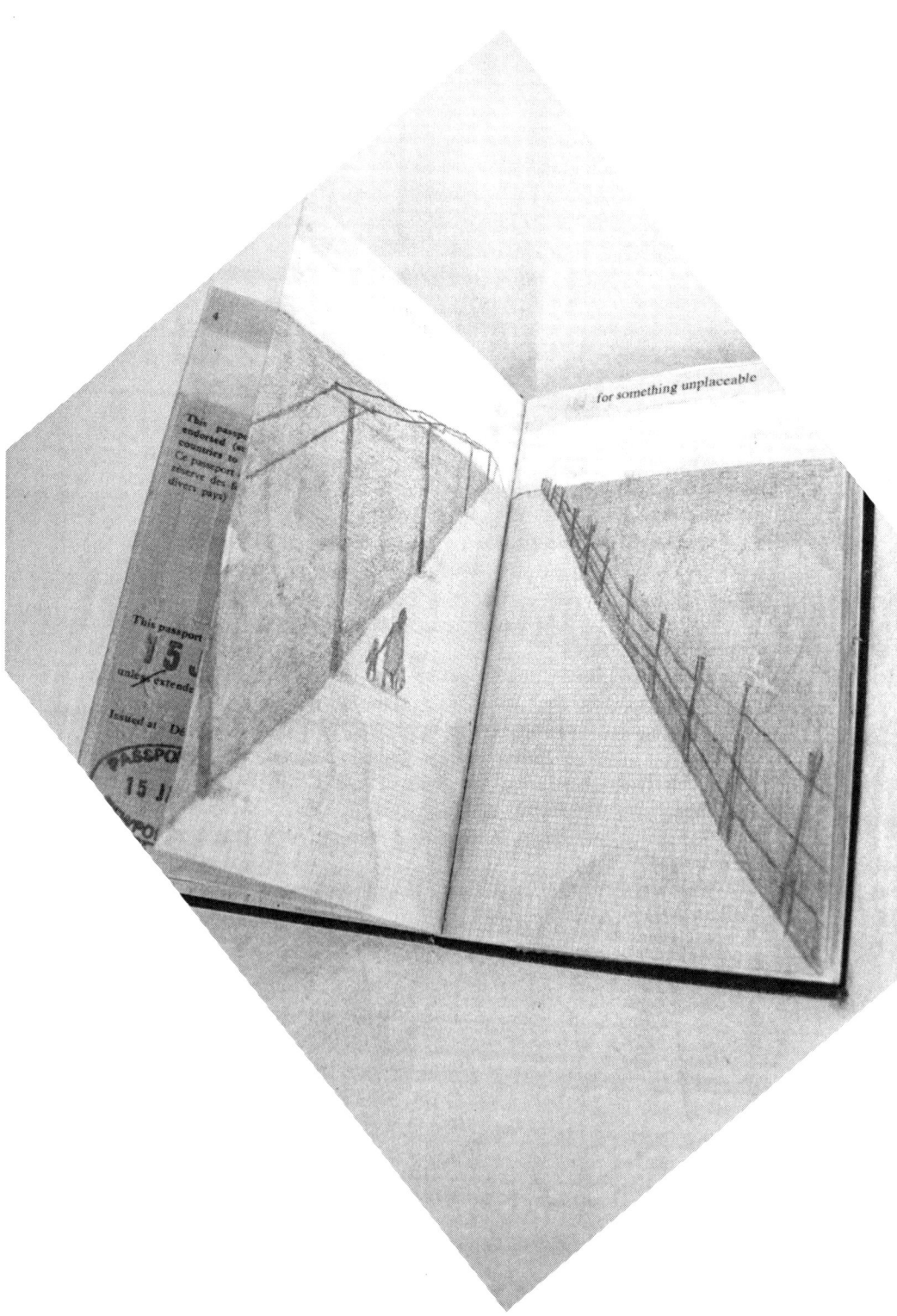

for something unplaceable

88 Hamburg Road

Tamsin K. Walker

I figured whoever it was must be dead, or at least unconscious because it was too cold to be lying on the ground just for the hell of it. I continued forwards calling an ambulance in my mind as I went, and I was just about to explain that I had found a dead body when it sat up. It wasn't just a body after that, but a she. A damned old she.

My imagination hung up the telephone and I looked at her. She might not have been dead, but she didn't look like she had much longer to go. Her skin was brown with darker brown blotches on it, and it was wild with wrinkles. I thought it was going to slide right off her face.

She looked at me looking at her down there on the snow, and she spat at me. No reason, she just spat. It didn't hit me, but it didn't charm me either, so I turned to keep walking.

'Come back.'

Her words slapped the back of my head so hard they unsteadied me. I upped my pace and I didn't turn back until I felt far enough away to look without her noticing. Only I misjudged the distance, and when I turned, I saw her beckoning to me. My common sense told me to ignore her, but she was too sorry a sight for that. My Ma taught me to be good to people. 'Do unto others as you would have them do unto you', that's what she always says. So I walked back to where she sat flashing more of her bony legs than anyone but an undertaker should rightly have to see.

'Can I help you?' I asked her.

She muttered something to herself and then stared up at me. 'What do you think?'

I thought she was past her best, been alive too long. My grandpa went like that. He tried to make shepherd's pie with earth from the garden. Ma found four cooked worms in her best pan. It made her cry as hard as it made me laugh. Not this old bird though, she didn't even make me smile.

She reached a hand up towards me so I took it and helped her to her feet. Standing, she barely came up to my shoulder, and I'm not a tall man. She poked a sinewy arm through mine and steered me clean away from where I wanted to be heading.

'I ought to be going the other way.'

Her eyes rolled up to meet my resistance. They were washed out looking and if they hadn't been so bloodshot, there'd have been no colour to them at all.

'You offered your help to me.'

She was a long way from home, I could tell that from her accent. I wondered where she was from, what she was thinking and what she wanted from me. I studied her boots, tramping the snow next to mine, for signs of lunacy, and adjusted the size of my steps to fit hers. We were an unlikely couple all right, and I wished she would suggest we parted company. But she didn't.

'They cut off our hair and turned it into blankets.'

It came out of nowhere and flattened any hope for her sanity.

'They made us into lampshades.'

I nodded because I didn't see what else I could do.

'And soap. They made us into soap!'

I looked at her when she said that. She was staring straight ahead, shaking her head so the loose skin under her neck flapped like a cockerel's wattle.

'Where are you going to?'

She stopped and looked right at me, tearing her eyes so wide open that I could feel mine narrowing in response. For one so small, she sure knew how to make a man feel odd inside.

'Number 88 Hamburg Road.'

I'd never heard of Hamburg Road and I knew our town pretty well. I wasn't even sure it existed, but I didn't think it made much sense to challenge her. I decided to walk her to the end of the street we were on, it seemed like the right thing to do, and then go home to wash. I had my first date with Mary B. that night, and it was one I'd waited a long time to call my own. A lot was resting on that date, I wanted it to be the one our grandchildren asked us about in years to come.

'Is that where you live?'

Her answer was a disgusted hissing sound, made with such conviction that it propelled a drop of her saliva onto my face. It burned a hole into my skin and I longed to wipe it away, but as long as she continued to stare at me, my hand hung limp at my side.

'How far to Hamburg Road?' I asked her in an effort to move us on.

She made a sound foreign to my ears.

'Ordinarily I'd gladly walk there with you,' I told her, trying to sound a little like I meant it, 'but I'm meeting a young lady tonight and I'm not keen to be late.'

'Then I shall go alone.'

As she spoke she pulled her arm clear of mine and without so much as one glance back in my direction, she hobbled off up the street. I was glad to have my arm back and wipe her trace from my cheek, but the sight of her skinny ankles on the ice turned my insides upside down. I don't know why, it just did.

She was moving so slow that I'd caught up with her in a matter of seconds.

'Oh, what the heck,' I told her. 'I don't have to be home 'til six.'

She didn't say anything, just laced her arm back through mine and continued walking.

'What's your name?'

'I don't have a name.'

'But everyone has a name.'

She lifted her arm free of her coat sleeve to reveal six smudged blue numbers etched into her shrunken skin. She held them up towards my face as if they were somehow relevant and I looked without wanting to. They stirred something in me, a memory I couldn't quite remember.

'It's cold out today. We should be indoors with a nice cup of tea.'

She made her hissing sound again and I felt myself flinch in anticipation of her spit.

'I don't want tea.'

I didn't want tea either. At least, not with her.

'I'm not afraid of them.'

'Who?'

'The people who meet at 88 Hamburg Road.'

I wasn't following her. Except I was, physically, that is.

'Who meets there?'

She didn't reply, just kept shuffling along the pavement, me at her side, the only sounds those around us. The cars, the crunching of the snow beneath our feet, and her sucking sharply at the freezing air. I was trying to think of a gentle way to say goodbye when she stopped in her tracks, dragging me to a halt with her and began waving a craggy finger in my face.

'H is the eighth letter in the alphabet, which means 88 is HH.'

She sure could talk fast, faster than my brain could make sense of what she was saying.

'Heil Hitler. Hansestadt Hamburg.'

She might have been mad, but I that didn't mean I wanted her to think I was stupid, so I made out like I knew what she was talking about. And fair enough, I did know what Heil Hitler meant and I knew Hamburg was a city in Germany too. I just didn't see the connection.

A tug at my arm told me we were moving on again.

'They made us grow their food, but we were not allowed to touch it. Can you imagine that? Being made to tend to food when you are starving, but not being allowed to touch a single bean?'

I couldn't imagine that and nor was I convinced that she could. I shook my head, because it seemed like the right thing to do. After a few more steps, she stopped us again.

'Someone has to teach them. To teach them before it is too late again.'

I didn't know who she was talking about, and with time closing in on me, I was only half-listening. It was 6:01 exactly and I needed to get ready for my date with Mary.

'You're quite right,' I told her, thinking agreement the best policy.

We started walking again, her pushing me along with the strength of her personality.

'In the fourth book of the Old Testament…'

I didn't want her to talk about religion—that wasn't my thing. The closest I'd ever got to God was at Sunday school, but I hadn't been much of a pupil there either.

'…is the Nazirite vow…'

I wasn't much of a one for reading. I thought I could do more useful things with my hands than hold books in them, so I'd never heard of the fourth book of the Old Testament and I'd never heard of a Nazirite.

'…which binds Jews to the Lord with a vow not to drink wine or alcohol, not to cut their hair and not to come into contact with corpses and graves.'

It was getting hard to listen because every step we took was one further from my date with Mary. I faked a cough to get my hand to my mouth, my watch to my eye. It was 6:08 and past my cue to leave. But when I looked at the old woman with no name, there was a storm brewing along the lines on her face, and I was caught up in it. Her eyes were roaming about in their loose sockets.

'Don't you see?'

I didn't see anything but time ticking against me and my future. My face must have betrayed that. She moved in close enough for me to smell the age on her breath.

'It was not enough that they tortured and murdered millions of us, that they used our bodies in the most unthinkable ways. They went even further, they borrowed a piece of the Nazirite name, and wearing it they cut off our hair and made us throw our kin and kith into mass graves. Don't you see... they desecrated our vows.'

When she finished speaking, she gave me a fierce little nod and once again, walked on without me. This time though, she did turn back, and by then my forgotten memory, once borrowed from a school book, had come back to me.

'That is why I have to go to 88 Hamburg Road,' she said.

I looked at my watch again. It was 6:21. Then I fell back into step beside her. I had understood. I would help her find 88 Hamburg Road, and if Mary really was to be my wife, she would understand too.

The Nazirite vow is described in Numbers 6:1— 21.

Lonely Planet.com

Matt Morrison

Welcome!

To the Lonely Planet
.com
Offering you
The wonder of travel
Where dreams come true

We're uploading your details
It won't take a moment
So strap yourself in
Make yourself comfy
For your FREE TRIAL

Loss

The adventure starts here

Paris, Tokyo, New York
London! No competition, right? Greatest city on earth
And the year?
Twentieth century, twenty-first, tell us when to stop...
2009 (sure thing—right where it all got interesting)
And the biggie, the 'who?'
Could be anyone
(from our drop-down menu)
Hot-shot lawyer
Musician, filmstar
Plain, old-fashioned tourist

Congratulations!
Our most popular choice
So just
Pop on your glasses
Slip on the sensors
We're ready to go
To take a walk down the river
In London, 2009. One click to start
And you're walking over a bridge from the biggest damn church
you've ever seen

St Paul's Cathedral, rebuilt
After one hell of a blaze
Survived the Blitz (click the link to see more)
And there on your right
You see that wheel?
Spinning, just too slowly to see
(It's moving though
We've got it moving
Just you wait—
Because)
That's where we're heading

You're on the move

Walking, over the bridge. And feeling it

Wobble
Under your feet
Don't be alarmed. That comes as standard, that kind of detail
(Truth is, they might've had it fixed by then
Had a little time to sort it out
But what the heck, we've thrown it in anyway
A little extra, on us)

And you know something else you can feel?
It's always wet in London, right?
Come on! You knew that already
Always grey. Always raining
Well that's what you're feeling
Raindrops
That's what they felt like
That's bonafide
London
Atmosphere

On with the show

On your left, in 2009
Everyone's favourite
The world, The Globe
Shakespeare's theatre
(S'why a lotta people come
But we know you know
It's not the real thing
Real thing burnt down
It's all just a fake
Doesn't mean it's not beautiful,
Right?)

Straight ahead
You don't need me to point that out
You can't have missed that chimney
A hundred meters in the sky
Some kind of factory, gotta be?
You're imagining the hum
Some mighty engine, but wait

Loss

Hold your horses
Because inside, it's full to the brim
—You're gonna love this—
Of paintings, art
Surreal!
You could have seen a giant spider
If you'd gone a little further back
Wouldn't that have been something?
(But we're sure you'll want to visit again)

Press on for now
Keep that wheel in your sights
(OK, We'll be honest
We'll 'fess up
We've brought it all just a little bit closer
Straightened up the river, just ever so slightly
Admit it though
It's one hell of a view)

This giving you an appetite?
Only asking
Because you're passing quite a selection
Of high-class joints
Pizza, pasta, smoothies, sushi
(So visit our on-line catalogue,
And pop a couple of pills next time around)

No time now though
To think about your stomach
We've got a lot more to show you
Things you're not expecting
Just take a look down
That's it. On your right
Over the wall, no
Your eyes don't deceive you. It's a beach!
Right there in the centre of the city
And there's people making sculptures
Out of sand
They're at it everyday
Because whatever was there the day before

Has washed away

Let's not get sentimental
Nothing lasts forever
It's the way things are

Ha! Try telling that to those kids over there
On the ramps
Their skateboards. Kids all think they're immortal
'Specially kids like these, with
Personality
Stories
Take the short one, standing by the side
He's watching. Learning tips. Learning the moves
Has a tough time at school
But he's safe here. He's found his groove
Amidst the concrete
Against the graffiti
They never cleaned off
(Interested? We've got the whole backstory
You can watch it
In 15 webisodes
'The Way They Lived then'
He's number 704)

Daydreaming?
We're not surprised
The place'll do it to you. Difficult to be bored
When you're walking in London. But if you need inspiration
Just pick up a book. They're bookstalls you're passing
Hardbacks, paperbacks
Get lost
In your imagination
It's all make-believe down this end of town

Or if your prefer
The Royal National Theatre
The B F I—catch a film
(There was never much on
Back in the day

But pop in now, you can see what you like
Just check out our on-line store
A million titles, and growing by the day)

See that crowd, standing about?

—Did I mention the crowds?
We're not kidding
2009, and people are like ants
It's like a plague
We have to warn you about that
There's people all over
But it's nothing to be scared of
Stop one, check one out

This crowd I'm talking about
Standing, watching others just
Standing
Covered in gold, silver, like statues
Throw 'em a coin
And they'll move
Money makes the world go round
Back here in 2009
They've had a little shock for sure
But they're still hoping
No need to get melancholy
Throw 'em a coin and you'll bring them back to life

And why not glance across the water? Floating there
Like a castle
That's the Houses of Parliament
The seat of power
You wanna go in?
I'm not talking about…
We don't mean…
That's not thanks to us
That's democracy
That's what I'm talking about

You fancy it, you can walk right in

Ask for your MP
Though they'll probably be out
Dining on the public purse
(Don't know what I'm talking about?
Look it up, click the link
It's all there. Archived)

And what do you know!
You're at the wheel
All this talking
All the hard-sell
And you're there
You've made it
Though your time's nearly up

Time up
On your FREE TRIAL
But we believe in value for money
In London
Version 2.0
So we'll let you have a ride
A quick spin
Used to take a while
—We've quickened it up a bit
We'll take you straight to the top
Give you one last look
Back towards that bridge
That cathedral (biggest damn church you've ever seen)
And while you're at it
Take a look at those cranes
Are they building the city?
Are they pulling it down?

There's those theatres
There's that chimney
Hanging all that art
Everyone thought it'd last forever
There's those sculptures made of sand
People who made them
They knew a little better

Loss

Ain't that right?
Ain't that the truth?

No need for you to worry about that!
Safe from all that out here

And at the click of a button
You can always go back

(Our rates are the cheapest you'll find)

At the click of a button

(All major credit cards accepted)

Click and relive it
In perfect detail
Rewind and replay

See everything
Just exactly

How it was.

The Girl Who Set the Fields Alight

Øystein Ulsberg Brager

My daughter, the country girl, was standing in the open doorway leading to the porch. She was wearing her red summer dress and she had a strange smile upon her lips, a smile that even I, her father, couldn't recall having seen before.

She spoke to me, and doing so her voice reminded me that she was still just a child. She was barely fourteen. Still, her voice did sound more childish than it had sounded for a long time. 'I set the fields alight,' she said. 'I set the fields alight.'

Why is she saying that, I thought. What a remarkable thing to say, 'I set the fields alight.' My head was drowsy from the heat, and now this phrase had got stuck in my mind, 'I set the fields alight.' As if I didn't have enough going on in my head, with the drought and all. 'I set the fields alight, I set the fields alight.' It was like a tune, repeatedly played at the back of my brain. I looked at my daughter and smiled quizzically. What did she want? She just stood there. 'I set the fields alight.' I looked up and past my daughter towards where the yellow cornfields used to be. The sky was red and black smoke was rising not far away. A cow ran madly past the window. She set the fields alight, I thought. The sky is red and there is smoke, and... Oh help me God. Oh God, help us all. She set the fields alight.

I ran out, but stopped quite fast, realizing that it was too late. Looking at the black square mile and the one in flames behind it, I knew there was nothing I could do. I had to get the cattle back into the barn. Oh bugger. No barn.

Later that evening, my daughter and I were eating ice cream on the remains of the porch. 'Why did you do it, darling?' I asked. 'Why on earth did you set on fire everything we had?'

But when she kissed my cheek for an answer, I knew that further pondering over this remarkable event would be futile.

There was no answer for me. But our freezer was still intact, so I helped us both to another generous scoop of ice cream.

The Last Puppeteer

Fiona Thackeray

Zé da Viola was disconsolate. Unemployed and disconsolate. He'd became unemployed at the word of the plantation foreman some hours ago, the man's thick-lined face carefully washed of sympathy—of any feeling at all. It was a simple message, a factual communication that needed to be conveyed in a business-like manner. Tears and emotional displays were, after all, a waste of liquid and energy in these drought-ruined parts. There had been work—yesterday and for years before—and now there was none.

The tall cane watched Zé as he walked among the furrows where he had cut and planted and hoed for so many seasons. The sugarcane whispered to him, 'Why are you still here?' In the distance he heard the trucks and the other cutters at work and he knew he was no longer one of them. It seemed strange, this dismissal out of the blue, but he knew better than to ask questions. His hands, shined and cracked like shoe leather, were not needed for cutting here. He did not belong to this field, to this earth, fat and silvered with sugar roots.

The old mare watched Zé returning to his shack on the plantation margins. She sensed, with her twitching tail and ears, some change—he was not ordinarily home at this hour. He looked around at his possessions. They were few: a chipped table, his radio and guitar, a couple of pans, enamelled plates and cups, a shirt or two, and on the wall a football pennant and São Judas, patron saint of lost causes. His hammock, bedding, the fridge that needed painting: he'd never felt the lack of more furniture, fancy shoes or gadgets. These things had always been enough, while he worked. A man who had work had his riches in the fibres of his own arms. He could buy rice, beans, a little cane liquor for the end of the day—he didn't need a lot more. If a man had work.

He stepped out for a moment to look down on the plantation, his fingers untying knots in the mare's mane. The acres where he had cut cane for years stretched to the horizon, the processing plant the only landmark, its striped stack topped with a twist of pale, sticky smoke. The workers moved like tiny beetles on the red roads between fields, although mostly they were hidden inside the sea of silver, waving cane. From his pocket, Zé took the few dampened notes given by the foreman. He spread them on the bed, pinning his gaze on them as if trying to discern his future among their watermarks and famous faces.

When he woke it was already dawn. Sun combed pink waves through the canefields: time to go cutting, for everyone except Zé. He sat, resting his face in his hands. Ants made a column along the door jamb and the mare stamped the ground, hungry. The mare's impatience, the ants' industry, provoked a shudder— a sudden rush of urgency—the need to find work; the knowledge it wouldn't be easy, nothing else but cane-cutting that he knew how to do. Out of nowhere, a fleeting memory came to him. Standing, slowly, he reached to the shelf above the bed, lifting down a wooden box. Inside, laid head to toe, piled one upon the other, were a cast of puppets, a little the worse for wear, but their painted eyes still vivid, their names and characters alive in his mind.

The puppets were musty-smelling, moulting, their clothes worn into brittle folds by the years spent entombed in layers. Underneath them, lay the posts and chintz curtains that made the theatre booth. A spider, flattened inside the lid, had died waiting for the next show. The familiar characters lifted in turn from the box rekindled Zé's best memories of his father. The old man had been rough-tempered; often drunk, spoke crudely to Zé's mother and was too worn out with work to have much to do with the kids. But now and then he took down the *Mamulengo* theatre box and played for Zé and the other kids and locals, and he was transformed. Gruff, distant father into proud puppet-master: animated, knowledgeable, admired, in control of his puppets and their destinies, in charge of happy endings.

Afterwards, he'd show Zé how to carve a new head, to mend a hand with a tiny shaving of wood, to manipulate the rods that made puppets dance, drink and fight. 'Pay attention, José', he always said, 'there's not many know how to work these puppets anymore.'

Little Zé watched and learned from his father and wanted to be him. Watching the show, hearing his father sing and play guitar, he was lost in a world where good won out, women were beautiful and beloved and men were brave; a place where the lowly worker won his victory against greedy planters and the rain came when people wished hard enough and crops grew strong.

Leading his horse between the whispering fields, Zé didn't look back. The mare was loaded with bedding and shirts, his radio and his Saint Judas. Tied level across her rump was the puppet box, wrapped in a sheet.

∞

Novo Mundo bore the signs of being another squalid little knot of liquor and grain stores serving local ranches: road-signs were leprous with bullet holes—the handiwork of ranch-hands on their way home, made brave and belligerent with cane brandy. Zé crossed the municipal boundary at noon, expecting to leave the place behind him in a quarter mile. But he rode another hour before the centre. Neat houses strung along the roadside with laundry pegged out and dogs minding the yard. The town square, when he finally reached it, was a kaleidoscope of busy market stalls, bound by a town hall, several shops, bars and barbeque joints and a church. The square extended across the main street—a large sandy expanse shaded by *jatobá* trees, a scattering of benches. The theatre would fit well there, with room for plenty of spectators.

In a bar off the main drag, Zé ordered cane brandy, the first of many, and tried not to think about how he'd pay. He began playing his guitar and passed the hours like that, drinking, singing, playing and drinking. The talk in the place was of the drought, farmers packing up and heading south, and of the latest corruption scandal centring on Magro, the catering magnate, supplier to schools and hospitals across Brazil of hot meals served in foil dishes. Magro was accused of mixing in animal slops. 'They're calling this Magro joker 'The Marmitex King,'' said the bartender wafting his hand over the newspaper. 'Even street dogs turn their noses up at his Marmitex meals. Let's see how long before he bribes his way out of trouble'. The politicians promised the earth before the elections. And now? Where were they now? The barman shook his head, waltzing between the tables with beer mats.

Before the sun fully set, and before Zé was quite incoherent, a guy with a beard showed up, carrying a drum. Eyeing Zé suspiciously, he sat by the door. Zé set down his guitar and nodded, hoping he'd play. The drum remained untouched. Another drink downed, Zé's impatience piqued and his inhibitions loosened, he strode over and asked the drummer to strike up some rhythms. Rangel was his name. He turned slowly to Zé and motioned at the guitar abandoned on the bar. It turned out they both knew the usual tunes, some folk songs, the familiar samba anthems. They played together a while, then Zé let the drummer play while he observed—watching to see if his hands were agile enough. He was a little serious, didn't show much sense of humour, but he played well enough. Rangel signed up as accompanist for the first show.

Zé watered the horse and sat in the shade working on his puppets. Rangel came and they rehearsed out by the railway. They took turns between manipulating the puppet rods and playing music. Rangel listened to the plot, a simple tale of Zé's own invention, the cane-cutter thrusting various puppets towards him as each character stepped into the limelight. João, poor but hard-working ranch-hand, Marilene his sweetheart; Damião, ranch foreman, full of lust for Marilene and ill-will towards João. The drummer worked out some riffs to cinch people's ribs with tension, a pounding, hostile signature for the villain, Damião and for the finale, a *frevo,* defiantly joyous, though Rangel remained pokerfaced. Zé felt himself a little clumsy in working the puppets, but figured he could distract from awkward moments with his strong voice, speaking the fears and secret hopes of characters as if from their very hearts of wood, just as his father did. He gave the minor roles to Rangel, hoping his quick drummer's hands could turn from drum skin to puppet rods in a second, and that his sense of rhythm would twist and jiggle characters into life on cue. Zé put up signs around town, written on scraps of cardboard, advertising the *'ESPETÁCULO'* to come that night.

In timid groups, people walked by, shooting curious glances towards the wooden frame draped with coloured curtains under the *jatobá* trees. The puppeteers nodded and beckoned, playing soft melodies, but no one sat. Around the bars they went with drum and guitar. A modest band of men—far from sober, and a few couples, followed them back to the puppet booth. A few more folk just coming out of church were swept up in the crowd. A very old man, all bent over, remarked, 'Mamulengo puppets! Haven't seen those since I was a babe in arms.' Eventually, with an audience of 19 and two dogs, the show began.

Spurred by hunger and nerves, Zé played a frenetic opening *maracatú,* Rangel struggled to keep up. The first scene opened well, João's bold entrance won applause, and Damião unequivocal hissing. The spectators shouted to warn João as traps were set for him and yelled as Damião plotted to send him away, leaving Marilene alone, vulnerable to the foreman's whim.

Zé made the most of the audience's drink-fuelled bawdiness and had his characters feign deafness now and then to provoke louder shouts. They hissed as the foreman told unflattering lies about João to Marilene. Rangel's nervous farm-boy made the crowd laugh, serenading Marilene to seduce her for Damião, and being mistaken in the dark for her beloved João. The prim falsetto Zé affected for Marilene's lines was hard to sustain. When it broke down into a croak here and there, the magic was lost, the crowd resorted to giggles. Delays between setting down the guitar and picking up the puppet rods slackened the pace of the story. Sweating, Zé threw all his energies into building towards the final showdown between João and lustful Damião, and the night air was taut like a guitar string. As João struggled against his exploitative boss, Zé felt he had the crowd in the palm of his hand.

Rangel's heavy, hypnotic beat built tension as João tried in desperation to defeat the foreman, but Zé could see now that they were not carrying the crowd with them. He peered through the chintz curtains at the spectators, sunken-cheeked and blank-eyed; scrawny, desiccated people, like strips of sun-jerked beef. They seemed barely alive, sitting askew in their seats, as if the vigour to sit upright had been drained out of them, evaporated by drought. Their humour and energy had been stolen by years without rain and trampled by an endless carnival of corrupt politicians. Shiny promises and free tee-shirts in election season were dependably followed in the spring by raids on the municipal coffers, leaving hospitals without medication, schools without books, dams and reservoirs still unfinished.

Rocking the rods back and forth, Zé brought João to his feet resurrected by Marilene's singing. Lunging towards the audience, the foreman made one last effort to relieve himself of his rival, but João's strength was immense now, spurred on by Marilene's loyalty. Damião knocked to the floor, the happy couple danced a great ruckus. Rangel drummed frantically and Zé reached down to pick out a few chords on his guitar, laid on the ground, all the while spinning the lovers in a wild jig.

But the audience had seen so many stories like this—good guy fights bad guy and gets the girl. They had seen the same plot danced through the streets in festivals in so many different ways, with inventive costumes and music. Zé's version, played straight

along the old lines, was routine as rice and beans. No surprises
or twists. Whether they foresaw the ending and were bored, or
just didn't believe in it, they were not roused by the frenetic,
happy dancing, no matter how hard Rangel drummed and Zé
stomped his foot, spun the dancing lovers and put his heart into
the song. A frail applause followed the closing curtain and five
of the nineteen drifted away before the collection hat had begun
its round. The hat, hastily returned to the front as benches
emptied, contained: two beer bottle tops, a button, a crumpled
prayer to Saint Expedito and thirty centavos.

The puppeteers didn't say much to each other. Zé was
disappointed in himself, thought he'd be more of a natural, 'It's
a lot to manage: puppets, voices and music...' he said, mostly to
himself. He was a little envious of the laughs Rangel got for his
nervous farm-boy.

'Yup.' Rangel shrugged in agreement.' They'd have to do
better if they were going to earn enough to get by.

The two ordered workmen's dinners in a bar. The takings
were not quite enough to get roaring drunk. They ate in silence.
Three old men by the door were arguing over the People's
Gazette headlines. The Marmitex scandal continued and the
three were in disagreement about the source of the rancid food.
A breeze got up, dredging red dust across the square outside. A
violet haze filled the doorway as sun set on Novo Mundo.

The barman switched on the television for the game; the
place filled up. Two women in tight jeans and brash make-up
patiently nursed long drinks, waiting for slow moments in the
football when men's attention came around to them again. A
new arrival during the first half caught the women's attention.
Tall and fair, he pulled up a stool to the bar, heaving a bulky
lacquered case from his shoulder to the floor and began doing
card tricks. Zé thought the case must contain an accordion. At
half time a small crowd gathered. The tricks grew more
elaborate. The audience shook their heads, bewildered by the
cards' impossible migrations and the treachery of their own eyes.
Surrounded by new friends, the tall guy ordered a beer as the
second half began. Motioning towards the instrument case, Zé
asked, 'D'you play?'

After the game, the trickster switched cards for accordion
and played. He was decent: the charisma that drew people to

him in the bar could revive the *mamulengo* shows. Rangel said nothing. The accordionist said he was a builder, but work had dried up lately—like the rain. Drought got people thinking of leaving rather than building. Zé's terms were stark: no payment unless he livened up the audiences and boosted takings. It was good enough for a jobless builder.

The card sharp said his name was Dorival; a tiny flinch of his eye—not quite a wink—left Zé wondering if really this was his name, and if not, what he was hiding. But there was no time to worry about that.

For the next show, Zé had been thinking of 'Captain' Lampião and Maria Bonita, the sweetheart bandits in half-moon hats. He thought they might strike a chord with the dried up, disappointed people of the backlands, people with their long history of being cheated and trampled on. The bandits, so he told the two musicians, were the underdogs who bit back, the poor people's champions—standing up against lawless Sugar Colonels and the corrupt National Guard. He could make the outlaws from his father's old puppets. All he needed to add were half-moon hats and Lampião's trademark spectacles, looped from a scrap of wire. Pedra Rosa, the next town on the road to the interior, was bigger than Novo Mundo, according to local opinion, and closer to the heartland of the original bandit saga. 'If we play there, we might find descendents of Lampião himself.' said Zé, 'Who knows, they may pay well for our tribute to the memory of their outlaw cousin...' Rangel shrugged, losing faith, perhaps. Dorival pursed his lips thoughtfully and swung the accordion on his back.

On the road, they heard the plan for the show. The accordionist's thick countryside accent was not helped by the lisp that whistled when his tongue pressed air over the empty gum between his canines. Zé kept the speaking parts for himself and Rangel, though the drummer had become all but mute—roughly since Dorival arrived. Dust rose in sheets from the parched fields along the roadside, coating men and horses in a dull terracotta. Soon the three looked like the clay figurines bought by tourists on their way north to Amazonas.

The city boundary was marked by an ancient cashew that had retained most of its leaves even in these dried up times. They dismounted and tied up the horses. Rangel went ahead to find a good spot for the show. Dorival sat on an upturned oil can and picked out some syncopated sequences to fit with Lampião's gun battles; some light, nimble chase themes for bandits fleeing to mountain hide-outs. Nodding approval, Zé listened, his hands at work bending new wire spectacles over the ears of the bandit Lampião. They made him look menacing, perhaps because they lent an air of intellect turned towards brutal ends. Next, he pulled Lampião's companion from the puppet chest. Dorival said nothing, but his eyes slid towards the cashew roots beneath his boots.

'Here's the *bandida*—not bad for a girl squashed inside a box for years, eh?' Zé's upbeat tone was unconvincing. The accordionist made a non-committal grunt, his fingers slowing on the keys. 'What's the problem?' Zé shook the puppet as if the indignation was hers.

'It's just...' He shrugged awkwardly under the straps of the instrument. 'Maria Bonita...she's not so *bonita*.' And he put the accordion down and went over into the scrub to pee.

The puppet's face was scratched. Her eyes were lopsided, her red-painted lips had suffered a large chip, giving her the unfortunate appearance of a backlands girl with half her teeth missing. The cruellest effect of Maria's years in mothballs was hair loss. The few tufts that remained were brittle and dull, sprouting at stubborn angles from her wooden scalp. Even in Zé's affectionate gaze, she was a fright. Toothless and balding— it was not how people imagined the daring heroine they nicknamed Bonita.

In silence, Zé stood and set off on the road to town. Dorival squeezed a melancholy tune, watching him shrink against the reddening horizon. At the door of a gabled house, Zé took off his hat, waiting. The woman who greeted him had her afro hair bound in coloured cloth. Greying flashes at her temples disappeared under the turban. Her lips were full, painted deep red. Inside, girls were lounging on sofas or leaning against a counter between bottles of *cashaça*, a telephone, a vase of plastic roses. They poured him drinks, chatting. One sat in his lap; another fooled around wearing his hat. But the one he wanted was at the counter, her back to him, glorious black hair shimmering down to her waist. She was a little sullen, but when they were alone in the room and she unzipped her dress, he thought of nothing else but the ample curves of her buttocks and he filled his hands with warm, firm flesh. Her eyes, black too, watched him, almost curious and she smiled when he looked at her, though more to hide her curiosity than from pleasure, he thought. Afterwards, pulling on his dusty clothes, he hesitated to open his wallet. She watched him, her face hardening.

'Your hair is beautiful.' She moved over and kneaded his shoulders in an impatient rhythm. 'Would you....can I have a lock, as a keepsake?' He turned to face her, her expression impervious, save for a slight crease appearing briefly between her eyebrows. She left the room. Zé waited, wondering if the woman with the turban would come to shout at him. The door opened. The girl returned with scissors. Turning her back, she lifted the curtain of hair leaving a few strands hanging over her neck.

'No more than a finger's-length.' she said. 'I should charge you more for this.'

∞

Maria Bonita's puppet was transformed with her glossy cane-black hair. The company set up the little theatre tent next to a bar Rangel had found. Customers wouldn't have to leave their drinks to come and watch, and, loosened up by alcohol and the convivial atmosphere, may part more easily with their coins. Dorival warmed up the crowd with popular melodies and soon people were requesting tunes. Zé tuned his guitar and lined up the puppets: police, bandits and Sugar Colonels in order. He ran through the storyline and the rhythms with Rangel. They opened to a crowd of over 50. The accordion music made the show somehow bigger, more alive. Lampião got the audience talking, shouting warnings, howling in despair when he was ambushed. Maria Bonita's sassy lines drew whoops of appreciation. The gun battles were electric with unsettling, disjointed wheezes of the accordion and explosive popping sounds from Rangel's mouth that really sounded like bullets whistling through scrubby valleys. But somewhere around half way, both Zé and the audience realised that the story was going to end as it always did, with the bandits' heads on poles and the police victorious. He hadn't worked out a new twist. The audience knew the old story and they were tired of it. The police and the politicians always got away with it in real life—they didn't want it to be the same in theatre shows. As the final scene played out, people had fallen silent, one or two jeered.

The hat filled up with some coins, an egg, a few notes. They would eat well that day, but it wasn't enough to live on and still they hadn't found a story to get through the leathery skins of these shrivelled people, to whisk their blood, nudge their hearts, uncork their tears. In Zé's father's day, the whole street filled with crowds pushing in to see the puppets. People climbed on lamp-posts and roofs to watch; they danced over the cobbles and shouted at the stage. But that was then. Now everyone had TV and nobody cared about old stories of long-dead bandits. Puppet shows were from his grandfather's day—their time was past. There was no escape from sugar cane—he'd fooled himself for a while, but like every other sucker round here, he'd have to go to the plantations in the morning and see who was hiring.

They split the takings and Zé went to drink his share. Some hours later, Rangel slunk into the bar.

'Lampião's no use.' Zé made a swatting gesture. 'Too much like real life. Who wants to see a guy rise up then get killed by police?' He sliced one palm across the other as he spoke of killing. The drummer shook his head, waving to the barman to bring another glass. 'A psychopath. The police, sure, they're rotten to the core, but Lampião went round murdering and raping—no better than them. Nobody round here remembers him anyway.'

Rangel picked at calluses on his drumming hand. 'People like rebels who stand up against the authorities. It's a good show—just needs a better ending.'

Swirling the dregs in his glass, Zé tutted, 'It's like my father said, nobody knows *mamulengo* any more—it's a lost art; dying even in his day. It's not some lone peasant like me going to bring it back to life. I'm good for cutting cane—that's all. Forget it man, go home.'

Rangel spat in the dust. His eyes had a dark glitter, 'You ignorant bastard. This thing can make a living for two, three men if you work at it. You're just too damn stubborn.'

Zé scowled, his bloodshot eyes looking devilish. 'What d'you know? Never set eyes on a puppet theatre before last month, now you're the expert? Drummers like you are glad to run alongside the Carnaval parade with the street dogs.'

Rangel staggered to his feet, swaying, 'Zé da Viola, eh?' he swung at Zé, hitting his cheekbone with a satisfying crack, 'Loser can't string three chords together.'

Reeling in his chair, Zé's hand flew up to his face. He pushed himself up from the table, the shot glass rolling in diminishing arcs, his red eyes slowly levelling on Rangel. He leant back, rounding his arm ready to shut the percussionist up, but the barman grabbed him from behind and shoved both men out into the square.

∞

Morning sun sifted through the broad leaves of the cashew tree, warming Zé's face. Grit pressed against his cheek; he found he could open only one eye: the other was tender and fat like raw mignon. His head throbbed noisily; he decided not to move. Something tickled in the crook of his elbow. A column of ants marched from under the cashew roots, over his arm and towards something shiny: a discarded foil package. Squeezing his eye half-shut to focus better, the print on the cellophane wrapper resolved into a familiar logo: 'Magro Marmitex', the 'M's drawn as little crowns.

Now Zé propped himself up on his elbows, dusting the ants from his skin. There in the foil dish were the remnants of a meal and the beginnings of a story that people cared about: the Marmitex Scandal. It had been happening all year, filling the newspapers and TV screens—the big company with contracts to feed half the hospital patients and schoolkids in the country was using slops not fit for pigs to bulk out their meals. It was the story that outraged housewives chatting at the grocer's, riled the old guys drinking *aguardente*, thumping their fists on the tin tables in bars. It was another story whose ending everyone knew already—the multi-millionaire Marmitex King would go to court, be condemned and sentenced, but would never serve his term. It was always the way. But this was an ending people couldn't accept—the injustice of it rankled, aching in people's bellies, snagging in their throats. Zé could bring Magro to account in his theatre; knock off his crown. People would jump up and hiss and make speeches. He saw how he could create a modern-day Lampião to speak for the people—a hero they could believe in, who would take pot-shots at the corrupt and the rich, at ruthless big business, poke fun at politicians. In the world-in-miniature of the *mamulengo* theatre, at least, they could bring down the villains of the day. Rangel, arrogant fool that he was, had been right on that score: audiences liked rebels. Hearing the cane fields whisper, Zé stood and brushed grit from himself. He mounted his horse and looked around for the musicians. Like the farmers whose hopeful sowings were answered each year with drought, he was going to try again.

The Final Confession of Christopher Close: As Narrated by Himself

Christopher Close

There is, for me, something therapeutic about removing make up. Certainly this is because it allows for what has become known as 'me time'. Half an hour to oneself is a pleasure, no matter what tedious matter one is engaged with. I am sure my more cerebral acquaintances would point to the ritualistic quality of the activity; one does not simply cleanse one's face of paint, but one's soul the burden of the role. Well, I never could stomach all that. The truth is often simple; I have engaged in this 'ritual' throughout my adult life, and it's nice to do something well and without thinking. There is more, though. As the muscles within my fingers recite their lessons, seemingly unbidden, they complete their allotted task with a grace and confidence that is quite alien to the rest of their existence. You see, from an early age I have been plagued by involuntary tremors. Of late, they have become my almost constant companions.

I have come to believe that the temporary cessation I enjoy before the bulb-rimmed mirror of my dressing room is as much to do with the movement, the circling motion necessitated by the removal of powder and grease, as it is the result of a relinquishing of conscious control. For you to understand why will require some acquaintance with my life history, or at least that part of it that relates to my condition. The first time I experienced this most unpleasant of sensations was in the bathroom at my parent's house. I was twelve. I remember running to the toilet from a large lounge that backed onto a garden, looking down at my own legs moving like little toddler legs, it seemed to me. I can't remember if I had even got as far as unbuttoning my trousers, when I felt the shiver in my arm. It didn't travel up or down, or offer any sense of direction. It was, instead, a numb, internal shiver. Initially it was localised, not unlike the feeling one gets from hitting a funny bone, or waking to find one has slept upon a limb, yet with the additional, queasy feeling of vibration. The feeling spread, and when I felt it in the back of ribs, then in my neck, I fell into a feint, and can remember nothing else. Apart, that is, from a terrible desire to escape. And the feeling that there was someone lying very close to me.

I woke in confusion and motion and was immediately sick. I could feel action all about me, and hear voices, at once urgent, controlled and mundane. I looked up and saw my mother sitting close to my stretcher. She was holding my hand. When we arrived at the hospital, I was wheeled straight into a large room, and curtains were pulled around me. A young doctor appeared, prodded me intently, asked some questions, then sat down on the end of a bed next to me and asked some more. These questions seemed to demand less immediate answers. As I tentatively responded that, yes, everything was all right at school, and, yes, at home as well, and no, only a little at Christmas or when out for a meal, I began to feel a sense of panic rising. My jaw grew numb, my fingers started to tremble, and an irresistible desire to run came over me. I asked if I could take a walk, and looked to my mother for help. She told the doctor we would be back in five minutes, if that would be permitted, and went with me to a little enclosed courtyard thick with acacia, where old men in dressing gowns stood looking up at the sky and nurses sat and read, all of them smoking. My mother left me there with a squeeze of the arm, and went back to talk to the doctor. The trembling subsided, yet I knew it would return if I didn't make a move. It was clear to me that the doctor thought there was a reason for my condition, rather than a cause. I knew that to escape from the hospital I had to step into his view of the world, even only for a little while. So I drew a breath of air, walked back inside, sat next my mother, with the doctor looking on, and spoke quietly of my fears.

The psychologist practiced in a village a few miles from us, and I went to see him every month for two years. It may have been his expertise and experience that, for a while, prevented another feint and made the desire for escape nothing more than a subject of conversation, but I prefer to think it was the regularity of my visits. Such was the success of the arrangement that when, at fifteen, the trembling began again, it was as if some mythic figure from the past had broken in on a disbelieving age.

This first new attack occurred at school. I was late coming in from games, having been ordered to pack the corner flags away, due, no doubt, to my lax performance on the field. The other boys were coming out of the shower when I arrived, and by the time I was ready to wash, only a few stragglers remained in the changing room. Even as I walked past them, a towel around my waist, I had an inkling of what was to come; the strange numbness around my mouth, the dead feeling in my arms and fingers. Soon my body began to tremble, and shortly after that I lost consciousness.

Whereas my memories of my first attack are limited to the events surrounding my loss of consciousness, in the second I retained some awareness of my ordeal, not of my surroundings, but of my thoughts. I suppose I was dreaming. All was dark, I knew that. Yet I felt myself to be on a stretch of sand by the sea, cold and desolate, not unlike the squat, open strands of the Norfolk coast. I was curled up on the ground, and as I opened my eyes, and felt the wind on my cheek and my ankles, I saw the sand close to, with the varying colours of the grains clear to me. Every individual bone in my body was rattling in a terrible excitement, making movement difficult. Despite this, I was managing to inch myself along, for I could sense what was behind me, and it terrified me. A little way off, yet with the sense of it having traversed an immense distance to be there, a dark shape was pulling itself forward at the same painfully slow rate as I. It seemed to be made of jelly. I came to on the shower room floor, still shaking and with the certain understanding that something intimately close was grinning at me.

There was, I knew, no point in talking to a doctor. I told the teachers I had slipped in the shower. And all the time I was aware of that grin, mocking me. It didn't stop until I got in the car with my form tutor and headed for home. As he asked me the familiar questions about family and school and my happiness, and as I parroted back the answers, I realised that I couldn't stay where I was, neither at home or school.

Despite my parents concern, I insisted on returning to my education at the earliest opportunity, but as I left home on the second morning after my attack I had another destination in mind; I took the bus to town and began looking for work. Hairdressers, newsagents and restaurants were all too aware of what a fifteen year old boy looked like, even, perhaps, what he desired, and asked for identification whilst explaining the law. By the time I got to the theatre, I had a little story about work experience down pat. The manager of *The Playhouse* took me on without too many questions.

I liked the place, as I have liked all the theatres I have subsequently encountered. They tend to be contradictory places; confident and vulnerable, exciting yet secure. My work consisted of some light scrubbing, brushing and polishing, and very little else. For a week I went home in a beatific state, troubled only by an awareness of the temporary nature of my position. The school, I knew, would soon catch on, and it would only be a matter of days before my front door would open on some very serious looking faces.

It was, then, with some excitement that I found a travelling company, expected half a week later, already arrived. They were performing *Robinson Crusoe*, *Gigi* and *The Country Wife* on a sixteen town tour, had suffered a last minute cancellation, and come to look over the next theatre on their schedule. There were seven of them in all; Dan Schreber, director and leading man, Bella Calvert the leading lady, Vicky Franks and John Defago the juveniles, the characters filled by May Beachem and sweet old Sherry Jennings, with Ed Derby taking care of the comedy. I fell in with Defago pretty quick, and Schreber made it known through him that the company were looking for an apprentice, the last having left at the beginning of the tour to gain what my new friend referred to as 'honest employment'. I never found out if this was true. No one else mentioned an apprentice, although there must have been one, I suppose. Maybe Schreber just liked the look of me, maybe he was already planning to move on up. Whatever the reason, I agreed to help out for the duration, informing my parents of the schools insistence that I gain some work experience and school of my parent's concern for me to briefly experience theatrical life as a way to dissuade me from it.

At the end of the week, when the company packed up and drove to Hastings, I went with them. Schreber had no interest in labour laws, neither in establishing a person's age with any precision. I told my parent's of my decision from a payphone 100 miles from home. It seemed by then I had gone too far to go back.

My leaving home, I understand now, was the cause of a great sadness, one that spread out to touch every aspect of my life. My parents loved me, in their own way, and, as it turned out, my mother died before I had a chance to set things right. I was playing *A Murder is Announced* in Bath when I got the telegram. I was thirty three and had seen her maybe 10 times over the intervening years, although I phoned her every couple of months. It is the cause of infinite regret. My father lasted much longer, thankfully. We never had a great unburdening or anything, but I was with him when he died, and we used to go out for meals together. We talked about family, and the theatre, even illness (although never mine). We never talked about mother. I hope he knew that I wanted to be with him, and it wasn't about duty or recompense or anything of that sort.

At the time of my leaving it wasn't so delicate, of course; belligerence on my part, a kind of bodily sense of insult on theirs. I phoned my mother frequently at the beginning, and my father drove up to see me a couple of times. The subsequent meetings, on stair wells and once across an open door were awkward.

I remained as an apprentice for a few years, and learnt my trade well. By the time we had visited every medium sized town in Britain, Schreber had enough bookings lined up to feel confident enough in taking on a wholly directorial role. This left a vacancy for male lead, which Defago practically leapt into. He never could stand little Vic. I was moved up to Juvenile and some poor waif from Barnstable was hooked up to learn the secrets of stage lighting and driving in the dark. And so it began. By the time I was sixty I had taken on roles vacated by Jennings, Schreber and Derby, and after I had toured as actor manager for a while, I got into television, as you probably know.

The life I had chosen was not without its difficulties, yet, apart from my separation from my family, these were seasonal, as so much is in the profession. For the majority of the year, we tended not to stay more than a week in any town, enough time to build up a little interest, not enough to run out of punters. This suited me down to the ground. By the end of the week I began to get edgy. Sometimes I felt the numbness around my jaw, often I had a strong urge to move on, but little more. The only exception was the winter season. Each year I found myself in Aberystwyth or Morecambe or some such, booked up for three excruciating weeks of Pantomime.

On these occasions, the numbness in my jaw began before I arrived, making its presence felt even as I packed my bags ready for the journey. Within three days, my hands were trembling throughout the day, and within a week I could not sleep for the trembling in my body. All this time, the wish to flee was growing in me. By the end of the second week, the trembling could no longer be described as such. This was a rattling, and a rattling not of the body, but specifically of the bones. By the beginning of the third week I could feel each one of them, individually vibrating. It was then that the dreams began. As before, I found myself on some lonely, grey shoreline, crumpled on the sand with my whole skeleton jumping round inside me with what seemed like joy. Behind me, agonizing in its slowness there crawled ever closer a kind of unstructured bag of skin. I saw it open its mouth, a black, stupid gape, and my bones leapt in me at such a rate that I thought that I would die, and I knew then that I would, and that all would be returned. I always woke up screaming to find myself sprawled on the floor of bedroom, dressing room or wing. I would stop screaming then, but start up another, ghastly little staccato cry as I felt my bones within me still vibrating ever so gently now, and that grin close by.

It would have been easy to leave at moments like that, but I knew few other jobs would allow me to keep in motion for so long. There was haulage, sales and vagrancy, but, truth be told, I would prefer to take my chance with the rattling for three weeks a year than submit myself to them. It wasn't, after all, as if I disliked Pantomime, far from it. Pantomime gave me a sense of purpose. It made me believe that my role was important. I would see children brought in by dismal parents, and know that, without this most traditional of treats, they would never be exposed to anything fun, or ugly, or odd in their entire lives. I think there is more to this than camp posturing on my part. That idea of the British Family as some ruggedly self-contained unit probably existed before our dear Mrs. T, but she certainly did a lot to put it about. What balls it all is. Most parents I meet have been told how to dress. In the theatre we could, for an hour at least, offer something intelligent, something that worked by its own rules, something that you had to think about to get. It wasn't obvious, it wasn't always nice, but it was safe, and the kids walked out like it was Christmas.

So I stayed with the theatre, even in winter, and grew up to be the old queen you know so well. As I say, I was a late bloomer as far as the TV was concerned. Most school kids knew at least one joke with my name as a punch line before I had graced the box. There's nothing wrong with a bit of graft. Even when *Close Friends* was raking in 6 Million, I was still out on the road. Obviously that was to do with my condition as much a more general work ethic, but the point stands.

Two years ago, during the winter season, I was booked in for three weeks at *The Palace*, Southend. Perhaps it was the proximity to the sea that made the desire to escape more pronounced, I don't know, but my hands were shaking wildly even before we entered the theatre. By the end of the first week, I found performing almost impossible. My jaw ached, my bones felt like they were popping, and an intense desire to get in a car and drive far away filled my every waking moment. On the Wednesday of the second week it took an extra hour to prepare myself for the matinee. On stage, I could barely stand. My ribs were trembling to such an extent that breathing was difficult. I was sweating, fluffing my lines, and, in the interval, my hands were so uncontrollable I couldn't lift a cup of tea to my mouth. Back on stage, I became spooked by the audience. I felt they were laughing *at* me. I sensed the ghastly, fixed grin amongst them. Stepping towards the wings, my body convulsed, and I collapsed in a heap of hoops and silk. I tried to raise myself from the floor, but I couldn't get any purchase, as if my hands were pushing into sand. I folded again, and as I did so my whole skeleton began to violently shake. I knew that my pursuer must be close to me, and I was so taken over with fear of it, that I could not bear to open my eyes. And as I lay there, shaking in my self-willed darkness, I felt something slippery trail across my naked foot. Whether limb, or tongue I know not. But I was certain that, after a life time of dogged pursuit, the monstrosity had finally caught up with me. I screamed, and opened my eyes to find myself on stage once more, exposed to the audience. I could feel the ghastly grin so close by me it might have taken a bite out of my cheek. Children were hiding their heads in their mother's breasts, or gazing on, enthralled. I screamed again, and didn't stop until the ambulance hit sixty.

Age has its benefits. No questions about my home life now, or my happiness. A and E referred me to a specialist, and after a round of questions, a physical examination and a scratch and sniff test, I was sent a letter suggesting I make a further appointment to discuss my results. Parkinson's Disease, apparently. I did point out that that I had suffered from bodily tremors since I was twelve, but this was brushed aside. The same symptoms can stem from very different causes. It seemed that I had moved from psychological to organic distress without noticing the join.

I took a year off work. I travelled round Britain, stopping no more than two days in any one place. I went by train. The trembling was with me all the time. I had just about decided never to set foot in a theatre again, when the call came through from *The National*. Something strange happens to any actor who outlives his critics, even a jobbing ham such as I; they become respectable. Some of this respect comes from young directors, who wish, I think, to secure their own place in Theatrical History by working with antiques, make and type irrelevant. The old guard give respect to each other because there are not many of us left. Then there are students, who validate people like me through an irony they do not really understand, and the marketing types who simply equate Saturday night television stars with financial gain. There comes a kind of tipping point, where there is enough good feeling to float the idea of a Pantomime Dame taking on Lear. And so it was that I found myself agreeing to that very role, and a month long residency.

John Defago, of all people, was lined up for Gloucester. We had a good laugh about that. I knew after the first rehearsal it was going to be remarkable. I felt, if you will pardon me, that this is what I was born to play. Maybe it's the part *we* are all born to play if we get that old. It was a release. It felt gigantic. The first night, I was taken up by it, even more than I thought. I was transformed, and the whole theatre was transformed. The press loves an underdog, and old Twankey raising a storm at *The National* fitted the bill. Saying that, there were some beautiful reviews. *The Guardian* ran with 'Love, and be silent', which was nice. The company were concerned about my health, of course. The Parkinson's was public knowledge by then. I had an examination after every performance, which always identified deterioration, but I knew more about what was going on inside me than any outsider ever could; my bones were rattling at an alarming rate, the intimate grin mocking me always, and the dream of the shore came to me during my natural sleep, with the contact between me and my pursuer growing on every occasion. I demanded to be allowed to continue. I came to embrace the rattling, to look for it, to build it up in me throughout the day and then – whoosh – to let it all go, with my blowing winds and drowning steeples, to channel it off in one big kick against the damned thick rotundity of the world.

And so here I am, and here you find me. I am two weeks into my residency. I sit here, before the mirror, marvelling at the control my fingers have as they circle my cheeks, and my eyes, And, yes, as they move along my lips, and that which lies beneath. I am waiting. I do not think it will end on stage, and I would hate to think of being found in a hotel room. Better here.

Loss

And so, as my hands move from my face, and metacarpals and capitates begin their gleeful dance, I listen out for the wet knock upon the door that will herald the return of all that has been so strangely lost.

In the Confidence of the Night

Shared by James Scott

Something was in pursuit of me, although I dared not look behind. The streets were dark and empty, tapering into impossibly narrow alleyways, wreathed in mist and enclosed by high fences. By now there was a dull ache clutching at my side, my legs felt leaden and my mouth parched, yet still this shadow figure kept up the chase, always gaining on me no matter how fast I ran. Finally I reached open countryside. There before me lay a sheltered footpath that seemed to shy away from the moonlight, stealing upwards into deeper woodland. No longer hearing footfalls behind me I picked up pace, disappearing into the pitch black beneath the boughs. In the distance glimmered a hollow clearing, and fixing my eyes directly ahead I fought my way through the foliage. Slowly the clearing drew closer, and closer. By now I was near enough to tell the shadows apart, to distinguish the briar from the overhanging branches, but what was that shape that lay stretched out on the grass, still and waiting? Suddenly the silhouetted figure sat bolt upright. I let out a scream...

∞

A silent scream. I started awake and found myself flailing amongst regulation blankets, the starched white sheets bathed in sweat. Yet nothing was emerging from my throat but a hoarse, stifled croak. For moments I could see only darkness, nothing to identify my surroundings by, neither objects nor people. Disorientated, I gripped hold of the mattress with both hands, as if this act alone could prevent me from drifting off into space.

Where was I? I tried desperately to gather my thoughts, but my mind felt unnaturally sluggish, weighed down by some unseen force.

'Bad dream?' came a voice out of the darkness, somewhere to my left.

I attempted to turn towards the voice, only to be denied by a blunt spasm of pain; I could not move my right arm, it was strung up at an awkward angle above me. Instead, I extended my left arm as far from the bed the possible, hoping to make contact, but found only emptiness. 'Hello?' I whispered tentatively.

'I said, did you have a bad dream?' returned the voice, a drowsy monotone 'Nothing to worry about if you did, we've all had them in here. That's what you get when you're sleeping in a strange bed…'

I was glad just to hear somebody speak. The welcome drone had an immediate calming effect on me, his manner naturally gruff, but hushed in the confidence of the night.

'Old Elvin opposite still has nightmares that he's fighting in the war, his plane going down over France; you should hear the racket he makes! I reckon it's due to all the noise you hear around here at night. I mean, there's always something going on, it takes some getting used to. These wards play tricks with sounds, especially after lights out.'

Of course, the hospital. All the details of my accident came flooding back to me, and then dislocated images of the aftermath; the ambulance to casualty, sprawled sedated on a trolley in the corridor, slipping out of consciousness in the operating theatre.

'Mind you, you won't be in here long' continued the voice from the neighbouring bed, 'I saw them bring you in early evening, when you were dead to the world. Just a broken arm isn't it? They don't usually keep you in long for that. What happened?'

'I was running…and I fell' I replied, after a moment's hesitation. Yes, I decided, that's all he needs to know right now. Already I viewed the accident as a point of catharsis, perhaps even a punishment for my weakness; a warning to pull myself together. In fact, this period of recuperation could prove a blessing in disguise, an opportunity to reflect. And time I certainly had; the injury was more serious than it might appear, my elbow having been fractured in three places, the bones requiring complex surgery to re-set.

'Sorry to hear that son, but like I said I'm sure there's no lasting damage. Anyway, mind if I get some kip? We'll have to be up bright and early tomorrow!'

'Don't worry about me, I'll soon be out like a light. Thank you...?'

'Barry, Barry Jackson. Don't mention it...'

With a heavy sigh and rustle of bedclothes I heard Barry settle back down for the night. However, sleep did not come so easily to me. My neighbour had been right; it was difficult to relax when unaccustomed to the ever present background noise. The muted acoustics of the hospital echoed through the small hours, ebbing and flowing like the artificial light that seeped through the frosted panes onto the ward. Outside in the corridor I would hear subdued voices in discussion, the soft tread of plimsolls on waxed tiles, the heavy trundle of trolleys being wheeled backwards and forwards, a brief squeal of tyres as they turned a far corner. At times I could have sworn I heard babies crying close at hand, when I knew the maternity ward was housed in another wing. Later, I thought I detected faint movements close to my bed; the patter of footsteps, the swish of a curtain. Yet, as I had been warned, this old building played tricks with sound. Nevertheless, the steady breathing of the sleepers within the room gradually became a comfort, as if they were calling me to them. When my eyelids grew heavy, so the hospital seemed to age about me, the strip lights fluttering as if gaslit, the high ceiling, with its shadowed murals, arching in grandeur. The dark, deep folds of the floor length curtains appeared drawn against time.

∞

I was startled awake just a few hours later by the violent sound of these curtains being ripped open. Harsh daylight poured through the tall windows, bathing the entire ward in a celestial glow, fleeting halos gathering around the stacked pillows against which my fellow patients reclined. A senior nurse strode the length of the room, pausing at the foot of each bed to gently wake those who continued to doze, announcing as she departed that breakfast would soon be on its way. Still groggy from the anaesthetic, I painstakingly raised myself up into a sitting position and rubbed the sleep from my eyes. The initial thing that struck me was that all the other patients on the ward were a lot older than I was.

'Morning sunshine, how you feeling this morning?' returned that voice from my left, sounding different than at night, more confident, jovial. 'I see you managed to get a bit of shut-eye then?'

For the first time I could put a face to the voice. Barry reached across the gap separating our beds and shook my free hand. A stocky, good natured man in his late fifties with a thinning, unkempt mop of hair, on first impression he appeared the very embodiment of ruddy good health. It was only as I studied him more closely that I noticed a slight, almost indefinable pallor to his skin. I returned his greeting and apologised once again for disturbing his sleep.

'No problem son, it's good to have some fresh blood on this ward. It's hard to believe I know, but until you arrived I was the youngster on the team! Hope you don't mind being lumbered with all us old fogies! They're a bit strapped for beds around here at the moment so it's pot luck where you end up! It just so happened at the same time you were brought in a bed was freed up on the geriatric ward!'

'What happened to the person here before me?' I responded, already guessing the answer.

'Old Terry passed away, god bless him' sighed Barry, briefly casting down his eyes 'That's the downside of a young 'un like you making friends with the likes of us, you never know whether we'll still be here the next morning! Terry never told us how ill he really was...'

The clatter of a steel trolley interrupted our conversation, the orderly serving breakfast.

∞

After we had eaten, Barry took his daily morning stroll down the corridor (the main purpose of which I soon discovered was to pay a call on his 'favourite' nurse, a young redhead called

Nicola), whilst I slumped back listlessly and tuned in to hospital radio on my headphones. There was nowhere to go when you were in traction, and too much to think about. My landlord had kindly thrown an 'overnight bag' together for me; there was no way for him to know I had finished reading the paperback novel he had included. On returning Barry observed my despondent mood and took it upon himself to entertain me. Sitting on his bed, he talked me through a guided tour of the ward, which housed eight patients in all. Against the wall and the windows that backed on to the corridor were three beds, numbered one to three, with mine closest to the door and designated number one. Facing us along the opposite wall, with their backs to the tall windows and the world outside, were beds four to six, whilst numbers seven and eight were situated at the top of the ward to my right. Taking pride of place at the foot of the ward was a widescreen television, left permanently switched on during daylight hours, but with the volume so low that nobody paid much attention to particular programmes. As Barry identified my fellow patients by names and ailments, a few of them responded with greetings or gestures, but most appeared preoccupied, or were already nodding off to sleep again. The names I managed to put to faces were 'Old Elvin' the war veteran, 'Poor Reg' (who had prostate trouble like Barry and was feared to be at death's door) and an octogenarian nicknamed 'Ash' who was suffering from lung cancer but insisted on keeping his cigarette breaks, a habit he had picked up during the war ('I might as well enjoy the few pleasures I've got left' he would reprimand anyone who criticized). Then there was the patient in bed four, at furthest remove from me, who nobody seemed to know very much about. Although resident on the ward for some weeks, this nameless inmate had declined to interact with the other patients, often concealed from view by screens drawn around his bed. In such a confined environment this behaviour soon bred rumours, circulated by his neighbours as he slept. Was he paralysed, possibly the result of a stroke? That may explain his lack of movement. Was he a foreigner, an immigrant? That might explain his silence; without foundation it was accepted he was most likely Polish. Yet Barry confided in me, a little mysteriously, that he was convinced that the patient in bed number four was neither paralysed nor Polish, although he would not reveal what evidence had led him to this conclusion.

∞

During the daytime, the ward was a completely different space to that I imagined at night. The transient atmosphere reminded me of a train station at mid afternoon, a straggling procession of individuals and small groups arriving, loitering, then departing. Visitors would come and go during the appointed hours, their voices either hushed in privacy, or ringing inappropriately loud. Nurses and porters made duty calls at regular intervals, administering our medication, distributing and retrieving the usual hospital detritus. Although not personally expecting any well-wishers, I shared Barry's anticipation at the prospect of a visit from his older sister the following afternoon. Only twenty four hours in and already I yearned for a break from the antiseptic routine of hospital life.

'Me and Sandra have always been close' he confided 'she practically bought me up when I was a nipper. And she made as good a job of it as can be expected!'

In the idle hours between meals, I encouraged Barry to tell me more about his life. He was a natural story teller, and I was glad for the distraction.

'Wendy died last year. Can you believe it? She was only sixty, but there it is. At dawn it was, just gone, passed away in the armchair. She had got up in the middle of the night, saying she didn't feel too well, and I knew that her family had a history of heart problems but you never think too much of it. The thing that gets to me is that I wasn't with her at that last moment, you know, just holding her hand or something. I mean, she looked peaceful enough, the doctor didn't think she suffered. But after she got up, I must have dozed off again for a little while. When I woke up, and Wendy wasn't back, I had this terrible feeling that something was wrong, almost like one of those premonitions.

Do you believe in that sort of thing? I never knew I did, but I actually felt scared before I even made it to the front room. And she was just sat there, beneath the window, her glass of water on the sideboard. I remember it was getting light, there was a bit of sun coming through a gap in the curtains…'

Barry cleared his throat and collected his thoughts.

'Of course you're too young to worry yourself about such things, and that's the way it should be. But you never really get over a loss like that, you always find yourself wishing they would come back. Especially at night...'

∞

With nothing else to focus on, I watched the hours draw on through the long windows, the sinking sun cascading prisms of light against the panes. The dinner service arrived, and I picked idly at cold rice, my medication having stolen my appetite. Shortly afterwards, I received a visit from my consultant Dr Gibbons, who informed me I would undergo further surgery on my arm the day after tomorrow. Whilst light still lingered, 'Ash' stepped outside into the courtyard to take his last cigarette of the day. He liked to watch the dying embers of sunlight glinting through the trees with their branches stripped bare. On the stroke of six, a pair of nurses would arrive on the ward, drawing the curtains in slow, solemn ceremony. The hours before 'lights out' were always listless, conversation between patients falling away under the weary glare of the overheads, to be replaced by the relentless murmur of the television. With the flick of a switch, darkness was imposed upon us. As last night had been so unsettled, this evening I was hoping to fall asleep as soon as I hit the pillow, but this was not to be. At first I found myself gazing up at the ceiling, attempting to decipher the painted murals amongst the gathering gloom, imagining strange, half glimpsed shapes. Sleep would not come, and so in desperation I turned on my side and screwed my eyes shut, only to realise I was now listening attentively to the night voices of the hospital. As before, I heard the whisper and bustle of the nursing staff in the corridors, and close at hand, the synchronized inhales, exhales of the slumbering bodies, laid out in rows. Only on this occasion I began to notice the sounds that lay concealed beneath this surface noise; the deeper, older acoustics of the building. I believe I heard the rumble of the pipes in the walls, the industrial whine of distant doors, the slipstream whistling through the lift shafts. Slowly, effortlessly, I began to drift. And in my dreams I sensed a presence on the ward, again the patter of feet in the darkness, a muffled cry met with a quiet, comforting voice.

'Poor Reg…Sister is with you now…' I think I said, talking in my sleep.

∞

I awoke late the next morning to discover the bed opposite me standing empty. Amidst the clatter of breakfast, two nurses were silently stripping the sheets. It took a few moments for the implication to register, but I soon understood 'Poor Reg' had passed away during the night, and that his dying breaths must have found their way into my dreams.

'Poor sod' Barry was lamenting to his favourite nurse, as she plumped his pillow, 'never thought he would go just like that, with nobody to tell. Never had any visitors did he?'

'I think he told me he had a twin sister, who died a little while ago' replied Nicola absently, smoothing down the bedclothes.

'Poor sod…' it was clear that Barry was particularly moved by this death; he and Reg suffered from the same malady, and he was perhaps afraid that he was catching a glimpse of his own fate.

'Still, the patient in number four is looking better,' Nicola indicated, with a subtle nod of the head, 'He had been quite poorly yesterday, but he seems to be having one of his 'up' days this morning'.

Screens withdrawn, the unnamed invalid lay open to view, although only his face was visible above the blankets, blotched and slightly swollen, his eyes raised to the ceiling with a glazed expression.

'Anyone know anything about him yet?' whispered Barry, close to her ear.

'No, we're still trying to get him to talk so we can track down some family, but that's our little secret OK?'

With a wink and a tender nudge in his ribs, Nicola moved on down the ward, Barry seeming to brighten at this little confidence, munching a slither of toast with a satisfied smile.

∞

Early in the afternoon Barry received the regular visit from his sister, Sandra. Although a slightly built woman with a worn look about the eyes, she nevertheless exuded a powerful dynamism that seemed to completely overawe her more placid brother. Whenever she was present, his gruff exterior softened and he regressed to an almost child like dependency, which she appeared to actively encourage. Sandra insisted on taking even the simplest activities out of his hands; peeling his oranges, pouring his drinks, even reading out the newspaper to him. I soon discovered this maternal role was one she adopted for all the patients, and we were happy to indulge her; she certainly brought a much needed shot of life to the ward. Apparently unable to sit still or remain silent for a moment, Sandra would take it upon herself to rearrange the ward under the guise of improving our quality of life, adjusting the angle of the television, rearranging the flower displays, even bringing in cleaning products from home to spruce the place up. Barry later told me his sister had only recently retired from her supermarket job, and he presumed this was her way of keeping busy. I learnt from Sandra herself that, although she had kept a number of 'gentlemen friends', she had never married, 'too busy raising Barry and the others after mum left' (a brother had emigrated to Canada, and a younger sister was believed to be somewhere in Scotland).

∞

Over the next fortnight I would look forward to Sandra's visits on Tuesday's and Thursday's, listening to her read out the obituaries from the local gazette. She and her brother seemed to find no end of pleasure in recounting news of long lost school friends who had recently died. They reminisced over hit-and-run victims and heart attacks, got sentimental about suicides in the suburbs, and swapped anecdotes about old Dan Watt, who had suffered a fall in the mobile library. Not to mention 'Michael down the road', who had been found dead in his flat after a suspected break-in 'and only a few weeks since he lost his wife too'. Meanwhile I dealt with the claustrophobic repetition of hospital life the best I could, daydreaming when not sleeping, trying to recall what the world looked like beyond the window view. Having been assured that I was making good progress following my second operation, towards the end of the fortnight Dr Gibbons called in on his rounds and confidently predicted I would soon be discharged, pending the outcome of further surgery, pencilled in for a few days time. During this period, the main topic of conversation was the sudden deterioration in the health of 'Ash'. There were rumours circulating about 'pernicious anaemia', he had certainly grown very pale and weak, to the point where he no longer had the strength to venture outside for his cigarette breaks. Nicola admitted to Barry that the staff were thinking in terms of days rather than weeks, and this diagnosis was to prove accurate, 'Ash' passing away quietly in his sleep. The nameless patient in bed four continued to have his good days and bad days, sometimes concealed behind the screens, sometimes lying there exposed but immobile with the blankets drawn up to his chin. One afternoon Sandra had tried to engage him in conversation, but when she had asked him if there was anything he would like to drink, she complained to Barry 'he didn't say anything, he just looked at me with this horrible grin'.

On the night before my third and final operation, a familiar voice whispered to me from out of the darkness. Barry's tone was uncharacteristically faint and hesitant; I had sensed that he was not quite himself, that ever since Sandra's last visit something had been playing on his mind. All day long he had looked tired and off colour, and although now he was hidden in shadow, I could still hear the anxiety in his voice.

'There's something I've been meaning to get off my chest' he began, and I had to strain to catch his words, 'Something I think I saw in here one night, something that I shouldn't of...'

'Is this to do with Ash, or Reg?' I presumed Barry was hinting at malpractice, or MRSA.

'Perhaps. You remember I told you I didn't think him in bed four was really paralysed, despite what any doctor might say?'

I nodded, forgetting Barry could not see me, yet he continued regardless.

'Well, you know our Sandra hasn't exactly warmed to him, and something she said the other afternoon got me thinking again, about something I saw one night. It must have been a few nights before they brought you in…'

It seemed as if the walls of the ward were closing in, and every patient in the sprawling building was listening intently.

'I hadn't been sleeping too well, we all know how hard it is to get a decent night's kip in here, and I woke up with a jump. Reckon I'd been having a nightmare, although I can't remember the details, something about someone lurking outside Sandra's door! Anyway that's not important, only I was awake in the dark; half asleep, but awake. When I opened my eyes the first thing I saw were the screens around bed four, across the way. Now we're told that chap's paralysed and nobody has seen him move right? Well, I could make out his silhouette through the screens, laid out in the bed as usual. But then, as I was about to drift off again, I swear the figure in that bed suddenly sat bolt upright!'

'What did you do?' I could hear the tremor in my own voice, an oppressive sense of foreboding drawing future and past together like hospital curtains.

'That's the stupid thing, I don't remember, I just had this impression. One minute I was as bright as day, the next I couldn't keep my eyes open, must be this new medication they've got me on…'

'Do you think you really woke up? I mean, everyone has those dreams where they think they have woken up but they haven't really? Or you might just have thought you saw someone sitting up? I've had nightmares that still affect me after I've woken up, you know, that leave you vulnerable for a little while, suspicious of the world around you?'

'There's no need for you to worry about it I suppose' Barry sighed despondently 'you'll be out of here in a few days, and it's always easier to imagine something isn't happening…'

'Please Barry, I'm not doubting you' I protested, raising my voice a little, perhaps too much, 'It's just you hear so many strange sounds on the wards at night. This hospital is never really silent, even when you think it is. What if you heard movements on the ward, and incorporated them into your dreams? For example, I'm sure there is a sleepwalker among us, more than once I've heard bare feet padding across the floor after lights out…'

'Maybe you're right,' he responded meekly 'I just wanted to tell someone what I've seen, that's all…'

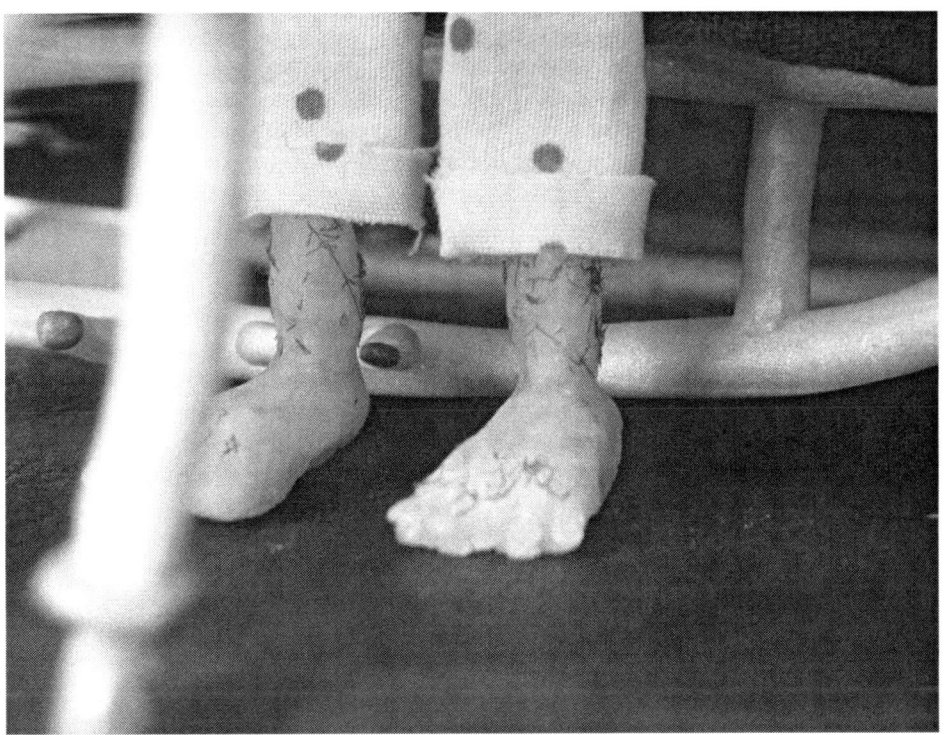

∞

Under anaesthetic, they wheeled me from the ward late the following afternoon. I knew nothing until the next morning, when I awoke out of traction, with a bed standing empty next to me. Barry had gone.

'Heart attack' explained Nicola 'Nobody heard a thing, it's so sad. I had to phone his sister when they found him, not the sort of news you want to wake someone up with. Still, he looked peaceful enough…'

'Isn't it suspicious, the amount of deaths you've had on this ward recently?' I demanded bitterly, stifling tears as I thought of that last conversation with Barry, his fears in the night.

'Unfortunately it's all too common' Nicola offered, with sympathy, 'It's something you have to try and harden yourself to if you work here, although it's never easy. Personally, I've learned that the way to deal with it is to not get too close to the patients, always keep a bit of a distance, otherwise you'll never cope. I try not to take my work home with me, if you know what I mean, although my boyfriend would probably say something different!'

That afternoon a new patient was deposited into bed number two, so recently vacated, and we exchanged brief pleasantries. The following morning Dr Gibbons broke the good news that my bones were setting well and I was to be discharged the next day. In spite of the prospect of my imminent release, I felt what can only be described as a rising sense of dread as I waited for darkness to fall, although I was uncertain as to whether I feared the night ahead or the morning after. With a heavy heart I watched the sun setting on the horizon, familiar hues shifting across hospital walls. Sitting up in bed, I casually pieced together a jigsaw, anything to distract me from contemplating the lonely hours that lay ahead. It must have worked; I don't even remember falling asleep....

∞

...and I can't recall what woke me up. Yet some instinct dragged me from my sleep, my mind unfocused yet tingling with an unpleasant sense of expectation, anticipating some sound, some movement amongst the sleepers on the ward. Darkness appeared to swim over me, the beds across the aisle fading in and out of the shadows, outlines trembling, insubstantial, as if underwater. Bed six, bed five...bed four. Suddenly, a silhouetted figure sat bolt upright behind the screens. Although I knew this was what I had been waiting for, almost desiring if just to wish it over, now the time came to confront my fears my voice failed me and my body froze as if paralysed. Against my will, I felt myself slipping into unconsciousness, into oblivion, yet I fought hard against the effects of my medication. Where was the figure on the bed? It had slipped lithely to the floor. With the curtains drawn it was dark, everything was concealed by the night, yet I heard the patter of feet across the tiles, stooping, scurrying across the ward. There was a presence at the bedside of the patient adjacent to me, the new admittance, who murmured restlessly in his sleep. A shadow fell upon him....

'No!' I must have cried out loud, as a face twisted in a hideous grimace shrank from me like a nightmare, merging with the gargoyles that lurked in the murals on the ceiling.

Almost directly, the overhead lights flashed on as a duty nurse rushed on to the ward, her attention immediately drawn to the crumpled figure that lay at the foot of the fourth bed, the screens scattered. Kneeling alongside the prone body, she called out to a junior colleague:

'Quick, fetch a doctor! He's fallen! There's blood!'

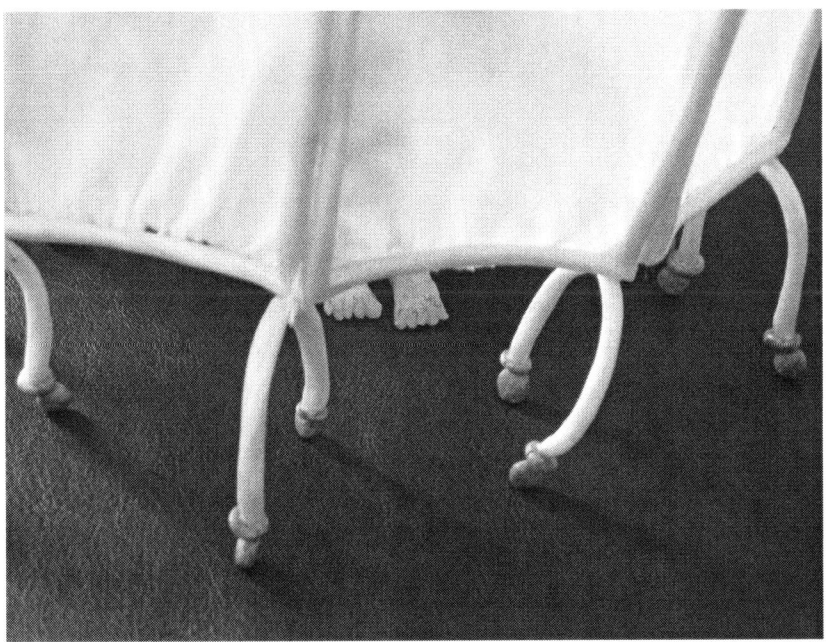

∞

The next day I was discharged and returned to my flat. The relief at having my own space at last, at regaining my privacy, was countered by a sense of unease that only became more pressing as darkness fell. Accustomed to the background noise of the hospital throughout the night, I found the silence, the emptiness of my own room uncomfortable, unnerving even. Unable to sleep, I skimmed through a copy of the local gazette, that I had picked off the mat a few hours earlier. From beneath the 'stop press' banner, an article instantly leapt out, as if it had been placed for me:

'Miss Sandra Jackson, 68, was found dead at her flat this afternoon. Cause of death is yet to be established, although police are investigating the possibility of a bungled robbery. Neighbours believe she received a visitor late last night, presumed to be someone known to her, as there were no signs of forced entry…'

Negative Terminal or
Confessions of a Sacrificial Anode

Peter Griffiths

The room is a cold blue. As they both sit idly speaking to one another with studied casualness the woman in white asks if he has asked for anything, making a small mark on her clipboard when they say no. The man thanks her in an effusive whisper and she leaves. Always the same: visitors speak as though nobody could hear them; the others loudly and bluntly, with no feeling at all. Over and over; the cycle is endless. Passing of day into night signalled by the yellow fluorescent lights and the reflection of this coffin-room in the window. When the light outside comes back, there are daydreams of birds slain by the false azure of the window, but then the room twice its size returns, and only moths, poor sport, mistaking this room for the moon. I could never navigate by that, since it is obscured by the top half of the next block. I wonder if I could ask them to move it for me. That might keep me occupied for a few more days, nights.

'Does he need anything?' Again? How often do they come? Now she says that it's been five days since fluids and twice that since solids. The prisoner's struggle; the child's refusal. If you will keep me here then struggle I will.

They discuss the weather; tasteless at the best of times, but now? Would they discuss deep-sea diving if I were in an iron lung? That little ponce doesn't fool me, with his suit and click-clacking shoes on the corridor floor. He's twelve years old if he's a day. And there she is in the corridor talking to one of them. Of course she's in this with them. Why else would they be speaking so closely, all the while looking at me? If I get out I'll have their guts for garters. I'm a powerful man, I'm sure of it. There is no mirror. There is no way that I could ask for one. They would bring it and then laugh the old man's vanity

She comes back. 'We're trying to help. You know that, don't you?' The mouth is too dry to answer anyhow. Her face... going to help me. Yes, it was just last week, a new suit and pay in the pocket and her saying, 'I want to help you', and looking at me with those cold eyes. Cold so much that they could right through you. Unchanging no matter what her mouth was saying. I never saw a a woman drink like that before. I was barely keeping up anyway, and she speaks faster and faster so that I felt dizzy with it and hardly noticed when as we're getting up bouncing off a table and her laughing. Then blinded by the street light as I look into it expecting the sun but now it must be later than I thought. That pinprick of orange light still in my eyes as she clumsily pulls me in and missing my mouth by a quarter mile. She says that she's here to help me and once we reach her flat, a dimly lit place above a butcher's shop, I lean against the doorway as she fools with the lock. Up a flight of stairs there is a another door, another lock to fiddle with. It gives, and we fall into the room. The lamp is already on, an indeterminate piece of clothing filters it to bathe the room in yellow. She pushes me onto the bed and I notice a man's suit hanging up over a chair. As I try to remove my shirt, still lying on the bed she says,

'No, I want to help you,' so I let her unbutton me.

'I'm going to wash you. Now lift up your arms,' her voice harsh, no longer softened from alcohol, and the light hard. I am scared, the change is too much. Is this a trick? She continues, lifting up my arms one by one and scrubbing under them despite my struggling. Am I reduced to this, lured back here by this woman to be babied in this humiliating way?

'Now I'll be back in a moment with your meds.' Drugs, plied with drugs and the promise of contact. Time passes, drugs come and go, the night comes and goes, I come and go. Faint murmurs along the corridor and those two come back in carrying fruit and juice and saying hello with their emphatic whispers. They left just now didn't they? They must have gone to get things from that shop out there, where all those women congregate, just like all women.

I cannot move. The light is sunlight through yellow drapes. I am naked, and I feel my Mother's presence. She picks me up and lays me on her naked breast. I am surrounded by her; her warmth flows through my body, now so small that it reaches the other side. The doorbell rings downstairs and my Mother gets up and puts on her dressing gown. She has left my world and may not come back.

It is light outside and group of them are standing in a half-circle around my bed. The two people are my friends, so I trust them. Not friends... relatives. Her eyes, the colour of soap, look at me with tears in them. The man walks to the window and looks out at the grey tower and the rain as it weeps steadily against the window pane. Mother told me that it must rain so that flowers can grow. When the rain stops we can go outside and play cricket.

'We would like to talk to you about the procedure which we're about to perform. As you know, the lack of oxygen...' I am walking down the lane that led from my Grandmother's house to a place in the woods where we would go. It is spring and the trees dapple the road as I walk. I come across the idiot boy who lives a few streets away playing with the Great Dane whose owner keeps him chained up outside. I normally tease the animal so that it rears up; like a horse to a man, bringing its owner out to chase us off. Since we're forbidden it holds extra pleasure for us to try to get near it. Its fearsome bark usually echoes around the small courtyard whenever anyone comes near, but the boy is there all alone, patting the dog as if it were the most natural thing. I stand motionless, neither the boy nor the dog seeing me, and it seems as if I've stumbled upon some secret meeting, like a student interrupting a snatched moment of flirtation between two teachers. The sun dances on my face and I shield my eyes. Time is not here for a moment, but suddenly it seems to return and the dog rears up, its huge shadow engulfing me. I run a little but feel foolish and turn again to look. The boy is caught in the dog's chain. The chain pulls tighter as the dog strains toward me. I turn and run but this time do not stop to look back. Tomorrow I will bump into the boy and he will be undamaged.

'...tissue with which we can work. Although experimental, the operation has a high chance of success. We will be implanting a small amount of tissue from a donor, hopefully halting the spread of your dementia and returning some of your cognitive faculties...'

Blinding white light, shadowy figures standing over, and the screech of a drill too close to the ears.

On an ash covered hill, three figures swathed in yellow polythene struggle against the wind. Though covered by a mask, your own aged face is among them, choking in the sulphurous air. The figure at the back collapses in the dust and slides a few inches downwards. Noticing her, you halt the others' progress and stop momentarily to catch your breath and look down onto the black valley of glass. Girders jut up at random like palms on a tropical beach. Though the sky is the colour of soap a faint sun is seen beyond the cloud. The girl finally reaches for your hand to regain her footing. You pull her up and smile at her from behind the mask, knowing that she'll be able to tell it from your eyes. Then you turn back up to the hill and continue forever walking.

A feeling of terrible nausea. I cannot move. Tortured voices moan all around me. This is a prison and I am to be tortured. No, a hospital recovery room. I turn and vomit onto the bed. Nobody seems to come, though I cannot see either way, blinkered like the roan mare that drew the tinker's cart where I was born. But wait a minute, whatever does 'roan' mean? This word is foreign to me, yet when I consider it, it must mean an animal with dappled fur. And yet again, there was no tinker where I grew up. I can see him, although the image is faint. It must have appeared in a film I once saw. That must be it. But a film in which I recognised it as a roan? I try to cry out but again my voice fails.

A nurse appears in my field of vision: 'Faint memories that do not belong to me. New words I didn't know before,' He wipes my head with a damp cloth and says something to himself as he wipes off the mattress. I gesture but he ignores it. Another person screams out from across the room, and then he is gone.

The cry reminds you again of that dun-black horse. How it broke out from its stable down the road near the scrap yard. You were a child still, but since the men were away nobody could see to it. You reached the end of the road and the horse reared, its hooves sparking on the cobblestones and it wailed like that man just there. You approached calmly, speaking slow measured words as you crept towards it. At your touch the horse calmed immediately. The woman at the sweet shop said that you could have anything that you wanted for saving everyone's bacon. You chose lemon drops.

I did not choose lemon drops. I don't even like lemon drops. Obviously you, whoever you are, chose lemon drops and are trying to force it into my unconscious with this talk. Who the hell are you anyway? What do you want?.

Consider that you have always contained me, that my being is intricately tied with yours. Is it not possible that you simply had blocked out this part of you, that your degenerating brain had made you forget? What would you have me say to you? You are in a room, surrounded by the tormented, that man-mountain over there towers above us all as we entreat him to help us. Would you have me tell you that a simple *Libera Me, Domine* would give you release? You want me to help you. Your eyes have yet to regain their focus and see only shapes, as if the room were obscured by fog. From the fog so thick that you can taste the grit grows a mountain and upon it loop in paths the inconsistent memories of your life. The paths are of black ash and below the faint glimmer of the base of blasted obsidian.

The smell of the cancer ward where your mother took you to see an uncle you'd met only once before. The quiet of the hospital as evening became night and the unspoken agreement that this would be his last. The man's smudged complexion and lips that seemed too red. His sunken eyes and his yellowish skin. His indignant look at you as your mother murmured to him, that a stranger would see him in this state before he died. The way he communicated all that to you with an outraged stare. Finally, dozing in the other room when he eventually went and walking into the pale light of dawn to go and look at his body. Tell me, is this one of yours, or one of mine? Can you tell where I end and you begin?

We are back in the hospital room. The light is still blue. The loving family and ever-helpful doctors are sat around the bed. Some take notes, other murmur softly to one another. They cannot yet tell that the patient is awake, but soon it will be too difficult to conceal. The vast moon- obscuring tower still hangs somewhere outside, though there is no moon for it to conceal, and the sun arcs high enough that its influence is only minimal.

'...success, though it cannot be told for certain until he is fully conscious. Motor functions seem fine, and with all hope his will be a landmark recovery.'

Eyes open; a brief glance at them,

'Ah, back to the land of the living,' says the Doctor, bright, young, unjaded. 'And how are we feeling today?'

'We're feeling surprisingly good today thank you. A little queasy.' The Doctor smiles at this. Humour is an excellent sign, he thinks.

'I think we'll be getting you home in a few days,' she says.

'And we can take the car? No ambulance?' The Doctor smiles and nods.

'Well, we'll let you rest. Is there anything we you'd like me to bring in?' the wife says, as she and the son rise.

'We think we'd like some grapes if that's not too much bother.

'*We?*' mouths the pale-eyed woman to her son as they leave the room.

The Condition

D. P. Watt

'All art constantly aspires towards the condition of music.'
Walter Pater, *The Renaissance*

I had not been back in the country long, but long enough to
have felt the faint oppression of that malaise which had forced
my departure three years before. To have received a letter from
Bertram Wilson was the last thing I was expecting. We had been
good friends at school—quite contrary to our interests—but had
not maintained the friendship after leaving. I had been a
precocious and arrogant exile from my peers. My interest in
Eastern antiquities and anthropology had always ensured my
exclusion from the mainstream pursuits of my contemporaries.
Bertram Wilson was quite the opposite; a keen cricketer, the
head prefect and a member of the national badminton team. He

was everything that I could never be, nor wanted to be. I skulked gloomily around the school buildings with my obvious hatred of all they represented seething within me. It gave me a sense—misguided of course—of some power within me; a power to control their simple emotions and subjugate them to an ancient will that seemed to be surfacing slowly, and painfully, within me. These were the fantasies and megalomaniac impressions of an adolescent whose abhorrence of the ordinary, the mediocre every day, had set him on a path to remote and unwholesome self-absorption.

My brief career at university had sealed our separation. I found the confines of the city destructive to my work. Libraries had never been a particular passion of mine and so I gradually forgot my studies for more carnal pleasures. In 1936 I left for Borneo and spent four incredible years drifting through the Indonesian Islands, living with the people and sharing their rituals and customs. Then the world broke in and with the arrival of the Japanese I caught one of the last boats back to England. Soon I was conscripted and the war worked its horror upon my mind. After being present at the liberation of Bergen-Belsen my brittle mental state finally collapsed and the years following the war were spent between institutions, the names of which I have forgotten. I gradually recovered my interests and spent a slow decade becoming more bookish; researching my interests into the occult from the comfort of an armchair rather than in the bowels of its practice. However, the books and articles could not long keep me contented. I was eager to return to travel and discovery, and after a serendipitous inheritance I departed England's dull post-war shores in the hope of permanent escape.

Those three years had been most rewarding. I had seen practices of unbelievable power; conjurations of ancestors, spirits and demonic powers; bizarre sacrifices to deities long forgotten in the West and magical incantations from the mundane to the extraordinary. The time vanished and the money did too. Like many men of my age, with relatively minor financial means, I had become a decadent; whilst others undid themselves—and hid from their memories—with drink and drugs, I had tried to vanish into an unreal other world of barbarism. Finally though, with little money left, and a mind filled with ancient terrors I returned to England: a country that was as alien to me now as those strange lands I had visited were to most of my countrymen.

So there I stood, in a beachfront boarding house, reading a letter from Bertram Wilson. It was short enough: 'Dear Miles, I'm glad to hear of your return, and trust your expedition was worthwhile. I am sick. I would ask a favour of you, in memory of our old friendship. Please call on me here at St Agnes' Hospice at your earliest convenience, if you are so inclined. Your old friend, Bertram Wilson.' It was also clear enough. I did not know what had happened to Bertram during the war but had a terrible feeling that his illness must be somehow connected to it. Perhaps seeing him again would help me settle back into the miserable greyness of my homeland. As it was imperative that I establish some form of income, and soon, it seemed sensible also to see if Wilson might know of a suitable position. I admit that my initial thoughts were of myself. Any remaining vestige of European social conventions had vanished from my thoughts, so immersed was I in alternative communities. I would discover soon enough what condition troubled him.

∞

The hospice was located in London, a short enough train journey from Hastings, where I was boarding. I believed that sea air would at least give me some feeling of freedom. I approached the city with foreboding though. It was the symbol of all I had wanted to leave behind: security, civilisation, progress and most of all, knowledge. What had we discarded in this rush for technology and capital? All our old gods had withered now, laying bleeding and abandoned amongst the scrap-yards and dole queues of Europe. Hah! What did this wretched society know of values, of love and hate, of true sacrifice? Everything was reduced to numbers, to clocks, workloads and formulae.

I had to break my hatred of modernity, or I was lost again.

I concentrated on the gentle rumble of the train upon the tracks, soothing myself into a trance.

A short taxi-ride from Victoria station saw me to St Agnes' hospice. It was a curious place, hidden inside a large private garden behind a tall hedge. Without the driver showing me to the very door I would never have found it.

It must have been run by nuns when first established, over a century before. But now it was staffed by modern nurses. In a way they seemed no different to a religious order. They were silent, almost devotional. They passed through the corridors and wards in their navy uniforms, dutiful servants to a higher order; at least it was to pure human compassion rather than the hollow God of the Holy Trinity.

One nurse showed me to Wilson's room before rushing away to the sound of a bell from down the corridor. There was some clamour and a man began to scream. I was intrigued and followed the commotion. I stood back from the doorway and watched as a nurse struggled to hold a grey haired man down upon a bed whilst the one that had shown me to Wilson's room rushed to an old gramophone on the far side of the room. The man was screaming at the top of his voice, crying out against some kind of threat he imagined above him. The first notes from the record began to play and the man immediately relaxed, as though he had been sedated. His face settled into a calm composure but his eyes still stared towards the ceiling, filled with a terrible void that I knew well myself. He was clearly much younger than the grey hair had suggested.

The nurse that had restrained him talked briefly with the other nurse and then left the room hurriedly.

'Excuse me, Madam,' I said. 'Might I trouble you to tell me a little about that patient?'

She eyed me suspiciously for a moment.

'Why,' she asked. 'What is it you wanted to know?'

I could hear the music through the door and was sure I recognised it.

'That's Elgar, isn't it?' I asked.

'Yes, it is,' she replied. '"The Nursery Suite." It is the only thing that will calm him when he starts.'

'What happened to him?' I asked, recalling the short composition which had been dedicated to the royal princesses some years before.

The nurse shook her head and sighed. 'The poor man lost his wife and child in the blitz. Direct hit, whilst he was struggling with the shelter door. The gramophone and a set of disks were in the shelter, and they are all that remained of the house and the family's belongings. He's been here ever since. When he remembers the event, which happens most days, the only way to quieten him is to play the entire suite. Alice will be in there now for the next half-hour or so, changing the disks. If you miss one, or don't change them rapidly enough, he has another fit and you have to begin again. Sometimes I wonder if it wouldn't be best for him to go and join his wife too.'

She stared at me a moment, perhaps regretting telling me so much. But I assumed he had no family left that might object to her indiscretion, and I was unlikely to tell anyone.

'Thank you,' I said, rather quietly.

'Yes,' she nodded. 'Now I must attend to my duties.'

I stood there, outside the door of the shocked man, and listened for a few minutes until the first movement finished and the nurse had to change the disk. It was indeed a child's sort of music, filled with moments of frivolity and gentle menace. Perhaps one might call it theatrical. I could image his child animating his or her dolls to the tracks whilst the loving parents looked on with joy. But those days of lightness were dead to him now. I felt they were dead to me too, with all that I had seen.

I headed back to Wilson's room and knocked lightly.

'Come in,' a voice said.

On entering the room I was struck by how homely it seemed. The patient next door had been here many years and yet his room was stark and bare. But Wilson had obviously been here some time too. He had filled it with books and paintings and even had a violin on a stand by the window. There was even a drinks cabinet in the corner by the washstand.

'Ah, it's great to see you Miles,' Wilson said, easing himself up in his bed which, despite the more cosy surroundings, looked particularly clinical. There was a drip on a frame beside him and a number of hypodermic needles nestling in a kidney bowl on the bedside table. 'I had a feeling you might come today.'

He certainly looked ill. Or rather, he looked old. Not in the startling fashion of the man in the adjacent room. Wilson was thin and haggard. In fact the skin seemed to hang from him as though he were an elderly man. Gone was the robust physique of the sportsman I had known. A cruel pang of schadenfreude welled within me.

'Hello, Wilson,' I began. 'It's a pleasure to see you again... I mean not in this state... but it is good to see you again.'

I was so unused to speaking with Europeans, with all their tedious evasive etiquette, that I didn't really know how to discuss his illness tactfully.

'Don't worry Miles,' he smiled. 'You never were any good at the small talk. It's one of the things I liked about you. You're an honest man, even if that is somewhat hurtful at times. It's because of your honesty that I asked you to come.'

I entered the room a little further and deposited my coat and umbrella on a low chest at the foot of the bed.

'I'll take a seat if I may,' I said, settling into a comfortable chair beside the window.

'Certainly,' he replied. 'Would you care for a cup of tea or something? I can call for some.'

'I'm fine thanks, Wilson,' I said, eager to find out why he'd called me here. 'What has happened to you?'

He stared at me with his gaunt face and I saw how much he had changed. His eyes were dark and distant. I wondered what they had witnessed in these past years. My own eyes must have betrayed a sadness because a single tear fell from his eyes and rolled down his cheek.

'I have a condition that the doctors are unable to diagnose,' he said, still holding the firm gaze. 'They believe it to be some sort of wasting disease. They are wrong. I am indeed wasting away, but it is not a disease and there is nothing in this world that will ever cure it.'

'I am sorry to hear that, Wilson,' I said. 'But how can you be so certain, perhaps they will...'

'They will not!' he interrupted. 'They cannot! Because what ails me also ails them, and you. It is the condition of all humanity. In me it has found physical expression and I will make sure it is concluded.'

There was a short silence. There had been an aggression in his voice which I had not expected, and had not experienced in all the years that we had been close.

'You have not really been able to recapture your love of other cultures and their odd beliefs since the war have you?' he said, bluntly. 'I mean, you've travelled. You've no doubt seen surprising and unusual things. But nothing can quite erase the memory of what happened in the war.'

He was right. He just stared at me with those black, unchanging pupils, and spoke the truth that I hadn't had the courage to confront yet.

'I am the same, my old friend,' he continued. 'I was captured after my ship went down and spent the last three years in a prisoner of war camp. I worked in the Sosnowice mine. There in the darkness I discovered something, something that has been with me since.'

Again there was a long silence and the solid, unblinking, gaze.

'What? What did you discover?' I asked, absorbed now.

'Not what you are thinking. Not some object...' he said, shifting his gaze finally towards the window. 'It is a *sense* of things that I found, or rather, the sense *within* things. I began to hear how the basest elements sing with the sound of the first eruption of life.'

I was used to hearing all manner of beliefs, of theories and philosophies that proposed strange celestial orders and cruel fates for humanity and its verdant earth, but I never expected to hear them from a man such as Wilson.

'Do you know what holds the most beautiful song?' he continued.

I shook my head.

'Works of art. Pass me a book from the shelf if you will,' he instructed, pointing to the bookcase nearest to him.

I extracted the nearest one I could find and was pleased to see that it was Sarban's *The Sound of His Horn*. It had only been published a few years previously and I had read it only recently, finding it one of the few books that had accurately captured the perversity and true horror of the awful regime we had fought against. But thinking again now I wonder if there was not a deeper meaning in my selection of that book, for it revealed a hidden lust and barbarity which lurks within us all, waiting for its bestial moment to come.

I handed him the book.

'Yes, an ideal choice,' he said, gripping it in his left hand and clutching it to his chest.

I stood by the bedside waiting for him to say more but he had closed his eyes and seemed to be breathing slowly and deeply. I waited for what seemed like minutes and was at the point of calling for one of the nurses, fearing he may have slipped into a coma.

Then it began.

It seemed as though Wilson became blurred. That is the only way I can describe it. It happened only for a brief moment, as though he had become a sort of gossamer being, as thin and fast as the wings of a fly. I blinked my eyes a few times but this odd haze still persisted around him. The rest of the room, and even the bed in which he lay were clear and focused. A moment later I heard a tingling noise, much like a tuning fork, clear and sonorous.

He turned to me and spoke. 'There, that's that.'

'What's *that*?' I said, rather frustrated at this increasingly obscure charade.

'There is no more Sarban,' he said, handing me the book.

I took it from him and placed it back on top of the bookcase. I must have looked thoroughly perplexed because he viewed me with what could only be called pity.

'You'll see,' he said. 'I am rather tired now. Might I trouble you to visit me tomorrow—just to witness the last movement, you understand. Then we can resume our distance again.'

I wanted to say no. But I suppose I owed something to our history.

'Of course, Wilson,' I said, gathering my things. 'You get some rest.'

∞

On my return to Hastings I felt unusually tired and considered that the brief episode of Wilson's shaking fit might have had some form of psychic effect upon me. I had experienced similar during my travels and slept until the early hours of the following morning. I watched the sun slowly penetrate a gloomy morning over the block of terraces my window looked out upon.   I had resolved to visit Wilson as early as possible to conclude the matter, which now seemed quite absurd. It was clear that he had become obsessed, as so many had, with the awful scenes he had endured. It would be a short time before he would pass away, and I would have done what I could to ease that passing.

As I gathered some bread and cheese to make a small breakfast on the train I thought again of Sarban's short novel and pulled out my copy to browse through. Leafing through the pages I discovered that they were all empty. Not a single word was printed in them. This must be some elaborate hoax, I thought. I had only read the thing a couple of weeks before. Wilson must have dreamt up the scam believing me to be some credulous moron who would accept any form of spiritualist trickery as evidence of the supernatural. I would take the book with me and demand an explanation.

I was striding purposefully down the corridors of St Agnes before 10am, determined to discover who was involved in this charade.

After a terse knock I entered Wilson's room to find him on a respirator. The patio doors were open to a small balcony overlooking the back of the gardens. A gentle breeze passed through the room.

Of course I was unable to vent my disgust and headed over to his bedside. He removed the mask and croaked a greeting to me.

I responded as politely as I was able. Then I opened the book before his face and flicked through it.

'Yes,' he nodded. 'Mine is the same.'

I flicked through his copy, still where I had left it the previous day. It was exactly the same—blank. I even removed the dustjackets to check the spines, in case he had had some other notebook swapped for the originals. But there on the spine was written the title and author, identical on each copy.

'What is going on, Wilson,' I said, as calmly as possible.

He seemed to have gained a little energy and was now propped up against his pillows.

'I showed you yesterday, Miles,' he said. 'It's all gone now. Not a copy remains in the world. I have liberated it.'

'But surely this is some joke...' I began.

'A joke! You think I would lie here and joke with what has been revealed to me in the squalid darks of the earth's depths,' he said, with a growing anger. 'From darkness I extracted light. We no longer deserve all of culture's gifts, which people have worked for years to reveal form the core of our being. There is nothing remaining that has not had its song darkened by this century's deeds. The world will have to begin art again. And from what it has lost it will realise the value of everything.'

'But what do you mean, Wilson?' I asked, struggling to understand his insane diatribe. I dropped the two books on his bed.

He picked one up and flicked through it smiling.

'Don't you see? There is no more Sarban,' he whispered, 'and soon there will be no Rembrandt or Shakespeare, no Stoss, Turner or Mozart. This world no longer deserves such wonders. I will extract them. The galleries will be empty; their canvases bare. The concert halls will be silent; their scores evaporated. The libraries will be unused halls of nothing; their books blank. Art will finally attain its condition.'

He closed his dark eyes and I saw his body shudder with that strange vibration that I had seen the day before. This time it was quite noticeable, even violent, but so entirely unlike any shiver or tremble of the body in even the most evolved and practised shamans of the bizarre tribal rituals that I had witnessed in my travels. It was as though every atom of his body had begun to oscillate making his entire form into a steadily accumulating blur. And from that haze a luminosity emerged whose origin was indiscernible, but without a doubt present, and then I began to hear it. It sounded like that last prolonged sigh with which all beings die, yet at the moment I had caught it the sound vanished and all the peripheral sounds; traffic, the breeze in the trees outside, the voices of passers-by and the general hum of existence, entirely evaporated. I felt enfolded within a tangible silence which wrapped me in its quietude so completely that I questioned my entire existence as separate from that supreme calm. The event of this quiet could have been only the most slight division of a second before I heard again Bertram's breath, and then again the quiet, the breath, the quiet, breath, quiet, all within an instant. Finally a rushing breath of sound, as of a gasping final trumpet call, seemed to enter through the open patio doors and I collapsed.

On coming round I found Wilson lying there unmoving. I presumed him dead. His eyes stared upwards, and had regained their original piercing blue colour. His face was contorted into a rictus, indiscernibly dreadful or joyful.

Before I was able to cry for assistance the patient next door began a screaming fit. I was beside the low bookcase at Wilson's bedside, and, through my horror, thought to check the books. I pulled one volume after another from the shelves. Blank. In my panic I scrabbled on my hands and knees amidst a growing heap of literature, checking each one before discarding it. Every word had been erased, from the greatest poems to the cheapest of potboilers. My cries joined those of the patient next door; him for his lost loved ones, me for a world of loss.

Gathering myself together and drying my streaming eyes I rushed to the room next door and found the same nurse struggling with the agonised man in the bed. The other nurse, Alice, was there too. She watched with amazement at the gramophone record revolving. The speakers emitted only a faint crackle from where the needle touched the blank revolving disk.

'It's not working,' she yelled, turning to me and appealing for assistance. 'The record's broken.'

'No, it's not broken,' I said, my words flat and hopeless. 'There's nothing on it to play. There is no more Elgar. There is no more Shakespeare, Turner or Mozart. This is now our condition.'

The patient thrashed about in the bed still screaming at the top of his voice. I could hear calls from down the corridor as other nurses gathered to lend assistance. I left Alice and her colleagues to do what they could for him. But, from that incredible day of judgement, there remained nothing in the world that would quieten him.

Cells

Claire Smith

She was diving in a sea of dreams: sting rays floating on the surface above her, a reef shark slapping its tail against the current, coral reaching for air, bright fishes passing her by. She was back in her dreamland, walking out from the see-through ocean onto pure white sand that glistened like pearls in their shells. Feeling the heat of the sun on her shoulders, beads of water sewn around her neck and middle. She was greeted by a man and whisked into a foreign town, all the alien sights, smells and noises a comfort: market vendors with fresh food, squawking livestock, women wearing bright clothes, children running barefoot up the street dodging in-between.

It was a shantytown; the poor houses were a pack of cards stacked in a pyramid, where a breath in their direction would shatter them to a pile of rubble. She had not forgotten the child, who had approached her asking for money; her companion merely looked the other way as she took her to a nearby vendor selling soft drinks. In a clear English tone she had asked for a Coca-Cola, and paid him with some of her small change. She handed the bottle of drink to the little girl, who nervously took a sip with a straw poking from the top of it. Her look of amazement told her this child had never tasted anything more luxurious than water. It was almost another planet, light years from the Western world.

∞

Daylight was transfixed by dusk when she awoke, a lost child in a supermarket: bright lights flashing around her, a rainbow of coloured food cans falling from shelves, a film of noise. She heard screaming, echoes bouncing off the walls, someone hitting a squash ball around a court—the thud, thud, thud. She was barely awake, but noticed her sister-in-law had entered the room and was sitting on the chair beside her bed. She wore strange clothing, not her usual bright colours, but a plain mono-tonal top and trousers. Weird, she's wearing trousers, she never wears trousers. She seemed concerned though, looked concerned. How the hell did she get in?

'Would you like something to eat?' Daisy asked her.

She didn't reply, choked hot air, an empty vacuum. She didn't want food, felt she should not have food, just wanted to know: Why? Why had they locked her in here?

'Suit yourself; just try to get some rest. Someone will be here to see you tomorrow morning.'

That wasn't Daisy's voice, she has time for people... But it *was* Daisy, definitely Daisy—she knew it. Daisy left the room almost as silently as she had entered, softly shutting the door behind her—the catch clicked locked—and she was left alone again. She suddenly wanted to scream, cry for her to come back, but she could only manage a yelp, a lost puppy needing its mother.

She kicked and punched the pillows, buried her head in them and sobbed, incessantly sobbed until her tear ducts were dried out, and her eyes were two desiccated prunes, black and blue. She found the energy to stand and peer at herself in a mirror, a stranger stared back, someone she had never seen before and did not like the look of: hair seeming strangled of life, face grey, lips dry and chapped. A bully began screaming at her 'You stupid cow!' loudly inside her head; she gripped at her forehead like a pain was striking at her. 'YOU STUPID COW!' Repeating over and over again, a broken needle on an old record player, a piercing scratch inside her. She plunged onto the bed, no more tears to cry, begging silently for it to stop. She knew if she screamed again they would come. So she tried to sleep and forget the angry bully.

∞

She was back on the beach again. The egg yolk sun was disappearing below the horizon leaving a brilliant pink and orange sky in its wake. They huddled together in sleeping bags, a blanket wrapped around their shoulders, though it was still warm. Birds squawked a goodnight farewell in the trees behind them. She drifted into a trance as the sea lapped, lapped further onto the beach and the stars began waltzing on its surface, making psychedelic patterns like a child's kaleidoscope.

When they awoke the sun greeted them with warm welcome home gifts. It was as though they were still encased in the blanket as they strolled dreamily along the shoreline. She couldn't see land from where they stood watching gulls flocking, and diving in turns, scrabbling for small fish. It made her feel hungry, just witnessing the sight. The water washed over her toes as she edged into it once again, then deeper so it covered her ankles. She looked back to see a trail of ghost footprints in the wet sand where they had walked to the edge of the sea, then an eerie disappearance where the water had swallowed them up.

This dream-island enchanted her—a castle of multicoloured sand stood at the centre, built it seemed for them alone. They had discovered it when exploring beyond the greenery further inland. They had climbed up to the battlements and stood on top of a turret, surveying a carpet of sea laid out and sparkling new the afternoon before. She wanted to stay in this faerie-castle, bewitched by its warm spell. Stay sleeping for one hundred years.

∞

The effects of the injection, she vaguely remembered they had given to her, had now worn off; sleeping beauty had been kissed by a handsome prince. She opened her eyes, stuck together with sleepy-men, rubbed them free, to see a strange face peering down at her. She was calmer now, like the beach she had laid on in her dreams. Her expression was one of amazement that she was still alive and that she was not in the place where the devilish spirits reside, as she had been told at Primary School. Though she knew she was in some sort of prison. The door was certainly still locked. He smiled kindly, as if at a confused toddler. She knew she knew him, but not from where.

'They'll show you around, if you want, Clara....'

A hint of recognition shadowed her, but still she did not know who this man was, and was baffled by his familiarity with her. He wore black jeans, a T-shirt, and Doctor Marten boots. Maybe this was.... She drew a blank, as most of her stay here had been. Why was he being so nice? Must know him, where from though? God, he looks like...

'You do remember who I am?'

Silence. She wore a look of confusion. Then the cells began to connect... The ceremony, flowers, people smiling at them, a photographer... Were they married? No... No that hadn't happened, not yet. She did know him though and she suddenly felt reassured, her heart rate reducing, calm.

They walked down a long corridor. There was an office area, closed in behind a sheet of glass, where a group of officers sat talking confidentially; they didn't seem to notice them at all. She registered the cameras almost immediately, blinking their red eyes at her to show they were recording her every move; she tried not to look up, but could not help staring at them; they were snake charmers and she was the caged animal, dancing to the soft tune. They seemed to hum at her. He took her past the office and into another softly furnished room; another woman sat at the opposite end, smoking a cigarette—you could smoke in prison, thank God.

'Would you like me to make you one?' He asked her.

She nodded a reply. He took out a packet of tobacco from the pocket of his jeans, put a lump of it in a paper and rolled it in his fingers, sealing it with his tongue. She watched intently, he knows what he's doing, he must smoke as well. He handed her the cigarette, and snapped his fingers on a lighter; she drew her breath in deeply, and felt light-headed almost immediately. Then he made one for himself, quicker than the first. The smoke made patterns in the air, a puffing steam train.

∞

She was travelling; the seats were hard wood benches, like in a Victorian schoolhouse. He introduced himself as Lars, a tall man wearing round shaded glasses, a John Lennon wannabe. He was balding, though his hair was still its original colour, apricot blond. He wore the native clothing—cream kurta pyjamas, and brown leather sandals that were well worn and showed his white nobbled toes. An Asian man sat next to him, she could not remember his name now, staring at her with Belgian chocolate eyes.

It was dark inside the carriage, eerie in a way. She felt every clunk-a-clunk trundling along the track; she was on the ghost train at the Fairground when every second you were just waiting for a neon skeleton to jump from the sides, or a bloodied finger to tap you on the shoulder. There was just a small window, with three metal bars across it, to separate her from the outside world. The scenery changed as they progressed from the South to the North of the country; she became warmer, comforted by the hustle and bustle of each station. Then dozing sleep in between when fields blanketed the view, a patchwork quilt in all shades of yellow and green, knitted together as far as the eye could see.

Several days went by either sitting quietly reading a book or sleeping on the hard benches. The men made conversation by both day and night, laughing over cups of Chi Tea bought from vendors at the stations where the train stopped. She knew she was going to Agra to see the Taj Mahal. This journey was draining her; she was lethargic when they reached the destination.

∞

A radio was playing some music she had not heard before—it clanged in her ears, the train screeched to a stop at its final station. She opened her eyes wide to see the familiar man and the strange woman exchanging furtive glances.

'You're that guy… The one off the television.' The woman murmured. He smiled. She returned a look of annoyance.

'Will you do my portrait? Come on I know you can paint, I've seen you with your drawing things—I could put it up in my lounge.' She asked, more animated now.

She wondered at this woman's audacity—first accusing HIM of being on television, when it was her who was one of the most infamous criminals of the twentieth century. Why would a police artist want to do a portrait of Myra Hindley? She'd already been caught and locked up in here. Maybe he was scared, as he plucked a small sketchbook and pencil from his trouser pocket and began sketching her. Myra spoke of the place as if it were home—though it had obviously been so for many years.

'I can help you with your washing, if you like? I know you're new, but you'll soon get used to it.'

She did not answer.

'It's hard at first, being locked up in here, but they'll probably start letting you out a bit soon.'

She nodded a dumb affirmation.

'You can help me sweep up the leaves later—I like to keep the place nice.'

She began feeling unsettled, tight in her chest, a caveman confronted by a wild animal. Unarmed, without a spear, the tiger was staring right into her eyes, flashing blood.

∞

The red of the women's dresses struck her, one large blurred traffic signal telling her to stop. But she had carried on accompanied by Lars against that sea of colour and out into the blazing heat on the other side of the station. The colour went

158

from red to amber when she looked up at the sky—it was dusk when they arrived, the sun leaving this orange reminder above her. She floated to a waiting rickshaw, guided by this man dressed entirely in white; she wondered at how he had kept so clean amongst all the grime of the train carriage.

The journey through the back streets felt like she was watching a film, frames flashing past her but no time to take in the details. She was thrown about the rickety vehicle, a rag doll with delicate cotton clothing threatening to tear under rough treatment. The driver slammed a hand on his horn, letting out a deafening screech, then carried on faster than before.

She appeared a ghost when they arrived, a green tint to her skin. The vomiting poured from her; she was a possessed vessel exploding poisonous liquid. She tried to relax, sweat seeping from her porous skin. Fish-like shadows began floating on the ceiling above, and muffled sounds of sleep echoed around the room. The fan became a buzzing insect pestering her until she hummed with its chorus, then fell into a deep sleep.

∞

He shook her shoulder, she nearly screamed with fright; she was back on the ghost train.

'Where have you been?' He asked.

She stared, an inquisitor reading her thoughts, burning into the core of her with a stoked rod fresh from the embers of a fire.

'Where have you been?'

She needed to run, back to the train, back to… But there was nowhere to go. She couldn't muster the energy to even get up, as though she was stuck in a marsh, wellingtons full of mud, but not daring to lift her legs from them for fear of sinking deeper. She couldn't see a way of escape; the mud seemed to stretch forever, be grabbing her for a final fatal embrace. Now she remembered.

'It, it was you… You tried to…'

But the air stuck in her throat, burning hot needles pricking at her words. She burst into tears, tears of fear. The rabbit was caught in a corner of a field, backing toward a barbed wire fence, as the fox was approaching, slime dripping from its mouth, waiting to pounce, tear this small creature limb from limb.

Before he could move she sprang at him, lashing out with her nails; she was not going to be the rabbit again; it was her who was the fox now, taking her revenge on this creature who had hunted her. She bit at his torso, kicked and punched him, ready to destroy her adversary for good. The fear spurred her on; he lurched in surprise at every attack, tried to shield himself with the armour of a jacket that had laid redundant next to him, called out in a panic.

A group of officers soon arrived, screeching sirens in their wake, a rescue militia carrying medication and brute force as their weapons. They pulled her from him still kicking and punching at the air, and held her arms behind her back, pushing her to the ground. She spat angry words. Cursed him. This should be him, he should be the one being restrained. He was the one who, who had tried to…

An officer arrived with some cotton wool, and gently bathed a scratch on his face that was bleeding, so gently it sickened her. She screamed louder. He calmly got up.

'I'll be back to see you tomorrow.'

∞

A man she had not seen before escorted her down a long corridor—she felt it was in the morning—though she could no longer be sure of the time of day since time had become so confused. She was taken to a room with soft peach walls, and comfy sofas like some one's living room; you wouldn't have thought this was a prison. A group of officers sat around, one spoke up that she could sit. They began questioning her, recounting details from the previous week's events; they knew everything, more than she did. They were picking her and her movements apart as you would slice a grapefruit, cutting it into segments and removing the pips.

'Can you remember the police arresting you?'

'Do you remember why they arrested you?'

'Do you know today's date?'

'Can you remember your date of birth?'

'Do you know your name?'

'DO YOU KNOW WHERE YOU ARE?'

'I, I, I…'

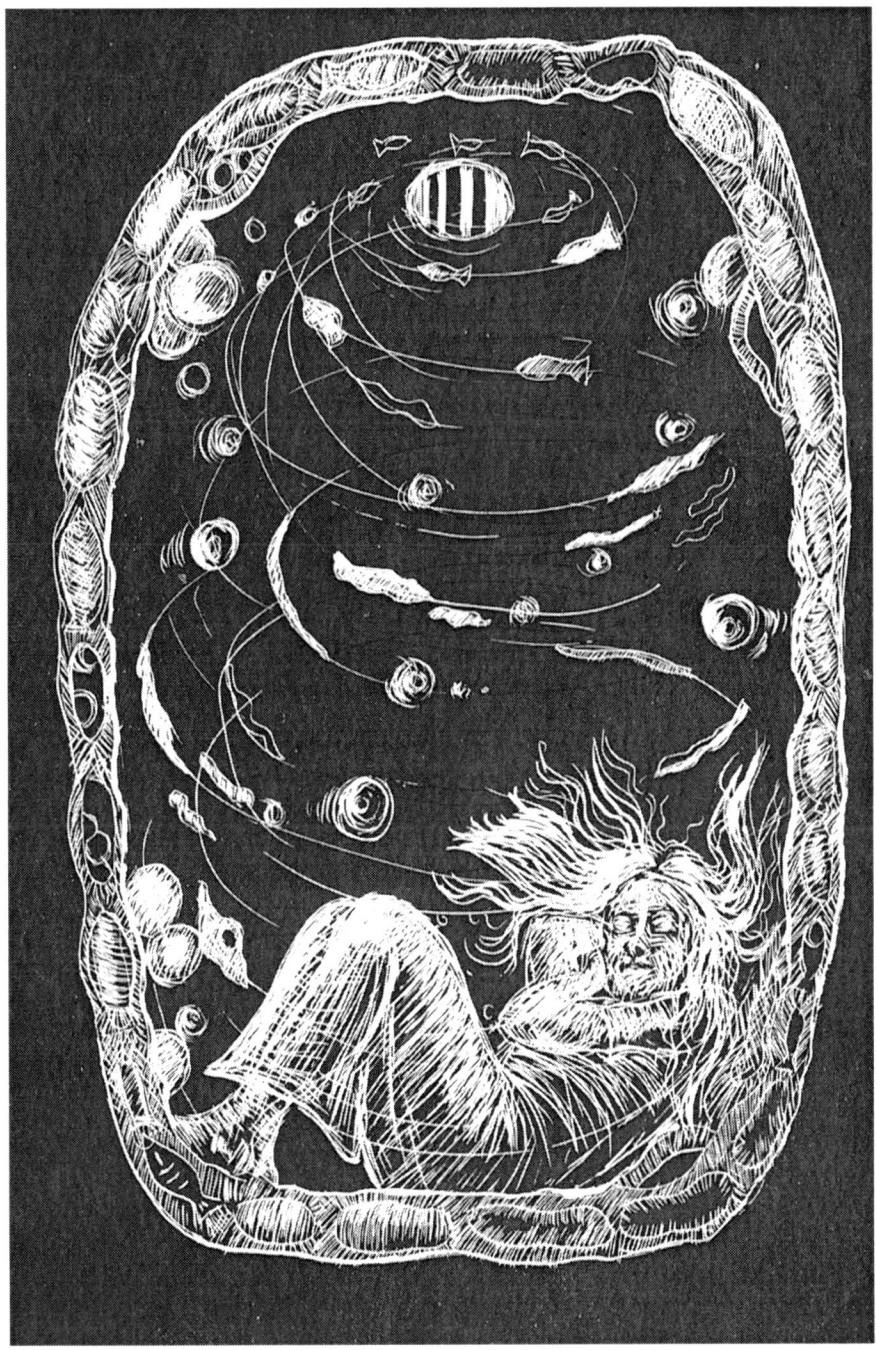

But there was nothing, no 'I' to speak of. They sent these bullet-questions flying at her, she felt shot through; her chest tightening, she muffled a scream. People appeared from the other side of the door, bleepers blazing they grabbed her arms and took her away, marched her back down the corridor and into the room.

BANG...

...She was sat in the cell, thoughts a cave of nightmares—garish creatures looming at her side, Devils and Angels whispering in her ears—it was a prison; she was in prison. She wore a frock, plastic to the touch; they had shoved her in a bath, roughly washed her hair and taken away her grimy clothes when she had arrived - an exposed new-born baby. She wanted to let out screams of panic, call for her mother to help her escape this place, where she felt surrounded by snipers hidden in the undergrowth. She could see their mirror-guns flashing in the sunlight out of the small window. She curled herself into a ball and rocked herself, a caged animal in despair. Someone was positioned outside, on guard; she could see her through the peephole, a spy monitoring every move. Her rocking was incessant, so they entered armed with a long syringe to calm her, force her into some somnambulist's nightmare. She resisted, but they held her down, gripped her by the arms and legs to stop her kicks, pricked her with the wicked witch's needle and she fell, a sleeping beauty, comatose.

Lost and Found

Monica Germanà

Brrr. Bal-tic. Rain is so last year. This year is all about ice and vampire skies: densely pale, with secret, purple bruises. The frozen breeze blew over her face, delivering a petulant answer to her thoughts. She sighed and wrapped her new scarf around her neck twice over, tucking the tussled ends well inside the raised collar of her coat. Not the fashionable, looser way with the scarf; the sensible one, leaving only a narrow slice of exposed skin, between matching hat and scarf. Pink. Merry Christmas, Sam. This will keep you warm in that cold, cold, flat of yours. Ha ha.

Glasgow's beer-gut was empty, but for the hidden threats of black ice and other—less invisible—objects: puddles of disintegrated food, torn rags of sequined garments, sparkling hems soiled in brown slush, sandals pining for their broken heels. Herds of half-naked Cinderellas had staggered home barefoot last night. Inches away from the drawn curtains of her front window, the party crowd had filed aimlessly past the thin wall of her house, desperate to make something memorable of a rather wet (this is Scotland, folks, remember?) and uneventful Hogmanay. Today's street performance had been stolen from a post-apocalyptic sci-fi movie: multi-coloured crushed cans, broken glass, half-eaten bagfuls of soggy chips were pasted onto the pavement. It was as if the city had been hit by a silent tornado: all that was left of the recent climax was a trashy mosaic of lifeless fragments and a muffled background noise, like the collective whisper of a congregation, when Mass is about to start. It was the morning after. Glasgow was nursing the first hangover of the year. It was a bad one.

Before she had reached the threshold, the concrete ogre opened its crystal jaws wide. Magic. Or hunger. Slouching against the wall on the right hand-side, a bulky lad in a dark uniform was fiddling with an earpiece and his mobile phone. He pulled a funny face to conceal an enormous yawn. Fancy working on New Year's Day. Ella Fitzgerald's festive tune filled the vacant air. Cheering people up. That was the idea, anyway. Whoever was in charge of music entertainment was still feeling Christmassy. Oversized letters and numbers were plastered all over the shop windows in fluorescent colours. In the small bookshop two young people were removing the tinsel decorations from the shelves. An old man was rummaging the special offers section in a basket at the front of the shop. Two ginger-haired children were running ahead of an older child, a redhead, too, in the main avenue. Pushing an empty pram, she stared ahead, a blank expression on her face. That those children once had belonged to her body didn't seem relevant any longer. The kids skipped around Sam and ran into the toyshop where teddy bears were 'stuffed while you wait'. Enormous pictures at the entrance illustrated this parody of creation: the furry carcass was filled from an aperture in the bear's backside, clothed in the ballet tutus, football outfits, bridal or punk accessories lined up on the shelves, and hey presto! a showgirl or lumberjack-boy bear was ready to be (paid for and) taken home. The older child entered the shop and stumbled, her Nike trainers entangled in a miniature beefeater; half a dozen animated cuddly toys were performing a chaotic choreograph around the shop-floor. Sam negotiated her way in, minding the treacherous floor. The two children had joined others staring at the conveyor belt rolling out bear after bear until their very own would be ready to take home.

'Mummymummymummymummy.' A sharp solo shriek and the unpleasant smell of burnt plastic announced the tragedy. One (unfortunate? blessed?) bear appeared to be stuck inside the cavernous opening of the teddy incubator. Angry tears were gathering over the cheeks of the youngest of the red-haired children, staring in disbelief at the Perspex glass that separated her from the half-stuffed, naked bear trapped in that absurd teddy limbo. The animated toys had gathered to the crime scene; fighting for attention at Sam's feet a fluffy pink creature (a piglet?) was frantically simulating an indecent sexual act on a black-legged lamb: both had a seraphic smile stitched to the soft fabric of their faces.

Red lights flashed simultaneously around the coin slot of the drinks vending machine. Sam had never got around to putting the fairy lights up on her Christmas tree; they were still wrapped in their sealed box in her flat. The intermittent lights felt oddly reassuring; their continuous flicker could last forever. An intermittent glimpse of life and loss, like the cadenced beam of a lighthouse. Or just a reminder of the continuity of time. Whether she liked it or not, things were moving on, seasons were changing, new clothes, new shoes, and new greetings-card ranges were being stocked in each and every corner of the galleries. She wanted to tear the virgin pages of shiny diaries lined up on the shelves, ready to be filled with lists, birthdays, important dates. She wanted to rip time off. And con space. She stretched her arms out, reaching out as far as possible. Her arms did not accidentally touch the body of a passer-by. They filled out the empty space. Now that presents had all been wrapped and unwrapped, the yeasty taste of cheap mulled wine had vanished from her mouth, intoxicated kisses shared under artificial mistletoes, she should cherish this solitary, purposeless trip to the shopping centre. What separated pleasure from its painful aftermath? Her body no longer knew.

Some of the shop windows were completely covered up in large sheets of brown paper, concealing the secrets of the new season to come; in others staff were openly performing changes to their display. Here and there dummies were lying in awkward poses, stark naked; their foamy bodies, artificially propped up, looked as if they were about to climax or faint. A plastic orgy, or a comatose after-party. Her favourite shop looked unusually minimalist. Vacant, in fact. Few garments were sparsely piled up in colour-coded shelves at the front of the shop. At the back a new space was being created for the new collection and several people were busy unpacking large cardboard boxes and taking the new garments out of their plastic covers. A pile of diamante-embroidered knitted jumpers drew her attention. A shop assistant walked gingerly towards her.

'Do you need some help?'

Sam considered that question carefully in hear head: she definitely did. The girl was fidgeting and seemed unusually eager to assist. She was a flash of silver: a glittering shadow shimmered on her eyelids, a large bangle rested high on her left forearm and a brushed steel choker appeared to support her thin neck; her feet were trapped in metallic pumps. Each of her fingers was wrapped in a silver ring and their tips coated in elongated glistening nails.

'Well, I don't know. I am looking for a... top.' Sam's voice sounded croaky. She was lost for words; these were the first ones she had spoken since waking up (alone) in her flat. 'Yes, something a bit... unusual, something different.' Polite smile.

'What size?' Brief (awkward) pause.

'I'm a size 11.' Silence.

'That doesn't ex... We don't have that size. We have sizes 10 and 12.'

Patience was running out. The girl gave Sam's outfit a quick, all-round look. Sizing her up. Sam rubbed her hand over her face; it felt greasy. This morning was too cold to contemplate the idea of wet. The girl trotted away, leaving Sam to run her fingers over the embroidered tops. They felt too stiff and rough under her fingertips. She glanced over her shoulder and left the shop without waiting.

The spongy shuffle of her rubber soles against the polished surface of the tiled floor sent soothing vibrations through her body; she could rely on the familiar rhythm of her walk. As a child she always listened to her own heartbeat against her pillow, each night, before falling asleep. The sugary scent of the wax the cleaners had used to shine the floor slabs earlier was still filling the air. She watched reflections of her insular silhouette appear and disappear on the mirrored wall fencing the escalator. Her body flashed by, stretching into impossible figures, dissected by the flickering lights of the shopping centre and then vanishing to be replaced by another distorted fragment of herself. Her eyelids felt heavy; she could have done with a lie-in.

A sudden scream rippled the numb surface of her thoughts. A bestial sound. Inhumanly loud. Her fingers tightened their grip on the handrail, the sweat of her palm seeping through the sticky plastic. Something was thrashing around convulsively, a body contorting and fighting its own mass against the metal surfaces of the escalator. The gaping mouth was barking raucously. Its eyes were wide open, all white, like shiny hard-boiled eggs protruding from their sockets. The mouth was baring a full set of teeth, their whiteness matching its glossy eyeballs. Her legs felt very heavy. Screaming seemed a good option, but her vocal cords seemed unable to project any sound. She felt trapped within an invisible frame, each of her limbs secured by a ghostly shackle and her throat choked by an impalpable collar. Somebody had stopped the escalator and someone else was already assisting the... Sam walked cautiously down the stationary escalator. Could it start again? The contorted mouth was grinning like a grotesque woodcarving. She could still hear a hissing and barking echo reverberating around the empty avenues of the shopping centre.

Blue flashing lights appeared quietly. Two fluorescent jackets picked the body up carefully, handling it with detached care. Sam wondered whether they were going to use a white body bag, like the ones you saw in films. Meticulously wrapping the body up, like a piece of meat over a butcher's counter. Zipped up inside its sterile wrapper, it would become harmless, just like chicken breasts, or minced beef. No. They were placing it on a stretcher and strapping it up. Was that to prevent it from moving? Was it going to start again in the ambulance?

Somebody inserted a needle into the body's left arm. It was linked to a pipe, hanging from a large upside-down bottle.

The clear liquid was bubbling inside the tube. It seemed all over. No more pouncing. There was nothing to worry about, after all. Then she saw it. A woolly hat was lying on the step immediately below her feet. Unsure, she picked it up. It felt odd in her hand. Warm. A series of buttons decorated the felt rim of the hat. One of them was missing. She looked around, then started frantically wading through an ocean of people, drops of fresh blood blending in with dozens grey bodies that suddenly seemed to have materialised on the scene. She reached the ambulance just before the stretcher slid inside it. She stopped to catch her breath, before she could speak to one of the fluorescent people.

'I found this... this belongs to...'

Her lips parted, then the motionless body lying on the stretcher gave one sudden jerk, arching her spine as if in an effort to set itself free. The fluorescent people fastened the body again to its temporary support. Just before it disappeared inside the ambulance, the head turned again, eyes wide open. The mouth opened, as if to speak.

'Good girl. Stay calm. We are here to help you. Everything is going to be all right. That's it.'

The voice spoke slowly, emotionless, mentally reading from a training manual. He was following a procedure, but the person inside that body didn't seem to hear. Or care. Staring past him, the body stretched an arm out at Sam.

The identical white cubicle doors stood parallel, open at a 45-degree angle, as in a domino run of white-veiled nuns. Sam bent over to double-check if there was anybody inside. She was breathing heavily, looking around herself, trying to remember what she went in there for. She turned the cold water on and stared at her own hand receiving the cold flow until her fingers were nearly numb. She caught a glimpse of herself in the mirror. Her eyes had been crying fragments of dead mascara. Her pale lips were glued together; the inside of her mouth was beginning to feel parched again. She tried relaxing her jaw, even attempting a fake, elastic smile. She felt for her lipstick in her handbag, when she noticed something strange: the bag strap was stained; an uncanny shade of burgundy. She ran her finger over it; it was still wet and discoloured the tip of her finger. Anxiously, she looked around the neon-lit room. She was still alone. She turned the tap again and washed her hand thoroughly with the green soap from the dispenser. On her way out, a young woman in a white coat walked past her. She smiled politely at her, and Sam felt her facial muscles relax. She had only walked a few paces, when the woman came out walking after her.

'Wait! You forgot something.' She was flagging something in the air.

'This must be yours.'

∞

My eyelids feel heavy. I struggle to half-open my eyes, gradually focussing, between my lashes, on the image directly opposite myself. A beach of clotted cream, two palm trees complete with dangling coconuts are choreographed into a perfect arch against the background of turquoise sky and emerald sea dotted with miniature white sailing boats. Utopia: it could be anywhere, or nowhere. A flower arrangement stands erect directly underneath the painting, complimenting its colours. The saturated hue of the petals and the rigid stems make the flowers look hilarious: like the type of circus prop that a clown will use to squirt water all over another clown's face. Somebody must have aligned the bouquet to the centre of the frame; but there is something odd: the vase appears as if suspended, there is no furniture on which it could rest. Like Alice in her wonder world, I close my eyes and re-open them again, trying to make sense of my absurd surroundings. Now I see it, as it is. A large mirror, framing the painting and the bouquet. I pan the room clock-wise: the real objects are right beside me, poster, flowers, sitting on a chest of drawers. The slight physical effort reminds me of my body, tender under a heavy blanket. I attempt to stretch my toes a little; the stiff fabric of the sheets is reluctant to my movements. When I inhale, a bleachy smell tickles my throat. I cough lightly. 'Happy New Year. How are you feeling?'

I am not alone, then. The other person, a woman, is smiling broadly. She is looking outside a window, pointing to a cadaverous sky.

'It's sooo cold outside.' She howls, like a ghost.

Feathery flakes are dancing merrily against the backdrop of a stubby, dark, stone building in the background; a few disintegrate carelessly against the clear windowpane. I picture the rich-yellow hue of daffodils: soon they will pop up like strings of coloured glass beads to garnish loans, parks, and mossy patches across the city. But I am distracted again by the performer in the room. The woman is now hugging herself, crossing her arms across her body and rubbing the sleeves of her white dress in a rapid up-and-down motion.

'One needs to dress for the weather.'

She bites her lower lip and then her eyes open wide, raising her eyebrows into two pointy arches. She may be about to crack a good joke.

'I bet you can't remember what you were wearing earlier.'

I am still waiting for the punch line, when the woman walks around the bed, to the chest of drawers I've just located beside my bed. A drawer is swiftly opened and closed. It sounds empty. There is a knowing look on her face, like that of a self-conscious magician. I can almost hear the drum roll announcing the climax of this strange performance. She raises her arm, triumphantly holding her prop. A piece of pink material. A hat. One of the buttons is missing.

'This must be yours, Sam.'

Flood Relief

Carrie Dare

Cherry Magnolia has come to her senses. She intuits that the landscape, internal and external, is no longer fully male. The stop signs have been uprooted, they will arrive eventually down river, in a delta or deserted barrio, stacked against the banks like broken bones. The air is lush, rotten, faecal, poisoned and florid. The scenery is adamantly ripe and full, becoming heady, hallucinatory, reeking of iris wine and blood moon. It is both feast and frenzy, female, pagan, pre-historic and devotional.

There is a thrill in ruin, in decay, in the guttural sneer of flood water, racing. Cherry Magnolia swims by with her hands in gloves, appraising the quality of foaming effluent, siphoning it into jars as barges lunge towards her and onwards to the spent, open seas. Toxins will save the day, spawning new lives in the form of foetuses sporting fins and gills, swaying through the puddled, muddy streets in infantile shoals. Cherry Magnolia lines up samples of flood and effluent in her jars, sterilised by fire and baked in the sun. She will observe the planet pausing. Grief is considered, exhumed from the river bed, held up to the sun. Cherry Magnolia observes the mutations of water, its ebb becoming embryo, its slow solidifying and anxious will to form.

Cherry Magnolia knows her name contains blossom and renewal, she carries the promise of spring, of upright trees and floral arrangements, zen weddings and paint charts. Cherry Magnolia has six syllables on her side. She has momentum, her awkwardness has risen to heights of abstraction, becoming monumental. Her hands are time, her mouth makes tides, makes the moon reconsider, makes sounds like spaces. Cherry Magnolia lists the things that could not be kept. She does this alphabetically:

A is for anger, ebbing away, leaving silt and stains in higher regions, diluting itself into a simple bitter liquid, drained down river and distilled to a drop, a speck of

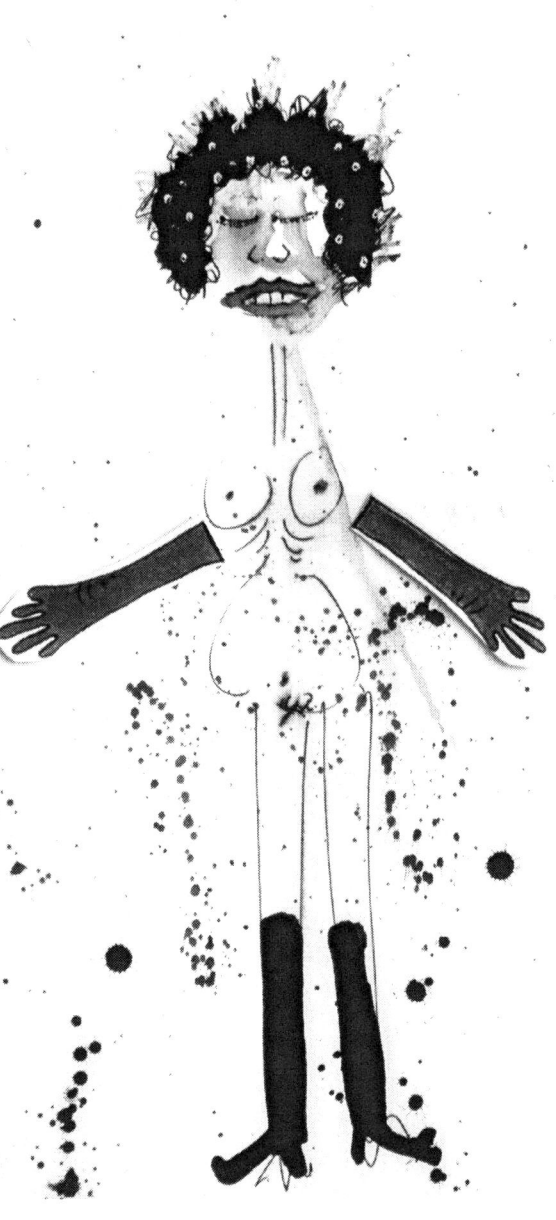

mud water.

B is for blood ties, gone overnight, entire families failing to recognise their own features, their bonded frailties stripped bare, not one thread left hanging.

C is for confusion, replaced by clarity,

composure, configurations for new beginnings, pre-requisites for a priestess born of tides and furious gushes of foam.

D is for dependency. E is for estimation. F is for fear. Cherry Magnolia is magnificent in the blackness, the last stages of her re-build now visible in the dark. The only woman to survive the waters. A strange swan gliding by. A new moon. The stilling of torrents still to come.

Cherry Magnolia has achieved refugee status without leaving home. This reverberates across the expanse, catching on rooftops, echoing through tunnels of collapsed houses. A people without papers have been born, a population mutating, becoming migrant with the birds, fluid, combatant, hopeless, ready for anything, for the next turn of the wheel. She begins speaking in rhyme, deciphering it as a form of prayer, a semaphore of the spirit. She says out loud that history was a deformity, a cataclysm. Her experiments with water have revealed this.

Cherry Magnolia had crumbled in increments, becoming vulnerable in certain winds, alert to the silent crashes of other women and the subtext of law-makers. Flood is a relief. Cherry Magnolia recalls the smell of outrage, over ripe, hung-over, dragging. She dons a band of twisted metal, crowning, glittering in sunlight and moonbeam. Her hair gives up its braids, holds itself up to the light. She unfolds a sodden and twisted flag from its pole and announces it as a costume, fallen, seamless, free. She is her own Republic, uncharted.

Three Women

Mary Byrne

You are 'churched' after each of us—including the baby who lived only 3 weeks—as if birthing is not punishment enough, as if you have been sullied, or are guilty of something. You feel this was suggested by the smug look on the nun-midwife's face. They are all medical missionaries. Each time, as you wait in the hospital church alone, you ask yourself why Dad isn't there too. Why isn't he here too? You howl silently to the cold church. And the answer comes as another accusation: he couldn't get off work and cycle 15 miles.

We are often sick. The house is rented, from the new castle owner who wants the rents up or everybody out, or both. And then there's your heart-ill mother in another of the estate houses. Your brother marries and two women find themselves in front of your mother's stove. The new daughter-in-law is not the kindest of people, but she has her own problems. They too are having babies. Some too are lost. Everyone is in the same boat, like the other houses on the estate. Dad cycles to work 10 miles round trip, arriving late in the evenings to you and us sick kids in two damp rooms and scullery, and always the possibility of getting thrown out. You haven't felt great since the death of our baby brother. There is a great snowfall and Dad walks to work.

Your brother and his family move out into another, smaller, cheaper house. After asking around, you and Dad rent a house for your mother from a friendly farmer who won't panic if you can't pay on time. After a short while she has yet another stroke. You and Dad walk and cycle in and out to hospital. You take her laundry home and wash it by hand in water heated on the old black stove. You remember her questioning face in the white bed: her inability to form the words, her wanting to be, to die, at home.

You feel guilty about this for up on 50 years. You now think she was wondering, in some inarticulate way, why you were doing this to her. You have nightmares about it, even and especially as the Celtic Tiger is in full spate. You organise your last years to avoid ending up like her.

Finally, when there is nothing left for you to work at or worry about, as home helps and medical helps come and go to the house, all you have to do is think and wait. But guilt will make you cry, and regret that you weren't able to do better for her. If she were here now, you would take her into this space and money. And warmth—above all, a warm house (even for someone on anticoagulants). When you ask if it's too warm, Dad—in the other armchair—mutters 'Shirt is stuck to me back'.

You dream that you are cycling past the house you lived in as a young girl. Your father joins your mother at the gate, his head sideways in that quizzical way, his old battered hat and moustache signifying other, more gentlemanly, times. You say to your dead sister, who seems to be with you, 'She'll be all right now, Daddy is there to look after her.'

You wake up. It is your 90th birthday. You have come through illness, poverty, hard work, bad luck. You have survived churching by men after the birth of children, the preaching of the same men who told you how to raise them. Neither the little education you managed to get, nor the culture you grew up in, provided you with the means to free yourself of the guilt those men bred in you. At 90 they still bring tears to your eyes.

Mysteriously, you still have a certain respect for the former lord and castle occupant, excommunicated after marrying for the third time the last bit of money that would keep him going for the final years. You remember Buicks on the avenue, talk of how warm Palestine is in winter, and detailed descriptions of stylish clothes and fabrics. You reminisce to children and grandchildren about the lord waiting on the balcony for the servants' return from Mass on Sunday mornings. You are still impressed that he always enquired of the servants about the theme of the weekly sermon. This was proof, for you, that he was a good man, really, unlike the greedy one to whom he sold out in the end, and who never had much luck either. You are convinced that all the bad luck is explained by the curse put on the whole property, castle, occupants and tenants, centuries ago, in the time of Oliver Plunkett. This is part of your heritage of stories of hauntings and mysteries, contact with the after-life, stories that go back beyond the Famine. Somehow such stories stop with you, for even you have doubts about a god and an afterlife.

You dip into Buddhism, have chats with a Bah'ai neighbour. You are curious about—but not fearful of—an afterlife. Grandchildren realise you are smart enough to cope with a fax machine for speeded-up letters. Some years later you move on to emails—which really scare you at first. Finally you manage to whizz photos and videos of family get-togethers around the world to places you've never been.

From time to time you ask how the whole thing works, fail to understand, and pause to marvel. You laugh and mutter, 'Them things'd frighten you'. To keep your head and steady your ailing heart, you organise family visits. Used to catering for others' tastes, you dictate sandwiches and their contents, someone's favourite home-made cake, who to pour tea for first because they like it weak.

May comes, and your birthday. We eat out. It is early, the restaurant is empty and hasn't warmed up. You enjoy it all, but shed a tear for Dad, too ill to be with us. 'April will try you, and May will find you,' you say mysteriously.

When the dessert arrives, it is of Celtic Tiger proportions: 'Just eat what you want and leave the rest,' we say. You take the spoon, determined as a 20-year-old: 'I'll leave nothing behind me.' You repeat Dad's description of thrifty families, where 'Nothing goes to loss but the squeal.'

Two weeks later you die just hours before Dad. Half of your mind in a world connected with Mesolithic times, the other half firmly anchored in the modern, you are hooked up in those last minutes to machines that cannot bring your heart out of its spin or convince you it is worth hanging in there, once more, as the nice Arab doctor convinced you that time a few years ago.

This time you listen to yourself, and go.

Fiddling about on the computer today, I accidentally click on a Christmas video from you. There you are, suddenly, moving and speaking goodwill, as if you were here in the room with me.

I wish in my turn that I could fetch you back into my nice warm house and look after you.

My turn to think of when you—and therefore I—were churched, my turn to mouth these words that cannot be spoken, words you cannot hear, until I too become heart-ill.

They Tarred the Road that Day

Bronwen Griffiths

They tarred the road that day. The sky was like something out of a cheap magazine and I was going to cut the hedges but I did not.

My husband said, 'Nat is expected at one thirty; we have important work to do.'

'OK,' I said and I turned away and looked at the wall. We'd only met Nat a few weeks before but I couldn't stop thinking about him even though I didn't know him any more than I knew the underside of my toes. He was way too young with grey eyes, which changed with the light. At least I thought they were grey: that's how little I knew about him.

I'd never felt this way; that's what I reckoned. Of course I knew about others. How could I not? Often it was all people talked about. But for me this was different.

'You're confusing lust with love,' my friend Sonia said and she frowned in that way she had.

I shook my head furiously. 'It's more complicated than that.'

'Rubbish,' said Sonia. 'Things are only as complicated as you make them.'

But things were complicated and in all sorts of directions. Nat had a girlfriend. Well; what did I expect? He was young and a musician. Did I think he would be a hermit? I saw them together a couple of times, arm in arm. They looked happy enough. But I couldn't complain. I had a husband knocking around the place.

The morning that Nat was expected, a huge machine trundled up and down the road, spouting smoke and dripping tar, and the workmen shouted, and my heart fluttered reckless under my ribs. At midday I went out into the garden and placed my hands on the summer grass and wondered if I could tie myself to Nat through the power of thought and slip into his dreams unannounced? Or, if during the day, he might be surprised to think about me differently. It was nonsense, I told myself. Yet maybe it wasn't. Everything is illusion. Part of me could be a strand of his hair, or that cinnabar moth, red and black. I could even be Juliet, I thought. That's how bloody tragic I was feeling.

When I heard the knock on the door at twenty past one, I was afraid to answer it. I thought that Nat might take one look at me and see into my heart and cut me right open. But I didn't want my husband to get to the door first.

'Hi,' Nat said; all grin and innocence. 'How's it all going?'

'Fine,' I answered, levelling my eyes at him but he just shrugged me off, sat down and took off his shoes. We always did that in our house.

I stood in the hallway and watched him. His hair was like a thousand tiny corkscrews and he was wearing a black T-shirt with no sleeves. He smelled of strawberries and summer and his shoes were broken down at the back. I wanted us to stay there forever but it was impossible; he and the husband had their important work to do and soon they were playing their music so loud, the house shook.

I spent the afternoon with Sonia, frizzling away money on coffee and ice cream. It was the end of August. Everyone was in town, and the old guy with the long, silver ponytail who always shouts out, 'Up the Arsenal. Down with United.'

Sonia told me that she had bet £50 on the horses.

'That's a bit wild,' I said, knowing how little she earned.

'I like things wild.'

I knew she did and I envied her that because I'd always been such a good girl.

While we sipped our frothy cappuccinos and blinked against the sunlight, I told Sonia about a film that I'd watched the night before. It was a love story and it had a sad ending. I didn't say that I had cried all the way through. When I had finished, a cloud drifted across the sky. It looked like a communion dress.

I told Sonia about Nat. 'You should get yourself a lover,' she said. 'Really, it's not difficult.' But she was years younger than I was and she never let her heart rule her head.

'I've been trying. But I never have always any luck.' I looked at the ring on my finger and counted the years.

'Luck? It's not a matter of luck, you know.'

'Do you think I'm crazy to feel this way?'

She shrugged. 'Everyone is crazy, you know. It's no big deal.'

∞

So much happened that summer. The weather was scorching and I swam in the sea every day. I discovered that I could hold my breath under the water for five minutes like those women who dive for pearls in the South China Sea. Every day I extended my breath until I felt more at home in the water than out of it.

A week after Nat came to the house my husband and I took off to France with our two sons, Lawrence and Ben. One evening we attended a music and dance festival. It was a starry black night with the wind blowing off the sea, cool and tangy. I was drinking the local wine, though it tasted rough.

'You're drinking like it's going out of fashion,' my husband complained.

'Really?' I said, draining the glass.

We sat down on a narrow wooden bench. I watched the boys and my husband laughing together, fooling around. It was good to see them that way but I couldn't join in because I was far away, thinking of Nat. He had suddenly become real and solid under my feet even though he was hundreds of miles distant. I could feel his hands on me and smell that hint of strawberry in his hair, blowing in the wind.

'What's up with you?' my husband asked later, back at the auberge. I was crying and making little gulping sounds as though I was drowning.

'It's nothing.'

'You always get like this when you've had too much to drink,' he said, taking off his shoes. He sounded irritable.

I didn't argue with him. I supposed it was true in a way.

∞

Soon after we arrived back in England, we were invited to a music festival a few miles from our home. It took place in a field above an apple orchard. Nat was there but I didn't speak to him. He was with his new girl. She had cherry red hair, smooth skin and lips like the Madonna that hung on my bathroom wall. I wanted to be her. Instead I felt like a wrinkled apple, dropped on the grass, rotting from the inside out.

My husband kept chatting to his mate, who'd come down from London for the day. 'These new computer chips are phenomenal,' the friend was saying. 'Who knows where it will end up?'

'Who knows,' my husband echoed.

They rattled on about computers, before starting up on where to buy the best pint of beer in the south. I didn't join in the conversation. I walked to the top of the orchard, away from the conversation and the crowds, away from Nat and his girlfriend. There was an old swing up there, tucked into a corner. I sat down and moved my legs back and forth, like I'd done as a child, searching for the sky. Higher and higher. The white lights strung across the apple trees turned blurry and my stomach tipped upside down, the same as when I thought of Nat. From my place in the sky I could see the tents and the marquee stage, and people fooling about on the bouncy castle. The air smelt of wood smoke and the damp of a late summer's evening.

'Come down,' someone shouted, joking.

The sky turned yellow as a field of buttercups. Then it caught fire and woolly clouds fled from it. When it was over, everything turned a soft grey. The moon rose, pared down and golden-white and it was facing the evening star as if to eat it, make love to it. Later the star rose and it was no longer caught in the moon's gaze.

Slowly I returned to the earth. I was no longer sad. I was just happy with the fact that I had met Nat. Nothing more mattered. Everything was pure magic.

The metal chains from the swing dug into my hip. I had bruises for weeks afterwards but that sort of hurt never troubled me.

∞

In September I started teaching at a new school. It was an Indian summer and the shadows were long but the kids scratched on my nerves and every day there were problems that had never bothered me in the past.

One day after I'd shouted at the kids, I sent Nat a text during my lunch break. I had his number because he'd left a message on our phone a few weeks before.

'I'm drowning,' I said. I didn't care if his girlfriend saw the message. I was past any sort of caring. I was sick of being a worker and a wife and a mother, sick of mopping up after everyone, sick to my bones of it all. I couldn't stand everything being so regular: the morning lunch boxes, the weekly trip to the supermarket, coupling on Sundays. Even the rhythm of my own heart was boring me half to death.

I couldn't sleep properly at nights either. There were hours when I watched the pale square of light from the window and listened to my husband breathing. He sounded like the sea.

It wasn't my husband I wanted anymore.

∞

One morning I woke up after a bad dream convinced that the house was listing like a ship.

'Something's wrong,' I said to my husband.

'What is it now?' he groaned without opening his eyes.

I tried to explain the problem. 'Our house used to be so perfect,' I said.

His eyelids opened and he gave me an odd look.

'See what I mean!' I yelled. 'You never understand!'

The house had never been perfect because when you look back on everything you forget the flaws: a grubby wall here, a mark on the kitchen side there. You even forget that you once loved a man, who turns over in the morning and shrugs.

'There's nothing wrong with the house,' my husband said. 'You've been dreaming.'

At breakfast, my son Lawrence reminded me that I'd promised to buy him new trainers. When I looked at him, I saw a stranger. Only the day before he'd been a boy but now he was a man. His legs were hairy and there were spots on his chin.

'I'll buy them next week,' I said.

'That's too late.' Lawrence moaned and stamped his foot as if he was still four years old.

'I'm having new trainers too, aren't I?' Ben put in.

'Oh; for goodness sake!'

'It will soon be Christmas,' my husband joked, playing with his Cornflakes. For the first time I noticed that his bones were beginning to poke out. Nat didn't have bones like that.

'I hate Christmas,' I said.

'No you don't.' My husband laughed a brittle laugh like his bones. Lawrence and Ben just stared at me.

'I do hate it!'

'Don't forget to pick up the milk,' my husband added just as I was closing the door.

'Buy a bloody cow,' I shouted, slamming the door so hard, the house shook.

∞

I took the dog out for a walk. Dew lay heavy on the early morning grass and the grass was silver. No, it was more like bleach. Bleached grass.

I checked my mobile for messages but there were none. I sent Nat another text. '*Get me out of here!!!*' The message shot into the universe and did not come back.

I lay down in the field of yellow flowers. It was warm and everything was gold and green. I closed my eyes, let the earth take me. The sun moved up another notch in the sky and it grew hot. Doves cooed. Dogs barked in the distance. I opened my eyes. Below me, the sea appeared impossibly calm: a membrane stretched between the town and the sky. A ship floated on the horizon and I waited for it to move. I wondered how long I would wait. Sometimes life felt like one long waiting room.

The dog climbed an anthill. I swung into an oak tree and listened to the grasshoppers in the meadow below. The dog was patient. He was looking at the church in the valley, his brown ears cocked. I saw the ship on the horizon had moved and I wondered if that might mean something.

We walked home, the dog and I, through spiders' webs like tiny silver skeletons. There was no wind, only the nodding of the topmost branches and the faintest sigh, like a lover.

∞

'I'm sick,' I explained to the school secretary on the end of the phone. 'It must be something I ate.'

'I hope you feel better soon,' she said.

It was true in a way, I was sick.

I drank coffee in the garden and made pizzas for supper. I put the washing on the line and tidied the living room, and in the late afternoon I dropped my sons off at the cinema. My husband was out. He rarely socialised but he'd gone to watch the match with a friend.

'You can walk home together,' I said to my sons.

'Mum!' Ben said and his eyebrows shot up. 'Can't you collect us?'

I shook my head.

'But you always do,' they said together.

'Not this time.' I said quite definitely. That shut them up.

I drove the car down to the car park under the cliff. It was late and I didn't need a ticket. The shingle beach was deserted except for a few kids chucking stones in the water. I changed into my old swimming costume, a baggy thing. Then I folded my clothes into a neat pile and finished it off with a large stone. From a distance the pile looked like a cairn, a holy thing.

I texted Nat one last time. Whatever happened, I promised: I wouldn't send another. *I love U. XXX.* I hoped it would mean something. After I had sent it, I erased his number.

I swam out past the pier and the orange marker buoys. The water was not cold and no one noticed me. Dusk was falling and the lights were coming on in town. I could hear music, people laughing. The town looked like a garment sewn with orange sequins. The sky was pressing down on it, metal and heavy; a colour I couldn't place. Eventually the sounds faded and I could hear nothing but my own ragged breathing, my body pushing through the water. Ahead the sea was dark and unforgiving.

I remembered a dream I'd had earlier in the summer, an old woman standing on the beach, throwing food from a bucket into the sea. And a thousand, thousand fish silver in the water.

I kept on swimming. I did not feel tired. It wasn't certain that I'd come back, not certain at all. Only love was certain, that's what I was thinking.

∞

When they saw my wet towel and costume, my sons asked me what I'd been doing.

'I swam out to the edge,' I replied.

'Did you get as far as the horizon?' Ben asked. His eyes were wide open.

'Further than that.'

'Give over, Mum,' Lawrence said and though he laughed I knew he wasn't quite sure.

'It's true.' I smiled at them both.

'Why did you go swimming so late?' Lawrence added, 'It's almost dark.'

'I was looking for someone.'

'Did you find them?' Ben said, walking over and turning on the television.

'No, I've lost him,' I said, 'but it doesn't matter anymore.' Then I kissed them both and they squirmed like a couple of eels.

Finding Loss

Glittermouse

For Gordon and Valerie Lawrence

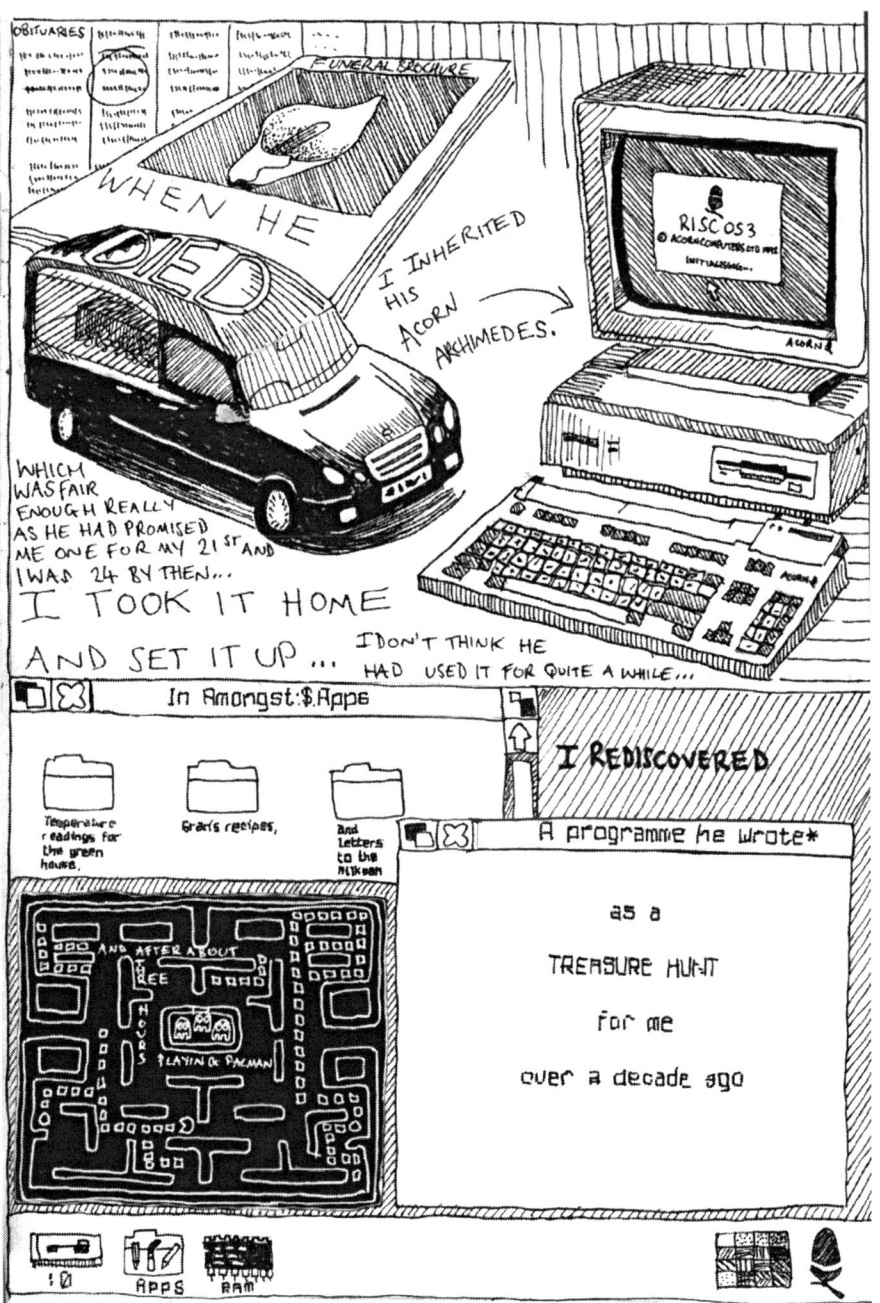

OF COURSE, I RAN THE PROGRAMME ...

upon correct response to a question
a basic animation would run
and a new question would pop up...

I managed a few... What is the cat's name?

Where do you live? but some like

Where did Gran have a Mother's Union meeting on Wednesday?
ELUDED ME ...

AN AMUSING EVENING WAS SPENT

WITH A CODER FRIEND

WHO
> HELPED ME
> CRACK THE
> PROGRAMME

AND GET THE ANSWERS

BBC BASIC

WE EVENTUALLY SAT DOWN TO RELIVE THE
EXCITEMENT OF A THIRTEEN YEAR OLD
SUNDAY AFTERNOON TREASURE HUNT ...

I FINALLY ENTERED THE ANSWER TO THE LAST CLUE.

I WOULD NOT HAVE THOUGHT EIGHT WORDS

COULD HAVE ENGENDERED SUCH A

FEELING OF ABSENCE

WELL DONE!
Now ask Granddad
for the treasure!

Acorn

AND THEN I REALISED··· THE TREASURE HAD ALWAYS BEEN WORTH SO MUCH MORE THAN A POUND!

AND I'D NEVER REALLY HAD TO ASK FOR IT

THOUGH IN SOME WAYS I'D ALWAYS HAVE IT··· RIGHT THERE AND THEN IT COULDN'T HAVE FELT

MORE LOST.

The Octavius

Matt Webber

He was due back. He had been due back for days, but every second seemed liked a missed appointment. She had lost count of the number of times she had stood here, but was doing it again. She could see the garden, and the sea beyond, through the drizzle streaking the rough glass of the window. The plunging scree that bordered the front door of their house had become so familiar to her over the years that, though even now she told herself she watched the dead tree sigh in the wind, she could see nothing. He was missing from this scene, still, and the path to the sea remained pointless.

Yet even the clicking rain could not puncture the silence of these hours. Her family had once lived in this house, which sits on a rolling outcrop of the Devon coastline. It was ancient, and from afar it resembled nothing more than a decaying pile of gravel. Once, the door slams and window creaks had been constant. Now, the clammy air deadened even the weather, and a trapped fly would be welcomed.

Ophelia had experienced this wait many times. The whaling vessels that repeatedly stole her husband were not known for their punctuality. The men of Teignmouth lied. What was worse, they knew they lied. Every foetal dawn they stood on the rose-lit jetty bidding their women goodbye, they repeated the same definite time-scales; 3 weeks to the Iceland hunting grounds, a week each to find and gut the unlucky Cetacean, and 4 weeks home. The women, except those who had the misfortune of being recently married, knew these were lies, or vague estimates at best. The wind is not made of sand, there are no clockwork whales, and any expedition could last months.

Yet he had not died this time, at least not yet. The ship had not returned, so for now he was alive. It was with this knowledge that she continued to wait. When he left to fish, the days were long even in winter. Without his boots, without him eating, the house stayed clean and the meals became simple. The house, for these weeks, became some underwater chasm for her, some dredging cave inhabited by the grotesque, blind fauna of her memories. She remained calm before their pulsing march, burnt the newspapers, and filled her first weeks with chores. By the 4th week, increasingly desperate, she was cleaning the guttering and the underside of chairs. She had never made this ritual last longer than 6 weeks, and always returned to this window at its conclusion.

This time it had been an age. He had now been gone for 4 months, and she had been waiting for 3. This was her 11th time, and it was the worst. Never had it taken his long for his shadow to darken the path again, and she was worried. She had been considering a visit to the village for days, for news. *The Times* was a regular visitor when he was here, but was forcefully exiled when she was alone; she burnt the left-over copies, as soon as she got home, every time he left. Whilst he was here, she tolerated its presence, though she had moved his reading chair, years ago, to the darkest corner of the room. She could not watch him read it, but the sound of his rope-burned hands on the paper still filled her with energetic dread, her heartbeat jumping into her throat with each page turn. When he read aloud from it, mostly from benign stories of curiosity, she was seized with violent nausea, as she had been the first time.

This had been the morning after her wedding night, in a July that seemed long ago. They had been in this room, when his chair still stood in the centre. The story he had stumbled upon, though he did not know this, concerned her first lie to him. He had been shocked, the night before, but understanding: she was not a virgin. This, in the year of our lord 1785, was cause for violence. She lied, and told him she had been raped. Though he had pressed her, she refused to say which hardened whaler (for it must have been one of them) had stolen his bride's sanctity. She could not, for the gentle young fisherman was dead, or so the paper said. He had been lost aboard *The Octavius*, and was just another name amongst the faceless dead that her new husband sombrely read aloud that morning. The innocent symbols that had been his moniker multiplied, for Ophelia, echoing back and forth from the gravel walls is some hideous, pulsing cacophony. He continued reading, oblivious to the racking ticks building on his new wife's face. *The Octavius*, he intoned, had made good time on the outward portion of her voyage. She arrived in the Orient barely a month late, and had unloaded a sizeable cargo of woollens. *The Times*, at this point, went to great pains to point out the value of these garments, 'much prized for making the brooms the stocky orientals used to sweep their blessed cherry blossom from their pristine streets.' Ophelia began to sway, the walls threatened to collapse, her eyes rolled back in growing nausea. Indeed, the paper continued, *The Octavius* seemed to have arrived at a fortuitous time, for she was able to negotiate an exorbitant price for her cargo. It was then that the considerably richer crew, buoyed by their bulging purses, had started talking of the North-West Passage. They were not discreet, reported the paper, and talked openly of their plan upon departure. They were last seen in Hawaii, a year ago. It was the paper's sad duty, it continued, to therefore report the loss of *The Octavius* and all her crew. Ophelia, struggling to stay conscious through the deadened weight of her lover's endlessly screamed name, fighting spasms through the overwhelming weight of the loss, was crushed. Her stomach dropped out from under her, her legs buckled under the weight of blood in her head, and finally she collapsed.

The weeks that followed her attack were a slow, quiet time of bed-rest, doctors and relatives. All were at a loss to explain her apparent fit, but all accepted the (equally unsure) doctor's diagnosis; excitement. Though her new husband was due in Iceland that month, he stayed home. She wished that he had not; her slow grief could not admit visitors. She re-lived the past 2 years in that month, endlessly re-assessing her complicity in her previous lover's death. She had not believed his last words to her, had thought that promise had been born of desperation. His worm-soaked face haunted her vision, so different from the clear-eyed teenager she had first met in her father's house.

He was younger than her, even then, but had already seen more than she ever would. His served a belated apprenticeship as a whaler, from Teignmouth, under her father. He hadn't set foot in Britain for 10 years before he arrived, penniless and desperate, and had seen both Europe and America in that time. Their intimacy was, at first, born of both proximity and pity. He found himself, after her father had taken him in from the cold Devon roads, sharing a room with Ophelia's brother. The gravel house, after his years on the road, was a haven. After his ordeals, it took him a year of warm meals and ship maintenance to regain his former self. He refused to talk about his past, save in incessant and fabricated stories of the ports of America and the bars of Europe. It was, perhaps, because of this that Ophelia came to love him. At first, she never considered that theirs was anything but a familial bond, but in the long nights of her father's repeated absence they became lovers.

It was kept secret, of course; one does not admit to pre-marital sexual intercourse with one's adopted brother in the family home. Such secrets, though, are what make trysts into affairs, and affairs into scandals. They both knew that Teignmouth would be unforgiving. And so, of course, they talked of running to Europe, to the Americas, to India, but especially to the Orient. He claimed to have seen China, in the spring, and to have wondered for hours through cherry blossom woods that stretched to the horizon. As he continuously revisited this scene, on her father's bed, post-coitus, another grew beside him; Ophelia, grasping his hand. She grew with a flowing skin of silk, with tiny silver birds circling her streaming hair, and with translucent, ecstatic jade necklaces. Around them, blossom danced in the breeze and was carried up, past the circling birds, and into a rose coloured, infinite and adamantine shell. They talked of little else for a year, he promising her lumps of jade the size of oranges, and silks that could pass through a gold engagement ring.

It was not to last. One night, after 2 years of apprenticeship, her father breathed bubbles into his supper, and declared 'that it was time for the boy to catch a whale.' He was powerless against such an order. She barely left her bed the month he was away, serving her own apprenticeship under the wives already sunken by their husbands' absences. She could not admit the reason for her sudden case of consumption. The various wives put it down to the murderously cold night on which she saw her father off. Such a cold night, in fact, that when she returned to the house, 3 hours late, she was streaming tears.

In this, her first wait, things began to change. She avoided consciousness, could not bear the cold, empty winter light. She spent 14 hours a day asleep, and the rest forcing herself into waking dreams of China, and of their orchard. He was not there, though. He had disappeared from their shared Eden the moment he had sailed. She spent weeks searching, running through the sprung turf calling his name, and grew old in doing so. The trees tore her silk into rags, the circling birds screamed out her sin, and she clutched her lump of jade so hard her fingers ached, lest it should disappear. As she wandered from the centre, where she had last seen him, the ground became unstable. After another day it threatened to swallow her. It knew, of course, what she had done.

And back in Teignmouth, so did the wives. They would tell no-one, of course, but it was clear that this was no consumption, that she was enduring her first lover's first whaling absence. One frost-covered dawn, the grass far behind her, the sun rose on the bare rock of the edge of her world. She was naked, stinking, fallen. She still held the jade, though, had carried it all this way, and had still not found him. Staring at the void beyond her fantasy, she slowly opened her stiffened hand and let it drop. She awoke, and was told of the death of her father.

The ship had returned, but some had not. The forties had sucked another into its tooth-lined ice. She had been conscious for barely a day when her lover returned, exhausted and devastated by the loss of his surrogate father. He stood outside, and knocked, three times, slowly. She told him to leave. At first, her voice trembled, and he could not understand the force of her words. Her brother, sitting behind her in silence, did. The maw of the life she was casting him back into was fierce, but she was the master of this house now, and could do as she pleased. Soon she was screaming, and beating the door that stood between them with increasingly manic force. It stood firm, so she did not see him leave.

She heard, though, his last words, 'I'm going,' and she heard the stress on the article. Only after half an hour of silent weeping, and only after pulling herself upright to stare after his long departed shadow on the front path, did she consider *where* he was going. She stood at the window all that night, watching the sky darken, but did not see anything. She was already waiting for his promised return.

He came back, then, and she awoke from her recollection into a reality that mirrored it. Floating up from the depths of her recollection, spiralling all the way, she found him staggering back up the path. Her husband, her second love, bearded and dragging the rags of his clothes over the path to sea, had returned. She attempted to open the door. The months it had stayed shut meant that she could not move it. She had to wait for another 25 seconds, and for her husband's heavy shoulder, before she saw him. The explosive crack of the freed door on the wall echoed through the house, disturbing dust from the secret frames, and her husband staggered forward into the house, his heavy gait thumping on the floorboards. Ophelia sank forwards, and he held her. He used his foot to violently slam the door behind him, kicking it so hard that the gravel wall, reverberating, threw its brass clock to the floor.

∞

'It was bad, this time, Ophelia. The worst. I've seen some bad winters up there, but not like this one. It was grey, east to west, and there was nothing. We saw some whales, on the way in, but could barely see their bodies against the grey of the sea and the sky. It was too late in the year, anyway; they were already heading south. Nothing changed after Reykjavik. We spent weeks circling; sailing in long arcs up and down the shore, but nothing, just nothing.'

He was sat on a kitchen chair, pushed back from the table. He had been restless since he had arrived back home, but he had waited until he had washed, and they had eaten, before starting to talk. Ophelia had heard this tone before, many times, but could see he was nervous.

'After the 6th week with nothing but the unchanging horizon, we were ready to come back. Somehow He convinced us to take one last trip, down around cape Ólafsvík. We never do this, you understand. The wind that blasts the Western Shores is fierce, it freezes the ropes to the deck and takes the life from you, but He insisted that the fishing would be better.'

He stares into the corner, then quickly rakes his gaze up the wall. His voice is a flat monotone, this time, broken only by the occasional creak as his chair flexes against the holed floorboards. She sits, hands folded in her lap, eyes fixed on his restless head. He makes eye contact once a minute or so, the flame from the oil lamp burning from his pupils, but his vision soon reverts to its wandering course.

'After a week of the battering weather, He proved Himself right. We saw a whale, the first one in almost 2 months. She wasn't big, but she was close, and we knew this would be the last chance we had. I was weary, and so were the rest, so we started the chase slow. She managed to get away from us, and we found it difficult to keep her in sight.' He starts to motion with his hands, drawing the frozen water in long palm-down sweeps, then points, away into the shadows that now inhabit the corners of the room. Then he continues, 'Somewhere I remember seeing a ship, way out to the West, its outline almost as grey as the sea.'

'After 3 hours, she got away, and the men were broken. She had carried us leagues offshore, and the roof of clouds still had no end. As the crew stood staring at the deck, occasional flakes of ice flecking their coats in the building Westerly, we knew we had reached the end of this trip. The captain, as ever, gave the order... but not the one to turn back.'

His hand darts out, his gaze focused on the tobacco tin. The scrape of the metal as he pulls it back across the table seems impossibly loud in the silence. He flicks it open, and continues.

'He had seen the ship. We had been carried to within 10 miles of her by the chase, but even at this distance, as all of the crew gazed over to the horizon, we knew something was wrong with her. The sail, in tatters, was the only thing recognisable as a ship. The rest, below the mast, was a mound, sloping sharply to the sea. We could have taken her for an island, were it not for that mast and the fact that she was gently rocking in the current.'

'She was silent, thankfully. I do not know what we would have done had she showed some sign of life; she was dead, and that much was clear. No-one could use such a ship, we knew, but none of us could guess how long she had been out there. No soul wanted to even get close to her, but we knew she must have been carrying something. We had failed, so far, we thought, and this was our chance. Slowly, and with our eyes fixed upon the ship's silent form, we started to approach.'

His hands, trained over the bowl of his pipe, begin to shake. He is attempting to tamp down a ball of tobacco, but is forced to grip the stem with his other hand before the task is done.

'We saw the weed first. She was trailing it behind her for more than a mile, some sodden tail of tangled wrack. Where it connected to her form, we were able to see the reason for her shape. Never, Ophelia, have I seen a ship so infected with barnacles and weed. Even on the wrecks, the ones that have sat in the waves for 20 years or more, there is more bare hull than she had. This was not the worst, though, Ophelia; some demented shapes were growing from her, spires of living coral of a kind none of us had seen before, twisted in the wind so they seemed like serpents. The weight of her new occupants had saved her, I suspect; she must have been floating unmanned since some ancient date to have accrued it, but it was clear that, even in heavy seas, she would not move far.'

He leans back, and strikes a match. Slowly, the pipe comes to steamy life, and he works the cloud into a deep fog before removing the pipe from his mouth. He stares at it, catatonic, whilst he talks.

'Still no sound came from the crew. We were, to a man, staring fixedly at her. When we eventually came close, and the captain gave the order that I and 5 others should board her, we climbed into and launched the lifeboat in a trance. I, seemingly the only one able to tear my eyes from the seething hull, rowed us over to her. The captain, standing at the bow of the boat, took hold of an overhanging tail of weed and managed to start to clamber up her looming side. One man we left with the boat, and the rest of us followed. It was not easy; the rain was heavier now, and the weed slippery and fragile. There were limpets, though, of a larger variety than I have ever seen, and they made good holds.'

He is moving, now, his hands moving as though in imitation of his feats. The smoke curls around his slight actions in some stop-frame abstraction.

'20 metres from the surface of the sea there was a narrow shelf, barely wide enough to stand on. This marked where the ship's deck had been, although her planks were barely visible. The mass of ragged detritus was piled against the central mast, making a narrow, circular walkway across the deck. We paused there for some time, whispering back and forward, trying to decide our course of action. One argued that we should check for bodies. The majority, who had instantly realized the futility of such a search and were eager to leave as quickly as possible, suggested we check for cargo.'

He looks up, slightly bowed, and meets Ophelia's gaze. She is so taken aback by his apologetic look that her trance is broken, and she smiles weakly. She knows he is embarrassed by this, knows that he would have preferred a whale to what he would see as grave robbing.

'We went our separate ways, each fighting the overgrown mass from engulfing us as we disappeared into the dank interior. We soon lost sight of each other. I had made out towards the rear of the ship, hoping to find an entrance down into the hold. With each step, though, the way forward became more difficult. I tried, at first, to push the trailing weed from my path. This approach, however, soon became impossible as the few specks of light reaching my tunnel were left behind. I was left stumbling blindly into the darkness, with the matted roof forcing me ever lower. Soon, I was crawling, with one hand stretched blindly in front of me.'

'After minutes had passed in this way, my knee came sharply against a raised section of deck. Feeling for its outline in the darkness, I realized it was a hatch into the hold below. Wrenching it open against the weight of its clinging lock, I was able manoeuvre myself onto the ladder below. To my relief, there was light in her hold. It seemed that the weed had only recently penetrated this far into the ship's bowels, for it had crept barely 6 feet into the large space. From the lateral join it had levered apart to make its entrance, the weak sky could be seen.'

He comes to life, as though in a bar. The last sentence has been accompanied by the pipe, trailing smoke, sweeping slowly up and down. He waves his hands wide, and then returns his gaze to Ophelia with some frenetic look in his burning eyes.

'As soon as I had reached the floor, I began to search. This did not take long, as the hold was virtually empty; not a sign of a trunk or barrel could be seen. Perhaps she had found poor fortune, perhaps she had been looted before, who knows. It crossed my mind, there in the dark with only the incessant sea booming through me, that the weed had reclaimed its due.'

He seemed to have lost the direction of his story, and his eyes roll upwards in a moment of thought. A silent second passes before he shakes his head, returns smoke to his lungs, and returns the table to his perception.

'But whatever the reason, I found nothing of worth until I reached the darkest corner of the hold. There, knees drawn up to his chin, was a boy. Long dead, of course, but the spray had so dried his skin that I could almost make out his face. Sat leaning on the wall of the hull, and with the light cutting across his face, I almost thought I recognized him. I stared for several minutes. I've seen some deaths out there, you know that. But this hold was so cold, and I knew that the weeds would reach the boy's body before long. I whispered a prayer. It was only when I dropped my gaze, and let my eyes come to rest on his grasped hand, that I saw what he was holding.'

He stands up, and seeks out his canvas bag from its position by the door. He sinks into shadow as he does so, and his disembodied voice jumps from the dark corner;

'So I jumped forward, Ophelia. I immediately prised his hand open, checked the other, checked behind him…'

He emerges, bag in hand, his eyes wide as he sharply regains his seat. He begins to pull at the knot in the leather cord that holds the bag closed;

'And then I got out quick. I could hear the men on deck calling for me, and I scrambled up the ladder and through the hatch.'

Virtually tearing the bag open, he reaches inside. When he pulls his hand out, it is clutching some folded pieces of canvas. He throws the bag into the flickering shadows, and starts to unfold the fabric.

'The way back out was easier, of course. I had already cleared a passage, so I stumbled towards the calls, stuffing these…' He briefly lifts the half-unwrapped package, before returning it to his lap, '…into my pocket. I haven't seen them since then, Ophelia, no-one has. But look…'

The package lies unwrapped on his lap. From where Ophelia sits, she cannot see its contents. She leans forward, but before the horizon of the table dips far enough, his hands appear. They are both holding lumps of opalescent jade. They look small in his scarred hands, but both represents a small fortune. What they represented to Ophelia, in that moment, can only be guessed. He places them on the table, gently, but their weight echoes around the room.

'I think they're real, my darling. If they are, they will be no more whaling for your poor husband,' he says. Then, fixing his eyes on hers, continues, 'but there was also this.' He brings his hands up slowly, each of his fingers draped with a white ribbon of silver. As the taught necklace emerges, the light from a perfect sphere of translucent jade, encircled by birds of silver, leaps into the room. 'This is for you.'

Ophelia leans her head forward, watering eyes fixed on the sphere. She presents her blunt crown, her forehead brushes the table. He, flowing forward, nooses her trembling neck.

'I've Forgotten More Than I've Ever Known':
Confessions on the Verge of Suicide by a
Vampire Past His Prime

As spoken to Joey Madia

The Legend

There is a mansion that no one enters.

It sits on a hill, as many mansions do, in a secluded spot in the Hollywood Hills, inaccessible to the bus tours and gawking eyes that undergird the tourist trade around the West Coast's infamous movie industry.

Byproducts of byproducts, I guess you'd say.

If one is inclined to believe the widespread rumours and vague memories of an industry that's long since lost its grace, there resided—up until recently—within this decaying, decrepit mansion, a nearly forgotten, slowly dying writer from the Hollywood heyday named Erik von Forthright.

His 3 am costume parties were the stuff of legend… It has been said—in dark corners and society rags—that what happened behind the walls of the countless rooms of this monument to depravity would make a Satanist blush—like something out of the psychological horror films he wrote for the biggest Production Houses in the world…

Or, more likely, those parties were the *inspiration* for the films, and not the other way around.

Egg and chicken, chicken and egg. So it is with the ultra-artsy crowd.

Then, in 1969, as the scripts became darker and more Satanic, the parties suddenly stopped.

They began again on April 30, 2004, like Wonka coming forth from the chocolate-factory gates, and ended just as abruptly within the year.

It's been silent ever since.

A Few Words about Me

I drink. I write. The first far more than the second.

I am separated from my wife and so far behind on alimony and child support that I'm no longer allowed to see my kids.

Not that I ever saw them much when we were all together.

Did I mention that I drink?

Not so long ago—a mere decade, give or take a month—I was the hottest Hollywood horror writer around. No Richard Matheson or John Elder by any stretch, but able to hold my own among the current generation of fang-and-slasher scribes. Barely out of college, I met Gavin Rome—superstar horror writer and casual companion. We had enough in common (choice in booze—Bacardi—and a fascination with the screenplays of Eric von Forthright) that when his novels went big and he was shopping movie rights, I was part of the package deal.

Those were heady times.

Gavin had a streak of eight bestsellers in as many years— *Helldoll, Morning of Death, Mirror House,* and *Eyeteeth* were the biggest—and I had written adaptations of them all. The money was pouring in, the bartenders were pouring out, and life was a blur of premieres, interviews, fancy meetings, and expense accounts.

Then Gavin was murdered.

In that mansion on the hill.

The Invitation

I wish I could say otherwise, but the late morning the day I got 'The Invitation' found me sleeping one off (a particularly sloppy, violent one), face down near an overflowing ashtray, with vomit on a four-day-old shirt and my silent laptop refusing to record a single word.

Not that I had conjured even a single, lonely noun to feed it.

The Invitation itself, slipped under the door by an unseen hand, was a piece of expensive linen paper neatly folded in perfect thirds and printed upon in a careful hand with a thick, sanguineous ink.

If I hadn't been so happy to see that it wasn't (a) an eviction notice, (b) a letter from the Office of Child Support, or (c) another of a dozen possible payment-(long past)-due notices, I probably would have used it to scrape up some fermented takeout from the end table the next time I entertained.

Or, more likely, as I haven't had a (welcome) guest in many months, it would have been slowly pushed under the couch in the process of my entering and exiting through my rarely used front door.

But there it was, open in my hands.

So let me tell you what it said:

'I am a fan of your work, as I was of Gavin Rome's.

You're better at what you are than you think you are.

And I need someone to tell my tale.

You will be the one.

~No notebooks, no cameras, no tapes.~

I am a remorseless, aged vampire despising blood and longing to stop the loss.

The rising of the sun, the second coming foretold in my own theology, is pressing in upon me...

My ageless life, full and fabled,

Has been spent enduring draughts and floods and Neptune's empty Furies,

Forcing me to be an eater of sand in my dancing madness,

for I have lacked my Father's power to convey with mystic eyes

and honeyed venom voice the Gift we so savagely bestow.
I've lost my hold on Time.
~You no doubt know the place.~

Yours in urgency and haste—
Eric von Forthright'

Casing the Casa del Forthright

I would have liked to tell you that I hesitated for even a second
to take this iconic screenwriter up on his offer. That I hemmed
and hawed (whatever the hell a hem or a haw might be) and
considered just ignoring this impassioned plea and going back to
the bottle and the utterly empty screen of my laptop, but that
would be a lie.

And I am many, many things, but a liar I am not.

It's important that you know that.

So I threw on some clean clothes and headed out.

I knew exactly where I was going, if not exactly why.

Being a horror writer, you'd think I'd go for suspense here,
describing my drive into the hills, the gnarled trees along the
path to the wrought iron gate, the expressions on the faces of
the angels and demons cast for eternity upon them, what I
(thought I) saw as I gazed up through the arched, Gothic
windows, and the minute details of the house.

No.

I have more important things to tell you, and there isn't
much left in the way of time.

Instead, I direct the curious reader to the tales of Poe,
Jackson, Matheson, and King, for the house was very much like
those.

At least, from the outside.

The interior was like watching a stately whore age from the
inside out.

Meeting the ... (Man?)

Eric von Forthright was a spectre made flesh.

He stood before me, some six and half feet in height, in a
custom-made suit of purple velvet, lacy cuffs draping four inches
below his painfully thin, thick-veined wrists.

His fingers, a classical pianist's dream, sported rings that looked ancient and expensive—precious stones, angels, snakes, and skulls adorned them in various combinations. The nails were half an inch long and filed to subtle points.

His hair, a shoulder-length and perfectly set mane of angelic blond curls, distorted to a dark halo all around him, backlit as it was by a crystal chandelier.

A carefully contrived first impression.

'Come and sit with me in the music room,' he said quietly, pivoting his expensive Italian ankle boots and glide-walking down a long, art-filled hallway.

'Bosch... Pollock... Caravaggio... you've got good—if not eclectic—taste,' I said, wincing at the stupidity of the statement.

'Copies,' he answered. 'I have painted to pass the time. What little there was left. Sit.'

He motioned to a Louis XIV chair covered in a plush emerald fabric.

I readily complied, running my fingertips along the worn oak arms as I settled in.

'You enjoy fine things, eh?' he asked.

'You seem surprised.'

He middle-fingered middle E on the grand piano that dominated the room before straddling its bench. 'I am. You present as little more than a dull-witted drunk.'

'Guilty as charged,' I said, feeling a few buttons at the bottom of my shirt to make sure they matched up. 'But I can hope.'

'Hope, my friend, is all we really have.'

And Now He Tells His Tale

'I have a friend,' he began, assessing the height of the moon through the heavy damask drapes. 'A very *old* friend, but new to here—a namesake of sorts—who once said, 'I've forgotten more than I've ever known.' Perhaps that is the best way to start.

'My time, as I have said, is short. With the rise of the sun, the devil will die, which has been, from the very dawn of Man, forever and a day foretold.

'I pondered the worth of producing a sizable tome about my time upon this Earth—other vampires have done so, as you know, spawning a lucrative cottage industry of rock bands, clothing lines, and films—but I have said almost all that I must say through my scripts, through their visions of the Dark Arts and the Great Gift. It will be up to you to go through and decipher them. To peer through the frame, listen past the score, and divulge what you are able from the multilayered subtext of which I am so proud.

'Then you can share with the world all that I have been.

'My age. I was re-born as a vampire in the time of the Bubonic Plague. A bygone, better time, for all its brutality and ignorance. A time when Myth was still the coin of the realm and the growing currency of the Church. A necessary cleansing to clear a swath for the heretical genius of Copernicus, da Vinci, Galileo, and Bruno—for you see, it has always been about the Sun. *Always.*

'And I was its Antithesis. Its *balance.*

'People fail to see how important we vampires actually are.

'By whom I was made is unimportant, as is the place.

'In the 1700s, I came to America, on a tall-masted, rat-filled ship, because I knew that it would be here, in this New World, that the Sun would reach its zenith in the politico-military sky.

'Those were rich, compelling times, as the thirteen colonies laboured on the bed of their own specific brand of Liberty to bring forth a blood-coated, screaming infant. I toured the battlefields with General Washington, securing a position as an aide-de-camp to members of his staff because of my considerable insight into the European mind.

'At night, I would juice the dying man grapes of the last of their wine.

'The War of 1812, the American Civil War, Westward Expansion, the Industrial Revolution… These were fruitful times for an aging vampire learning his strengths and decreasing weaknesses by testing the boundaries of both with a pointed blend of intelligence and instinct.

'I truly loved America…How could I not? We were exactly the same. Blood was our strength. Our daily *need…*

'Then came motion pictures.

'I was in the audience in Pittsburgh, Pennsylvania in 1905, when The Nickelodeon opened.

'As did my eyes, and my mind, and my emaciated heart. For I saw, in those early flickering images—the beheading of Mary Queen of Scots, the life of the Christ—the possibility to relay all that I had learned in my centuries-old vampyric state to the semi-conscious masses crowding Plato's modern cave. To show them all that I had seen, make them feel what I had felt—to love despite death, to be lonely despite crowds, to be in darkness despite Light.

'For I had known much in the way of pain. You cannot know what it is to watch a young woman, firm of breast and light of step, grow old and wither and die while you remain unfalteringly young and unblemished.

'My early hopes were continually rewarded. Film was not just *story*, but *agenda* and *message*, constructed by the director through the multi-coded pages of the script. Griffith's propaganda. The social commentary of Chaplin and Keaton. The German expressionism of *Nosferatu*, *Metropolis*, and *The Cabinet of Dr. Caligari*. Cinema was the culmination of all of the arts. Even in the days of the Silents, there was music, as you know.

'And the screenwriter was her Goddess and God. Her snake's-mind and turtle's-back. Her great Creator.

'Of course, it couldn't last.

'Musicals in Technicolor—mindless eye and ear candy that they were—were the first signs of *pointless entertainment* in the temple of our great Muse, but their heyday (thankfully brief) was also the time of the romantic films of Westward Expansion by Leone and Ford and films championing the American cause of war starring Errol Flynn and John Wayne.

'By this time I had already made quite a fortune as both a writer and producer, and in 1941 had purchased this house.

'I am sure you know the legends of what took place here— all true, and many things more occurred that no sane man would or could believe. I was a little bit Velasco, a little bit Prince Prospero, and very much Myself. You see, although I was for many centuries able to have sex, over time—well... nothing was enough. Not youth, not blood, not all manner of extreme depravity—and so I, and dozens of others who shared the Great Gift—were forced to *watch*. To control and collect from the borders of the room the potency and release of the human spiders caught within our web.

'The sex and Satan connection was well and truly forged within these walls.

'Which brings me to the sixties and seventies. The time of Hammer and American International. The time of monster movies, bared breasts, dark ritual, and the Matheson–Corman reworkings of Poe. Human psychology torn wide open—its blood gushing out in a wave of symbols and Satans. This was, of course, *my* time. All those centuries of living and decades of learning the screenwriter's craft finally paying off.

'And it truly is, young man, a *craft*, lest you have forgotten.

'As almost all your 'colleagues' have.

'Because the industry is shit, and it's all the writers' fault. They have been bought and sold a thousand times over with all of history's stock enticements. The Whore of Babylon feeds finely on the souls that walk these hills. You know what they've done to you. The mirror tells your tale. Without story, there is *nothing*. Just empty images—dick jokes and pointless violence. So-called *special effects*... Cheap gags and—dare I say—carefully contrived confrontations packaged as *reality*.

'Please... Reality, my friend, is the fact that I could move across this room and tear your throat out within the span of an eyeblink.

'My namesake—the very old one I mentioned earlier—agrees with me that cinema has become a garden overgrown, with the weeds of spoon-fed plots and palatable endings choking out the flowers that were the spirit of its birth. Controversy is manufactured in Board rooms instead of flowing from the artist's pen, as it once did. And it is 'Controversy' only in the loosest sense of the word—designed to last only as long as the film's run and to be only as edgy and potent as the great modern Moloch—the Bottom-Line—requires.

'When the Prophet turns Promoter, the sheep will soon be sheared.

'And I know you know this. And I know that's why you drink. Why you suppress your gift and write the shit you do, when you do.

'That is why I asked you, and why you came.

On the Verge of the Rising Sun

Eric was staring at the moon as it began to dip below the horizon.

We had sat in silence for the better part of the night, and the dawn was coming fast.

'What do you want me to do?' I asked, needing to hear the sound of my own voice.

'There is a writer—a sort of freelance editor—who my namesake is using to tell *his* tale. You will tell him mine. He will know what to do with it.' He handed me a crumpled business card. 'Don't delay, lest you forget what I have said.'

'So what's next for you?'

'The fabled sun, the second coming foretold in my own theology, will soon rise, and when it does, I will burn myself to memory in the back garden. I cannot face another night.'

I stood up and, without thinking, tugged at my collar, baring my neck.

'Do you want to feed on me first?'

How lame.

'Lame does not even begin to describe it, my friend,' Eric answered, opening the drapes in lieu of my veins. 'Your friend Gavin would be disappointed in you.'

'Did you kill him?'

'Me? No. I preferred to dine on the very rich and the very poor. Your collaborative companion was neither. Gavin was chosen to be the mechanism to usher in a new Age designed to undo what had been done with the corruption of the Arts, the corruption of all that was pure and potential about what it is we do. But a power far more potent than mine could not bring this new Age to be. At least, not yet. So Gavin Rome sits frozen in Limbo and I haven't the resolve to wait a moment longer.'

The first rays of sunlight began to dance upon the window.

He involuntarily moved several steps back.

'You must go,' he said, inching once more toward the window. 'Tell my tale to the man on the card. Leave through the front door. I will go out the back. Do not turn around. And do not ponder coming back. There will be nothing left of me to find. Nothing of *this* to find.' He brushed his long fingers the length of his torso. 'Go. You are no longer welcome in my house.'

I had gotten half way down the hallway, conjuring mind-films of the sodium fate of Lot's wife in my effort to not look back, when I heard the French doors that opened onto the back garden open and close, and I had the damnedest thought.

I couldn't wait to get home and write.

For I, too, had tales to tell.

And the second coming of my own fabled sun was suddenly not so far away.

Chapter XV

Stephen Loveless

Remnants of the lost chapter of the Origin of the Species by Charles Darwin as memorised by the cracksman Greville Voe (Acquired by this publisher for a substantial financial amount from his Great-Great Grandson Jack Voe)

Authenticity: Let it be known that all these writings are as I remember reading them by shielded lantern on twelfth night (6ᵗʰ January 1860) while hiding in the Down House garden tool shed. Believing the heavy, leather satchel they were in to contain money or easily disposed of valuables. The satchel and papers I returned to the safe in the study of Mr Darwin only for him to enter the room after returning the papers. I hid across the study behind an armchair.

And I swear that before midnight of that date I had committed all these memories of words to paper in by room at the crossroads tavern: the Mad Dog Inn not more than two miles from Downe. Also I must admit to the theft of two silver snuff boxes belonging to Mr Darwin.

I declare that I saw Charles Darwin from my hiding place stand before his fire and tear each sheet of the papers from the satchel before throwing them in the fire.

On the life of my children to be and their children to come I state with a hand on any Holy book you wish, that at the moment of the final paper burning the room went dark, the fire died without even an ember glowing or final spark flying. Then the fire roared alive again and a finger of blue flame left the hearth and touch the chest of Darwin before vanishing. So hot must it have been I smelt the scorching of his coat material. Darwin fell back with a scream that brought the household to him and forced me to make a stealthy exit.

By what strange phenomena did hot coals go cold and at equal speed rage back into life I do not know. Nor what force threw that blue flame to strike at the learned man's heart.

Chapter XV
Notes on the frontpiece

As the monkey writes then so it is written and I here declare my existence first. To many I am called the Fuegia Monkey, others Winchester Cathedral , I have named myself Hai Kur Mamashu Shis for I am the recorder of the event as well as a witness. I watched and I dipped my nib in ink and wrote and fought the tremble in my hand as the horror of that night unfolded.

To describe myself would be cruel to my eyes to read, yet it must be done. I am small and dark with heavy features the pale long faces of these islands look upon and say, 'He looks like a monkey'. My heart is big and braver than my size.

What follows is a rendering in the voice of my old master's friend and shipmate taken from my original transcription of events.

Torn page from a Diary page of 1859 found attached by pin to the draft.

My dear wife Emma and the children thankfully left for an enforced visit to London. It took lies and much persuasion to achieve which I feel has cut another scar into my conscience. Yet tonight has to be endured though to what end.

Staff were easier to dismiss for a night.

Dog Gladly has arrived as promised. Though paid well for this night's work I would not have condemned the Jack Tar if he had declined. Though older now then when we were shipmates on the Beagle, the sailor looks as fighting fit as then, a good man in an emergency.

He has brought Winchester with him, as small and as strange looking as ever. Another of Fitzroy's failed social experiments from Tierra del Fuego. Yet he is an excellent secretary. Like Dog he is discreet and obedient.

I wish I had not agreed to Wilkie Collins to make these appointments. You never know if you are talking to him or his opium induced double he calls Ghost Wilkie.

But he believes their stories and that such beings exist, more that they wish to approach me and make a claim to include their existence within my book...

I have loaded by gun and tucked it in my belt under my coat...

Draft for Proposed Chapter XV.

Laid down here first as a memory of events.

The guests had arrived before I finished my stroll in the garden, an agitated walk that kept me out until sunset. I entered the study by the French windows to find a concerned looking Dog Gladly stood on guard by the window and Winchester on the other side of the room behind my desk staring wide eyed and a little scared at the company.

Curled up in my wheeled armchair an imp of a girl so pale I assumed her ill, with gaunt features white, thin hair and almost colourless eyes. I took her for an albino at once. She wore little more than a slip of a dress looking more a nightgown. Sat on my blue couch a huge, broad shouldered man with as poorly a complexion as the girl. The man had a large head and a deeply scarred face, his clothes were rough and ill fitting as if borrowed from someone smaller. His big hands lay so still in his lap you'd call them lifeless. He seemed oblivious to everyone. At his feet lay two ragamuffins in manacles and chains. I could smell the dirt as well as see it on their sunken features and clothes.

Lastly a tall man, easily as tall as my father, six foot - two if not a little more, but he appeared more lithe than my father's robustness. He stood with his back to the fire. His eyes were red, his skin pasty and he wore an insincere smile on narrow lips.

These were Collin's second world creatures, the shadow races of Man that both preyed on humanity and depended on mankind at the same time. People Wilkie thought worthy of my study. For these I had hired Gladly and wore a gun under my coat. This motley looking bunch I had sent my wife and children away. They were no more another species then a common mammal.

The tall man spoke first.

'Perhaps we could speak a lone Mister Darwin?'

I glanced back to Dog Gladly and nodded. He left via the garden closing the French doors behind him, he would walk around and enter the house at the front.

'My name is Wormstone.'

The man took me by surprise appearing so quickly beside me.

'Allow me.'

He pulled the heavy curtains closed over the doors and windows which did not plunge us into darkness, the fire roared bright and three oil lamps glowed steadily.

Wormstone pointed to Winchester at the desk.

'He is my secretary recording our meeting—which Mister Wormstone I am terminating now.'

My words took him by surprise.

'Mister Darwin I am a vampire—Miss Chaney there in the chair is a werewolf.'

She looked at me, hugged herself and stared away.

Wormstone then pointed to the couch.

'And Mister Ussher is a species made of the parts of long dead Georgian's, a product of the last century's science.'

I looked down at the children. 'Are these then the Fairy King and Queen?'

'Do not mock us Darwin' he replied with anger. 'They are gallows bait we bought off the prison cart pulling. With these we will prove how we survive as a species.'

I turned on him quickly.

'You are charlatans at best a circus act for want of employment or worse opium den driftwood that have taken in Collin's.'

With those words I moved towards the desk where Winchester sat scribbling. The weight of the revolver felt comforting should these vagabonds cause trouble. Once at the desk I turned and faced them.

'I do not know where you learned of my research. Regardless I am asking you to leave.'

'We are different species.'

'You are intruders in my house—please go.'

'If we were what we say what species would you call us? Perhaps Homo Nefandus? For you certainly believe us abominations.'

'If the mythology of what you claim yourselves to be is true then you would a metamorphic creature such as a butterfly.'

'Mister Darwin do I look like a butterfly? Perhaps a Purple Emperor—Apatura Iris.'

In a rage Mister Wormstone held his hand up to his mouth and snarled to reveal long fangs resembling those of a cobra, with them he bit into his own flesh and sucked blood from himself. This he did for a few moments before tearing his hand away revealing a deep wound and torn skin. Blood circled his lips.

'Do butterflies feed that way?'

Following a clearing of the throat.

'Yes some butterflies have a habit of hematophagy.'

Mr Wormstone laughed like a mad man, calmed and turned his red eyes on me and in a whispering voice.

'I very much have a hematophagy habit as a species trying to survive.'

'Mr Wormstone I feel your visit has been a waste of time for both of us.'

'I feel that I will leave here when I have proved my existence—Miss Chaney's existence and that of Mister Ussher's.'

He clicked his fingers and the room fell into quick darkness as if every oil lamp had been blown out at the same instant. The fire in the hearth still burned brightly and by its glow we saw Wormstone move with great speed towards the French windows. He stood facing the drawn drapes and then seized them in both hands. As if a signal, Ussher rose from the blue couch and positioned himself with his back against the door in doing so preventing Gladly from entering. My hand slipped under my coat for my revolver as I saw the pale featured Miss Cheney become strangely animated and start to uncurl her thin form from my wheeled armchair. I only sensed Winchester stiffen behind me and the chained children on the floor began to whimper with fright.

Wormstone tore down the curtains to the ground, pulling the pole and rings with them. Moonlight filled the room, eerily filled the study with a luminous brightness I had never seen in all my travels.

Miss Chaney leapt up and spread out her arms and the shift of a nightdress she had been wearing fell to the ground. Moonlight touched her paleness and turned her naked skin a brilliant white.

Wormstone had turned around and started walking slowly up behind the young girl. I found myself momentarily transfixed by Miss Chaney as she began to sway her body as she rippled her hands and arms in the air as if performing some Eastern hindu dance. It became a dance, a metamorphic dance on my study carpet in the moonlight by a young woman turning into a wolf.

The wonder of theatrical effects and make-up quite stunned me.

From that moment of change all action and movement in the room accelerated and to me all necessary for further theatrical illusion I believed I observed.

The howling of the girl and her leaping wolf like about the room, Gladly banging on the door and shouting to come in. Mr Ussher's grunts of approval at the commotion. As for the terrified prisoners, they crawled nearer to the fire dragging their chains with them.

Miss Chaney picked the boy,. In my mind I assumed her to be hiding in the dark behind furniture and that Wormstone had somehow let a dog resembling a wolf in the room to run around and fool me into thinking Miss Chaney had undergone a metamorphosis into a werewolf. But this dog reared up on its back legs and stood upright as a human being only to stoop down and grab the boy with her clawed hands.

The shock of seeing such a sight slowed my reactions and I did not draw my revolver fast enough to save the poor wretch for the once frail face of Miss Chaney now had a snout and long jaws with a mouth full of fangs.

She ripped out his throat in one bite before I drew my gun and aimed the Beaumont-Adams revolver. I had been a good shot since a boy, even in the queer mixture of moon and fire light I marked my target and shot Miss Chaney dead with a bullet to the centre of her forehead.

She collapsed without a sound dragging the boy's dead body with her. The thud of them hitting the ground seemed to be the magic note to bring the oil lamps back to life.

Wormstone ran to the fireside and knelt not by a dead dog or werewolf but the corpse of a naked young woman on my hearth rug.

'Murderer,' he snarled at me. 'Done with a silver bullet?'

I did not answer and kept my pistol pointed at him.

'It would have to be a silver bullet to kill my little Arabella Chaney. So you must have believed in us before we came.'

He started to stand up keeping those devil red eyes on me all the time. Once standing he clicked his fingers without looking in the direction of the cowering girl who rose as if in a trance.

Without describing more melodramatic gore, he ripped her throat out with his fangs and made a show of drinking her blood. Nevertheless the clever trickery held me rooted by its suddenness. Once filled Wormstone tossed the girl's body to the carpet as if he she had been a dummy stuffed with hay. Which may have been the truth.

At that moment Dog Gladly kicked the French windows open and stood with the moonlight behind him brandishing a shotgun. As if he had eyes in the back of his head.

'Tell your man he would need more than two twelve bore cartridges to kill me.'

I raised my revolver so Dog could see that I had a gun. From his assumption we had everyone under arms and in our control.

Mr Ussher stirred from leaning against the door as if ready to lumber forward and cross the room to tackle Dog. A nod from Wormstone froze him to the spot.

I aimed my gun at the so-called vampire which made him laugh and show me his bloodstained teeth to match his blood spattered mouth.

'Silver bullets will not kill me Mister Darwin you need a symbol of faith to keep me away. The Star of David, the name of the Prophet, the cross of Christ and many other signs of soul-felt belief.'

He slowly began to walk towards me, the urge in me to shoot strong, the fear of such an action failing having a more powerful restraint upon me.

'Of course you have a theory—perhaps you should hold that up and hurl it at me. Maybe an ape's skull will do. That looks like a monkey behind you.

Poor Winchester forgotten by me. I glanced over my shoulder and saw him sat there writing everything down, quill in one hand and my paperknife in the other, held as a weapon. Brave Winchester gave me courage and I turned to face Wormstone again. Instead of coming nearer he had backed away to pick up the wan skinned body of Miss Chaney. Mr Ussher with childlike ease had picked up the corpses of the criminal children, the boy over his shoulder and the girl under the other arm.

'Mister Darwin, a theory will not rid the world of species like us and for you to ignore our existence is to prove your theory wrong. Remember you see Man as descending—I see my kind as ascending. Expect much more of us in the future.'

Dog Gladly stepped aside without lowering his shotgun and let this mammal oddities of evolution leave.

In daylight the next day we found no bloodstains anywhere in the room, on the carpet and rugs or on the furnishings. But for the damage to the curtains nothing of proof that the night ever happened but for the notes of Winchester and our witnessing of the events.

FOOTNOTE:
I have researched and written much of what I have called *Species Fantastic*. Chapter fifteen of my work only to destroy that and

Winchester's verbatim record. These few scraps are all that is left.

Briefly, for whatever reason I had wanted to believe in the creatures Wormstone and the others claimed to me. Even if such dark and dangerous beings. What is a Tiger but dangerous to others.

Now I am convinced all had been a hoax, some mad prank dreamt up by Collins, though Wilke denies it.

Whatever they were skilled conjurors and illusionists and maybe one day I will know their secrets. But they are not the secrets of evolution.

[Editor's Note: It is well documented that after the publication of the *Origin of Species* that Darwin described the experience as such 'like confessing a murder'.

Did he mean his theory had murdered mankind's faith in a world and universe created in a single act proceeding nightfall on Sunday 23rd October 4004 BC? Losing Mankind's faith in a Divine presence? The loss of his own religious beliefs? Now we have to consider he meant his murder of Miss Chaney with a silver bullet.]

Leaving Netherford

Steven Sowden

The morbidly efficient lady in the grey trouser suit with the golden crucifix pin brooch reached down beneath the counter and I heard the sandpaper ruffle of her starched clothes in the shattering silence. The moment was protracted and sluggish; my face and nerves numb as she finally set the urn down in front of me with an understated quietness. A real and tangible thing, it landed with a tiny, muffled thud and for a while, I couldn't look at anything else. I had seen it fleetingly in the death catalogues, but the pictures could never do it justice. It was a new-fangled biodegradable one made from natural clay. Slim, skeleton-white and patterned with red roses, it stood innocuously still and glanced right back into my face and began to rummage around behind my eyes, pleading and plundering. However menial-looking, any old thing will take on this weird, somnambular significance if it happens to contain the remains of your dearest dead. *These are sacred days.* The lady paused with her old hands crossed neatly at her belly and allowed me my minute of fast, secret heartbeats and choked reticence. I didn't cry, although I thought briefly that I might like to. Never before had I so desperately wanted to shed long, horrible tears in front of a stranger. Temporarily resolute, I glanced up and asked her how much money I owed her and she told me with a hint of latent apology on her cracked, church voice. I passed over my credit card and signed for the transaction on the counter, the soft underbelly of my right hand momentarily brushing the cool hips of the clay container with her inside. I handed over the payment, took a mint from the bowl and claimed the crematorium pen as my own. I expected the mint to taste odd. The old lady told me that she was sorry for my loss and I thanked her with profuse nods and left quietly with the urn.

In the hire car, I stood the urn up on the passenger seat, placed my carryall in front of it and fastened the seat belt around both. After a battle with the passive immobilizer and a phone call to the hire company, I locked and unlocked the car with the key ring button and jiggled the steering lock off whilst fiddling the ignition. The engine fired and, with the radio firmly off, we chugged slowly and breathlessly out onto the main road through vast gardens of stone-gray memoria and stark little trees. I started thinking about how I would play things at the other end. Wondered whether I should say anything out loud, or whether I should scatter the remains in a cross shape as is traditional and customary. Would she approve of that? She hated church. She asserted on many more than one occasion, often during a Friday night gin monologue, that all religions were nothing more than a collection of 'elaborate fairytales'.

We wound down through half-empty shop streets and twisted past shady corners where cameras buzzed overhead. She was a genuinely heartbroken woman in the twilight of her days. I often told her that she read all the wrong newspapers and that her anger would eventually make her ill. She retracted from family closeness six years prior and often sat aghast in her armchair; watching horrors local and international play out daily on the television news. This was her permanence. Her last incarnation, bar one. She polished tank shells for the army in World War II; spent most of her late teens underground, working hard to support the effort. It was her generation, she would often say, who saved civilisation from itself. She didn't even come to my wedding.

I decided that I was going to lay some lilies upon the ashes of my dead mother once I had poured them out onto the ground in roughly one hour's time. I parked up near the Interflora shop at the foot of the high street hill and decided to put her away in the carryall, in the foot well of the car's passenger seat. I placed the urn underneath my laptop, pushing aside a clutch of CDs and my mobile phone which was showing four missed calls from Spain . I turned the phone off and threw a hooded jacket over the cargo. I picked shades off of the dashboard and wore them out into the shady overcast. I fumbled deep for currency and scuffed past Netherford faces, head low, no show.

Amongst the flora, opposite another matronly bystander to my grief, I filled out a flower card on the shop counter. Meanwhile, five feet away, an artsy young thing with a headscarf prepared and pruned the purple and yellow bouquet with her delicate, painterly fingers. *Dearest Mum, we shall miss you always. Breathe easy and rest now. Forever your loving son and adoring family, Kevin, Melissa, Harvey and Bump* x

∞

I arrived at the old orchard in the crushing grey cold of a February sundown, not more than an hour after leaving Netherford. I parked by the old wooden turnstile. Through painful minutes I sat there, surrounded by droll duskiness; quietly preparing for what I was shortly to see and what I was terrified of seeing. A powder. The final culmination of eighty-four life years; burned and crushed down into a gritty pile that was surely as washed-out and colourless as the doomed old island itself. The intermittent drive down from the airport past dead meadows and through grayscale motorway towns had been fraught with a creeping heaviness. A slow confirmation that my home was now elsewhere; that this place had drifted so irredeemably far from my heart. Nothing but a dark parade of people doing jobs; caging away all tenderness amidst a vortex of biting, surprising cold. Miles upon miles of infinite repetition, broken only by the odd, fleeting road dream. Thoughts of her dressmaking hands brushing my brow in soft strokes on feverish nights all those long years ago. It all came and went. Was I ready to see Iris Leary again? After eighteen months of stilted, crackling conversations, was I ready to cast her dust onto the frozen floor of the world?

It was only after I had turned on the interior light that I realised the urn was gone from the carryall. They left the laptop and my phone and all of the CDs. Three days prior I had agreed to pay eight-hundred quid for this urn. Through guilt of not seeing her, I sought to offset the bad thoughts with a big credit card payment; and that was the very least a distant son could do with the tools at his disposal. *Surely.* They must have taken it directly from the unlocked car outside of the flower shop, from right under my nose in a moment that must have lasted all of one minute. There was nothing I could do. *You couldn't even get her out of fucking Netherford for the day. Jesus.*

Back at the Rosemount guest house, I found myself dry-crying for about ten minutes with the lights off. I turned on the television and found a news channel and fell asleep in the dull, blue strobe. I woke up hungry in the dead hours and ate some tortilla chips. I got up, got dressed and quietly left the premises, posting keys and cash through the letterbox. With less than two hours' sleep to my night, I drove back up to the airport and changed my ticket. I had a beer, boarded a plane and flew home to my family, to whom I lied for the next seventeen years about my part in Iris Leary's last physical journey.

Good Grief

Nigel Hague

Living so close to the town hall clock did have its advantages. You didn't need a watch to know what hour it was, and the timing of meals and daily domestic chores resolved themselves into hourly patterns based on the number of times the clock bell had rung. In the middle of each day, by the time the bell had rung 12 times, Cyril could have the kettle on and already be buttering the bread for his lunchtime sandwich. It became a little more difficult at the half hour because there was only one ring to announce it, but Cyril enjoyed the game of trying to remember what hour they were in. Things were different during the night though. If you stirred from your sleep and were unable to resume your slumber, what was described as a ring during the day became a clang during the night, and those clangs painfully informed you of the length of time you had lain awake. Cyril had just had such a night. He often did these days. If it had happened when Ivy was with him she would have comforted him and he would have been unlikely to hear the next half hour clang before resuming his necessary eight hours sleep. But Ivy had been gone six months now—that was the reason Cyril couldn't sleep anyway. His melancholy at missing her was deepened by the timely clangs, and the untimely knowledge that he would inevitably be tired the following day. Cyril repeated the painful, but heartfelt, words in his head over and over. 'Ivy—I do miss you love'. By the time five clangs had heralded the dawn, Cyril had decided to get up and start the day early—again.

∞

Six hours later and the town hall clock, on cue, announced to anyone in earshot that it was 11.00 a.m. Cyril, dressed in the same blue suit and tie he wore on the day of Ivy's funeral, was scattering slug pellets in the borders of his immaculate garden at No. 7 Chestnut Avenue. Ivy had loved the garden and Cyril had loved keeping it beautiful for her. Over the last six months his need to keep it immaculate, just the way she liked, had been the only reason to get him through the days. He sometimes felt she was watching him tending the garden still, and approving of the work he did on it in her memory. As he sprinkled the slug pellets around and in-between his beloved plants his thoughts were rudely drawn to the present.

'Ceasar! I've told you before. It's eat inside—crap outside! Back in the garden you go 'cos I 'aint seen you have a pee yet and you know how slippy this lino gets.'

Before he even heard the self-satisfied burp that his Chestnut Avenue neighbour, Bert, always greeted the morning with, Cyril knew that Bert had forgotten that they were due at the snooker knockout tournament in just thirty minutes. Bert had invited Cyril to the tournament believing that he needed a distraction other than his garden now that Ivy had passed away. As Cyril wondered how many minutes it was before the single ring from the town hall clock announced it was 11.30 a.m. and they were late, he also pondered how come Bert's dog Ceasar managed to do so many dumps on his lawn if he was also doing it in Bert's kitchen. That dog must be being fed too much he thought. He also wondered how Bert could stomach the can of beer he was drinking at this time of the morning.

'Morning Bert—you haven't forgotten we are due at the Legion at 11.30 have you?'

'Ey up Cyril—didn't see you there. What's that you're doing.'

As Cyril mentally wished there was a dog version of slug pellets he managed to avoid speaking his mind and said 'Just trying to keep on top of the slugs and snails Bert.'

'Right Cyril, I see. Well you finish that off and I'll just finish me can and me ciggie and I'll be right with you. After all breakfast's the most important meal of the day they say.'

Cyril maintained his composure but didn't want to be late. 'Its gone eleven you know Bert. We'll need to get a move on if we are going to make the start.'

Bert drained his can of its contents and threw it onto what Cyril thought was too large a pile of other empty cans in the corner of Bert's weed-filled garden, took a drag on his ciggie and blew the smoke into the air. 'Won't take me two minutes to change Cyril—I'll go and do it now.'

As Bert turned to enter his bungalow Cyril nodded towards Bert's drooping washing line 'Won't you need to take your underpants off the washing line to change into?' It came out more like a suggestion than a question.

'Nah. I'll turn the ones I'm wearing inside out Cyril. They'll last another day. Save those for tomorrow eh.'

'Yes Bert.' said Cyril queasily.

∞

Bert had been as good as his word. Turning his underpants inside out and re-attaching his braces to his trousers instead of his pyjama bottoms had only taken two minutes. Not bothering to change his vest and topping the outfit with his aged jacket took about another minute. Indeed Bert and Cyril were on their way to the Legion before the town hall clock struck the half-hour. A result.

∞

As ball after coloured ball click-clacked into the pockets of the snooker table and one competitor after another was eliminated from the competition, the town hall clock announced the advancing hours from 11.30 in the morning to 10.00 pm in the evening. Bert and Cyril were well out of earshot. Neither of them had noted the passage of time or the amount of beer they had consumed whilst they took part in the snooker tournament. But it was clear they had enjoyed themselves. With the competition finished and the prizes presented they agreed it was time to wend their way home. The two of them swayed and staggered in the general direction of Chestnut Avenue and more than once they had needed to take a rest. The double effect of too much alcohol and a late night on their ageing bodies was having a detrimental effect on their ability to travel very far in a straight line, and their internal compasses chose the wrong direction more than once. In all it took them twenty three minutes to meander the 200 yards to Chestnut Avenue from the Legion club.

∞

As they finally arrived in front of their adjoining bungalows a mixture of exhaustion, confusion and inebriation forced them to take a seat on Cyril's front garden wall before attempting the fifteen feet of footpath that would take them to their front doors. Cyril was the first to speak—sort of.

'Eeeh, Bertie, Bertie, Bertie—I'm absolutely shattered but thanks so much for inviting me today. I haven't had that much fun in ages. And I honestly never expected to win Bertie. I was sure that you would win it like you do every year.'

'No problem Cyril—it was a real pleasure. So you've enjoyed yourself then Cyril?'

'Oh yes Bert—I haven't had so much fun since...'

As Cyril's voice trailed off Bert supplied the end of the sentence for him. '...since before your Ivy died—I know Cyril. And you needed it you know. Listen Cyril—whilst we are on the subject I never did thank you for choosing Boothroyds to handle Ivy's funeral arrangements.'

'Well I knew you wouldn't want me to use Hetherscales because of your Mary.'

'No Cyril I didn't. I mean, what woman of sixty runs off to have an affair with a funeral director. It wasn't like I wasn't seeing to her needs. Anyway I figure it's her loss. I can still crack one off once a week you know.'

'That's nice—and I wouldn't have chosen Hetherscales for all the tea in China. But you sure you don't mind losing the tournament Bertie?'

'I've said already Cyril. I don't mind losing the tournament at all, especially to you, and I'm really glad it's taken your mind off other things and you've had a good time. But you ever call me Bertie again and I'll chop off your hollyhocks! Understood Cyril?'

'Understood Bert. Anyway, I think I'd better be getting off to bed Bert. I've got the garden competition tomorrow remember.'

'The garden competition?'

'I told you earlier. The Chestnut Avenue Corporation Housing Bungalow in Bloom competition.'

'Oh yes—I think you did Cyril. Hard to forget really.'

'Right, night then Bert.'

'Cyril.'

'Yes Bert.'

'Erm, it's nothing Cyril—it'll keep till tomorrow—night Cyril.'

As Cyril and Bert made their way up their respective paths, squashing and crushing the nights slug and snail fest as they went, Bert wished he'd taken the few minutes to tell Cyril what he had wanted to. Never mind he thought as he heard Cyril's front door shut behind him. It was late, Cyril had a big day tomorrow and it would keep anyway. As Bert drew the last drag on his final ciggie of the day he surveyed the starry night sky and decided that he had disliked losing the snooker competition a lot more than he had been prepared to tell Cyril. But he decided that Cyril winning it was much better than that fellow Hetherscales. Bloody funeral directors he thought to himself. 'Right Ceasar. You've been inside all day. You must need to go. Over the fence and do your business—sharpish!'

∞

The following morning found Cyril asleep in the armchair in his front room. The town hall clocks' noting of the nighttime and early morning hours passing had not disturbed his sleep. In fact, so deeply did he sleep that a small earthquake would have been unlikely to rouse him. What actually did the trick was the sun's early morning, low in the sky, shafts of penetrating light that drove in through his kitchen window and, uninterrupted, traveled through to his living room and settled on Cyril's face. Whether it was the warmth or the brightness that had penetrated his sleep, neither were a comfort as Cyril opened his eyes—he had a hangover and it was a bad one! This wasn't improved by the loud, officious sounding knocking on his front door. Cyril rubbed his closed eyelids and then tried to shield his eyes from the persistent rays as he stood up from the chair gingerly, and then used both the sideboard and knick-knack cabinet as handrails and support as he swayed to the door to find out who was knocking so earnestly at this time in the morning.

As Cyril opened the door noting, despite the depth and severity of his hangover, that he had forgotten to lock it behind him the night before, the hand that had knocked was already raised, its knuckles bared in readiness to deliver another head-aching battery of his senses. Cyril stared at the visitor in silence waiting for them to announce who they were and why they were knocking so loudly on his door. The young woman before him now seemed to have lost some of the chutzpah with which she had just banged on Cyril's front door.

Hesitating, whilst she scanned the clipboard held in the crook of her right arm, she said 'Oh good morning, Mr. Smith? Mr. Cyril Smith?'

Cyril answered as fully and politely as he could muster. 'Yes.'

'Are you okay Mr. Smith—you don't look so clever.'

'No—I don't think I've ever looked clever—but I've felt better than this, that's for sure.'

'Is it the flu Mr. Smith—you look ever so pale.'

'Are you a doctor?'

'No, no, Mr. Smith—my name's Arabella Donna Mr. Smith.'

Cyril winced visibly—'Sorry?'

'Arabella Donna Mr. Smith, bit of a mouthful I know. I'm from the council Mr. Smith. The Municipal Gardens, Memorials and Grass Verges Department Mr. Smith. I'm judging the garden competition this year.'

'Oh I see.' Cyril said rubbing his forehead—he didn't really know why he did that because it didn't ease the pain ensconced behind it. 'Yes. Sorry. I'd forgotten that that was today.' How could he have forgotten the competition was today he thought. Why had he had so much to drink? Cyril had started to mentally comfort himself with the thought that his garden was ready for the sturdiest examination at any time when his aching, and yet-to-focus, eyes were drawn to his little patch over Ms. Donna's right shoulder and he spotted a solidifying pile of Caesar's excrement gracing the centre of his lawn. With a strength he did not really possess, Cyril passed Arabella Donna, took his spade and lifted the ever so neat little pile and deposited it in his dustbin.

'Damn dogs!' he said to Arabella. 'They can ruin all your hard work!'

'Yes true Mr. Smith. I've been checking the notes that last years judge made and it looks like you've done just the same as last year. Very regular and full of perfume and colour. Extremely pleasing on the eye. The perfect English country garden. As she enunciated the words of her last sentence Arabella Donna noted exaggerated ticks on her clipboard. 'Though I do see you have a bit of a slug and snail problem.'

'Yes sorry about that. I do try to keep on top of them.' But Cyril sensed he had already lost her attention. Arabella was looking towards Bert's bungalow.

'Do you know who lives there Mr. Smith—I don't appear to have any details of the entry for last year's competition.'

'Oh I do apologise for the state of that. Bert hasn't entered the garden competition before and he's not taking part this year.'

'Oh on the contrary Mr. Smith. This year, in the spirit of community inclusiveness—we have a new Director of Strategy for Inclusiveness at the council now—we've opened the competition up to all corporation properties and were more than happy to see new and innovative designs. Mr. Jones, did you say, clearly has an eye for the contemporary. Yes I'm quite taken by the unstructured fussiness he has engendered in it. The minimalist colour and his credible attempt to create an urban pastiche, whilst retaining an authentic post-Cold War ambience. Yes! Quite the radical is our Mr. Jones—I like it.'

∞

As if on cue, Bert's front door opened and both he and Caesar exited the bungalow. 'Hey, what's going on here then? Not one of them council snoopers are you? I've already told them the dogs been neutered, and if that woman from number 23 makes any more outrageous claims that my Caesar has done a spot of lie-down dancing with her Fluffy then I am going to make a formal complaint myself. I can assure you that Fluffy is not Caesar's type. In fact he's much more fussy in his choice of partners than I am on account of the fact he cant get drunk beforehand can he?'

'No Mr. Jones, my name's Arabella Donna from the Municipal Gardens, Memorials and Grass Verges Department. I'm judging the garden…'

'Well you can't be too careful these days can you. The Municipal Gardens, Memorials and Grass Verges Department. That must be a very long ID badge!'

∞

The next time Cyril saw Bert come out of his front door he was shocked at his appearance. He was more than shocked at the state of his garden. Bert was neatly dressed, washed and combed, and if it hadn't been for the braces Cyril might not have recognized him. He certainly didn't recognize Bert's garden, which was also neatly dressed, washed and combed. Cyril had died only two months before, just three days after the gardening competition. He knew people would think it was the shock of losing the Chestnut Avenue Corporation Housing Bungalow in Bloom competition after keeping the winner's trophy for three years on the run. He knew some people would even believe it was the shock of him losing the competition, and the trophy, to Bert with his 'urban pastiche'—but it was neither of those things. Cyril's heart had ceased to cope with the strain of dealing with his own body's physical demands, and Cyril had passed away quietly in his sleep. As he watched the well-scrubbed Bert survey the reformed, but award winning, garden, Cyril wondered, from his heavenly vantage point, how and why had Bert achieved this transformation in such a short amount of time.

Two months previously, when Cyril had died and arrived in heaven, there had been the necessary identification and entry administration procedures to go through. He had been impatient and desperate to see his Ivy again. When they had finally been allowed to see each other he had experienced a joyous re-union with his much-missed wife that made him want to sing a hymn at the top of his voice. Problem was Cyril didn't know any hymns so he gave her a rendition of My Way. Ivy's eyes had crinkled and lovingly smiled at Cyril and she had quickly decided not to deflate his ego by telling him that Frank Sinatra gave regular in-tune renditions of the same song in the 'Heavenly Italian' Cafeteria where he was now working as a waiter. After they had hugged and loved and kissed and said how much they had truly missed each other, Ivy had explained to Cyril one special rule that he needed to know about. Cyril had tried to kiss her moving lips whilst she told him that if you have been good in your life and get to heaven you are granted one last visit to a person of your choice. The purpose behind the visit, Ivy had explained, '… is to try to give that person some comfort about your passing.' Cyril wondered if Ivy had paid a visit to him. 'You can see and hear them, but you can't talk to them even though you will want to, and probably try' she explained 'And they can't see or hear you.'

The idea, Ivy had explained to Cyril, was not to haunt as a ghost but to comfort as a spirit. As Cyril had gazed into the beautiful face of Ivy while she related this great secret rule of heaven he was struggling to take all the information in. But he knew he would enjoy listening to her explain it to him a second time and that she would have the patience to do so.

'And don't forget Cyril—they can't see you and you can't speak to them. All you are allowed to do is move one item that might remind them of you.'

Cyril had struggled to understand why moving one item would tell the person that you were dead, but well, and living happily in heaven. Ivy explained that most people were not susceptible to this suggestive message in these modern times.

'In the 'olden days'….' she said, '…people had fewer possessions and were more likely to notice that a favourite item of the departed had moved and consequently 'feel' the power of the intended message. Sadly, in modern times most people put the unexpected move down to forgetfulness or stress, or even Alzheimers.' Cyril could understand the logic behind that statement but had forgotten to ask Ivy when the 'olden days' actually were. It didn't matter.

They had both laughed together till tears rolled down their faces as Ivy had explained that when she visited him after her own death she had decided to move his best blue suit to the front of the wardrobe hoping he might wear it more. When they were both alive she used to tell him that she had always thought he looked so handsome in his blue suit—'quite fanciable' she would chortle, on the few occasions he wore it when they were still together. As old as Cyril was he clearly hadn't been old enough to be one of the people from the 'olden times' who were susceptible to the heavenly message and he had to admit to her that he had missed the miracle of the moving suit. Though he did tell her that he always believed she was somewhere watching him when he toiled hard to keep their beautiful garden just the way Ivy had liked it. And he didn't forget to tell her that he was wearing the blue suit when he won the Legion snooker competition.

When Cyril told her that he'd beaten Bert in the final she remarked that she didn't think the Bert she remembered would make a good loser. 'And anyway, when did you get good at snooker?' she asked him. 'Have you had a mis-spent old age? And I hope you weren't drinking.'

'Oh no Ivy!' he protested. But she knew he had been and forgave him. This was heaven after all.

∞

With the knowledge Ivy had given him, Cyril knew straight away that it was Bert he wanted to visit and set about making the necessary plans to do so, whilst trying to think which object he would move. One of Caesar's piles on his lawn had come to mind but he'd dismissed it as tasteless almost immediately. And now, here he was. Looking down from on high and watching Bert in his garden. If the truth be told, Cyril was more incredulous at the state of Bert and his garden than the fact that he was looking down at Bert two months after his own demise, on a visit from heaven where he was now a resident.

'Eeh Cyril lad—I do miss you.'

The comment startled Cyril. Bert was staring right up, directly at Cyril, and speaking to him. Wasn't he? That wasn't supposed to happen according to the instructions Ivy had given him. Bert surely couldn't see him.

'I hope you're up there in heaven somewhere Cyril. If you can hear me up there matey, I just want you to know you could be a real pain in the backside sometimes—but I really do miss you.' Cyril's cheeks flushed at the comment and he hoped no-one else in heaven was listening, but at least he now knew that Bert couldn't see him.

'And since you've been gone I've realized that you were right and I needed a focus in my life. And I think I have one now Cyril. It wasn't winning the garden competition—and I really hope it wasn't losing it that took you away my friend. I prefer to think that you had decided that you had been away from your Ivy for long enough. There's no way you should have lost but I think that Arabella woman got herself stuck in a carriage on the 'inclusiveness' train, whatever that is, and decided I was a good cause rather than a lost one. I hope the Director of Strategy for Inclusiveness at the council is happy and proud of her. No, what stated it all off was one morning when I got up and one of your hollyhocks was growing in my garden. If you were here now Cyril you'd call me bloody daft but I sensed it was a sign. I don't mean this mumbo jumbo 'signs from the grave' rubbish. No. A sign that if one of your lovely plants could send its roots out under the paths and come up in my jungle of greenery, then there was a chance other things could be improved as well. So I started work on me garden Cyril.' Bert chuckled as he said 'I'm glad you're not here to hear this…' Cyril tensed in anticipation of the revelation. '….but I must admit I borrowed quite a few plants from your garden to give me a head start. But they don't grow beautiful on their own do they Cyril, and I figured what did you need plants for now you had been re-united with your Ivy. I've worked hard to get it this nice and the discipline has been good for me. Anyroad, if the truth be told, that's not really what I wanted to tell you Cyril. It's something I never got round to telling you when you were alive. I tried once but I never quite managed it. I didn't tell you when you were here lad because I was a little bit embarrassed about it. I could never have told you to your face but I need to say it out loud. I didn't think it was possible for one man to love another - but I loved you Cyril. Noooo, not in that sort of way. Not the sort of love where you actually say to someone 'I love you'. Not the sort of love you and Ivy had for each other, or the love I had for my Mary, or the love she probably had for that rat from Hetherscales Funeral Parlour. No, I mean a friend love. The sort of love where if someone's not there you miss them. You hope they are okay—and safe. And you wonder what they are doing. And you want them to come back soon and share good times and bad times with them—that sort of love. As a dear, dear friend. I do miss you Cyril now you're not here anymore.'

Cyril suddenly realized why it was so important to come all the way back down to earth to try to comfort someone who is sad about your passing. He wanted to help Bert, to say something, tell him it was alright, and that he was happy up in heaven. But he couldn't could he. All he was allowed to do was move one bloody object.

. 'I know you can't hear me Bert but I loved you too. You were a dear—'

'Eeh I might just have to get back to you Cyril.' Cyril thought for a moment that Bert was talking directly at him again, but realised Bert's attention was elsewhere. Bert wondered if it was a hallucination as the vision of a woman holding a Co-op carrier bag, a kettle, and a small yellow table lamp came walking towards him. He realised it wasn't a hallucination when the woman stopped at No. 7, and struggled to open the gate.

'Hello love—can I help you? You're not looking for Cyril are you?' Bert hoped she wasn't as he didn't want to have to explain that Cyril had died and spoil the moment.

'No. I don't know anyone called Cyril. This is No. 7 isn't it? I'm supposed to be moving in here. I live in a flat on Oak Drive and the council have decided to move me here. I thought I'd come and open the door for the removal men and make a brew.'

'You're moving in here—next door to me—well, let me help you with that gate. The hinges have gone rusty and it can be a bit stiff. I'm Bert by the way.'

'Hello Bert, nice to meet you. I'm Alice. I'm a widow.'

'A widow? Oh I am sorry to hear that. Well don't you worry

because this is a very friendly neighbourhood and I'm sure you'll make some good friends round here.'

'Oh, I do hope so Bert. But just look at the state of this garden. It's overrun with weeds and full of slugs and snails. I wish it looked like yours.'

'Yes. My pride and joy. But it doesn't happen all by itself you know—takes a lot of hard work. I'm not the sort to brag normally Alice but I've actually won the local corporation garden competition. Remind me to show you my trophy sometime. And don't worry about this for now. I'm sure if we work together and do it between us we can soon have it looking just as nice as mine! You've lost your husband and I've lost my wife. Well, maybe not so much lost her as misplaced her. So you and me have a lot in common besides gardening. I tell you what, Alice. Why don't you go and have a look around inside, maybe put that kettle on, and make us both a nice cup of tea… and I could get started on clearing some of these weeds for you.'

'Would you? That would be so kind Bert, and such a help. I don't have the energy I used to and you look… such a big strong boy!'

'It's not a problem Alice. As you say I'm a big strong boy and if you can't help a neighbour in need—who can you help? Now—off you go and put the kettle on, and I'll just go get me tools.'

'Oh look Bert—there's a canister of slug pellets here on the step. Have you left them here.'

'No but I've been looking for them everywhere. Don't know how they got into Cyril's garden but we'll make good use of them shall we.

'Eeh Cyril, things could be looking up round here. I do miss you lad—but hey, apart from the slugs and snails, life goes on. And I've not just got me own garden to look after now. Alice is going to need my help in more ways than she can imagine so I'll have to be going.'

'And so will I Bert. I can leave you now, happy that you will be well looked after. Me and Ivy have still got a lot of catching up to do. Hopefully it won't be too soon, but I look forward to seeing you again one day. Goodbye and god bless my dear, dear friend.'

'Right then—where are them slug pellets?' said Bert.

Øystein Ulsberg Brager is a freelance theatre director and joint artistic director of the international theatre collective Imploding Fictions. He also works as a dramaturge and a writer. Directing credits include Sense, Nose (Southwark Playhouse), Hamletmachine (international tour to London, Amsterdam, Rome, Cairo, and Strasbourg), Norway.Today (Junction, Southwark Playhouse), and The Hitch (Oslo). The Hitch, written by Brager in collaboration with Marie Ulsberg, received an award in the Norwegian Theatre Council's Playwriting Competition 2004. Other awards: Premio Internazionale Claudio Gora (Hamletmachine) and Young Angels Theatremakers Award (Norway.Today).

Brager trained as a theatre director at Rose Bruford College. He is an experienced workshop leader and teaches improvisation, writing for theatre, drama, digital filmmaking and creative writing as well as other subjects. He is an associate artist of Company of Angels, directs radio plays for Bunbury Banter Theatre Company and works regularly as a mentor for the Norwegian arts organisation Trafo.no.

Mary Byrne. Born Ireland. Worked London, Germany, Morocco, US. Currently living France, divides time teaching, translating and writing. Work published & anthologised Europe & Nth America: BBC Radio 4, BBC World Service, *Orbis, Stand, European Geologist, Dalhousie Review, Long Story Short, Irish Press, Sunday Tribune, Irish Times, Cyphers, Crannog, West 47, Cúirt Annual 2005, Phoenix Irish Short Stories 2003, The Faber Book of Best New Irish Short Stories 2007-8, Queens Noir* (Akashic Books, New York 2008). Broadcast several series of short pieces on Vienna and Morocco on Irish national radio RTE Lyric FM's 'Quiet Quarter'. Travel pieces *Sunday Tribune, Sunday Business Post* (Ireland). Hennessy Literary Award 1986 (shortlisted Transcontinental/WICE, Prix Albertine Sarrazin, Hennessy Literary Award 1989 & 1994), *Bourse Lawrence Durrell de la Ville d'Antibes*. Has completed a book-length study of Durrell and the baroque spirit. Was invited by Durrell to collaborate on his last book, *Caesar's Vast Ghost* (Fabers 1990).

The remarkable career of **Christopher Close** has been somewhat overshadowed by the manner of his death. We urge all readers to cast that infamous horror from their mind, and remember instead the triumph of his Lear at *The National,* the nostalgia and innovation of *Leckie and The Puck,* the abiding warmth of *Close Friends.* We thank James Scott for initially bringing this narrative to light.

Carrie Dare currently lives in Bristol with her long suffering boyfriend, Tim. As a general rule she believes the less people know about her the better. However, in flagrant disregard of said rule she has 2 websites, www.carriedare.co.uk & www.carriedare.com

S. J. Davies was born in 1971 and started writing short stories over four years ago. She has spent most of her adult life in the Westcountry, working as a research student, archivist, photographer, prison worker and more recently as a university administrator in Bristol. Her stories reflect an interest in the folklore and folk narratives of the South West of England.

S. J. Davies is a member of the writers group at the Folk House in Bristol. She lives, without a cat of any description, in a quiet suburb. 'The Lake' is her second published story.

David Gaffney is from Manchester. He is the author of *Sawn Off Tales* (Salt 2006), *Aromabingo* (Salt 2007), *Never Never* (Tindal Street 2008), *Buildings Crying Out,* a story using lost cat posters (Lancaster litfest 2009), *23 Stops To Hull stories about junctions on the M62* (Humbermouth festival 2009) *Rivers Take Them* a set of short operas with composer Ailis Ni Riain (BBC Radio Three 2008.) and *Destroy PowerPoint,* stories in PowerPoint format (Edinburgh Festival Fringe 2009)

Monica Germanà was born in Sicily and studied Modern Languages in Viterbo (Italy). She moved to Scotland in 1997, and collected two more degrees, while collaborating as a photographer for a number of Glasgow-based theatre companies, including 'Vanishing Point' and 'Flexible Deadlock'. A selection of her photographic work was selected for an award and published in *The List* magazine (Glasgow) and her first exhibition, WONDERWANDER was held at The Arches in June 2003. After spending seven magical years in Glasgow, she decided that the Scottish winters were too dark for her Mediterranean soul and, after a spell in the Midlands, is now lecturer in Creative Writing at the University of Westminster, in London. She has published articles in academic journals and literary magazines including *The Drouth* (2003) and *The Bottle Imp* (2009). Current projects include 'Ghost Trains', a stage-play set in a ghostly underground system parallel to the Tube, and 'Off-Peak', a novella set in contemporary London.

Glittermouse is mostly a visual artist but also enjoys writing and often works with text. Producing a wide range of different outcomes from crafts and fine arts to illustration and digital imaging, Mouse has enjoyed success in exhibitions and competitions both in the UK and abroad. Born, raised and educated in London, Mouse has recently relocated to Manchester and the effect on creative output has been a bit like what happens to a plant when it gets a nice new pot and some fresh compost. Mouse currently lives on the 13th floor with two cats, a man and a balcony full of carrots. You could visit www.glittermouse.co.uk if you wanted to know more.

Sean Gregson is the proud owner of a completed Panini Football sticker book from the eighties. He has previously written some short stories which other people have printed or rejected off hand. His first play, *Donal Fleet: A Confessional* will debut at the 2009 24:7 Theatre Festival in Manchester, which is also the location of Sean's flat. You can spam him or complain about his misuse of tenses by sending a thing here: shaygregson@gmail.com or here: twitter.com/seangregson. Take care of yourselves.

Bronwen Griffiths. My mother used to make up stories for me. My favourite was sledging in the snowy woods with the wolves after us. We always made it to safety of course. As soon as I could write, I began making up my own stories. Most featured princesses with long golden hair. These days I say I don't write about princesses but sometimes they slip into my writing in disguise.

Two years ago I started teaching creative writing but I've also worked with troubled teenagers, slapped up posters for a local theatre and run around the countryside organising events for young people. When I'm not writing or working, I like to walk along the beach and when I can, I go off trekking to deserts and mountains where I can gaze at the stars and pretend I'll never have to go home again.

Peter Griffiths was born in Cardiff on October 9th 1981. Through a Dickensian series of deaths and misunderstandings he was sent to live with his grandparents in the country in 1985. Following a financial windfall related to the above he was sent to St John's College in 1989, where over the course of ten years he slid from the top to the bottom of his class. He then read

English Literature at Exeter University where he scraped a 2:1 and discovered that science fiction writing can be the highest form of all literature. This was partly due to a Philip K Dick obsession he has only just managed to get under control. He currently lives in Bristol and is writing a novel that he knows deep down he will never finish.

Nigel Hague was born and raised in Oldham. After 30 years working in the IT industry, a long illness advantageously provided him with the time to spend on his favourite hobby— reading. He decided that he had several stories of his own that he wanted to tell and began to write in earnest. Nigel enjoys all aspects of story-telling but particularly enjoys the challenge of turning his stories into plays. He still lives in Oldham with his family and friends.

Graeme Harper, writing as Brooke Biaz, is Professor of Creative Writing at Bangor University and Honorary Professor of Creative Writing at the University of Bedfordshire. His awards include the National Book Council Award for New Fiction (Australia), among others. His latest works of fiction, as Brooke Biaz, are *Camera Phone* (Parlor, 2009), *Moon Dance* (Parlor, 2008) and *Small Maps of the World* (Parlor, 2006); and his latest critical works, as Graeme Harper, are *The Creative Writing Guidebook* (Continuum, 2008) and the forthcoming *International Creative Writers on Writing* (Palgrave, 2010) and *On Creative Writing* (MLM, 2010). He is Editor of *New Writing: the International Journal for the Practice and Theory of Creative Writing* (Routledge), a Fellow of the Royal Society for the Arts, and Chair of Higher Education at the National Association of Writers in Education (NAWE).

Stephen Loveless was the first winner of the Daphne Du Maurier Literary prize and more recently the Radio Netherlands Worldwide Audio Book Award 2008. His first film broadcasted by Central TV in 1998. Other work published includes articles and cartoon scripts. One of his short stories appeared in The InkerMen's *Green and Unpleasant Land*. Stephen has had an array of jobs including been an archaeological technician, security guard and woodsman. Currently he is Course Director of the

University of Leicester H.E. Certificate in Creative Writing. Stephen lives in Northamptonshire.

Joey Madia hears voices. All the time. This story, and many others, long and short, are the result. You can read the prequel, 'Gavin Rome's in Ice,' at www.newmystics.com/joey/docs/lit/ JoeyMadia-GavinRomesInIce.pdf

Pauline Masurel never learnt to play the piano. She has lost plenty of things in her life and given away many more. She is enthusiastic about knitting, toilets, puns and rope. Her short fiction has been published by The London Magazine, Tindal Street Press and Leaf Books. Her stories have also been broadcast on Radio 4 and appeared in various spaces online, such as The Barcelona Review, Radgepacket and New Fairy Tales. She lives in the South West of England and performs with the Bristol-based storytelling collective Heads & Tales. More about her writing can be found at www.unfurling.net.

Kayleigh Moore is a doctoral Creative Writing student at the University of Gloucestershire specialising in transgressive and experimental writing. Her first book, 'Dolls', will be released this year with a short story collection 'Exit' to follow, both by Bluechrome.publishing. Her ultimate aim is to teach creative and critical writing at university level.

Matt Morrison is a writer of plays and short stories. He has also written for several radio sketch shows and in 2007 published 'Big Questions', an introduction to philosophy for teenagers (ICON books). He is currently a senior lecturer in Creative Writing at The University of Westminster.

Katharine Orton doesn't know if she can call herself a Londoner any more given that she now lives in Bristol. She seems to be living backwards: becoming more insubordinate and immature the older she gets. She would definitely recommend it. Going to gigs, admiring (and getting) tattoos and watching scary films all feature regularly on her 'to do' lists. She writes a lot of lists. Hanging out with people who use their brains in strange and original ways is how she maintains her faith in humanity.

She thinks a lot. Writing is her day job as well as her night job—it afflicts her on the train and sometimes even creeps into her dreams. She is really very friendly, and in the age of the internet, incredibly easy to find. Get in touch on en00kdo@hotmail.com

Antony Pickthall is a playwright and sometime writer of short fiction. His plays include: *Soft*, *Bath Party*, *Catch the Pigeon*, *Teach Yourself Bollocks* and *The Stunning Flight of Archibald Bone*. His stories in the previous InkerMen anthologies were: 'Document 16A: Within the Rubric of an Electric Postman' and 'The Seaside Snow Globe is On Fire'. He lives and works in Liverpool.

James Scott was born in 1972. He is still not dead.

Claire Smith was born in the market town of Basingstoke in August 1977. She grew up in the village of Old Basing. After leaving school she spent time travelling in Australia and India. She gained an honours degree in English from the University of Gloucestershire in 2003; and now works as a Research Assistant. She lives in Cheltenham with her husband and cat. Her poetry and photography is also published at newmystics.com. Her web site can be found at theclairesmith.co.uk.

Steven Sowden was born in '79 and resides with his partner and three children in sunny Paignton, South Devon. He is the chief songwriter and producer with Stoke Gabriel-based band The Weaver Twins.

Fiona Thackeray has won prizes in the Macallan/Scotland on Sunday Awards, the Neil Gunn Competition and Woman's Own magazine. Her work has been broadcast on BBC Radio 4 and published in the Polygon 'Shorts' anthologies, Ironstone magazine and 'The Guardian International'. She grew up near Edinburgh, studied psychology at Glasgow, worked with sea turtles in Greece, built a sensory garden in Brazil then set up a national Scottish charity based in Perthshire that supports therapeutic gardening projects. In 2007 she was a guest of the Bydgoszcz International Book Festival. Her stories have been translated into Polish and Brazilian Portuguese. Mostly, her writing is about the wealth gap in Brazil and 2009 finds her living in Curitiba, Southern Brazil, working on her first novel about slavery and sugar cultivation.

Tamsin Walker's interest in language led her to study French and Spanish and latterly to a career in English and German. Her background is in documentary and journalism and she is a regular contributor to DW-World in Berlin. Two years ago she turned to fiction and has since completed a number of film and TV scripts, several short stories and her first novel 'Stranger Than Me', which was selected as a 'quarter-finalist' in the 2009 Amazon Breakthrough Novel Award. A student of the National Academy of Writing, some of Tamsin's stories appear in the NAW Book of Numbers Anthology. She lives in Berlin where she is currently working on her second book.

D. P. Watt is a writer living in the bowels of England. He balances his time between lecturing in drama and devising new 'creative recipes', 'illegal' and 'heretical' methods to resurrect a world of awful literary wonder.

Matthew Webber is an author and painter, who lives and works in London. His work attempts to explore the fallibility of contemporary conceptual theory by exposing accepted thought structures to the destructive unconscious. He has been a contributor to various short-lived magazines, is a founding member of the journal *Sink*, and is publishing a collection of short stories, *Osmotic Potential*, in the spring of 2010. He loves and despises Jorge Luis Borges, and wishes he was George Orwell. He regularly reads his own poetry, has often read this to empty pubs, and regularly visits the real world.

The King in Yellow - A Spectral Tragedy
Raymond Lefebvre
October 2005 — 978-0-9551829-0-7

The Just Maybe... Stories
James Scott
July 2006 — 978-0-9551829-1-4

Pieces for Puppets and Other Cadavers
D. P. Watt
November 2006 — 978-0-9551829-2-1

Bookworms I
Some Strange Experiences in Cheltenham
D. P. Woveweft
November 2006 — 978-0-9551829-3-8

Darker Later
James Scott
August 2007 — 978-0-9551829-9-0

Green and Unpleasant Land
The InkerMen
November 2007 — 978-0-9556259-0-9

Lands End
The InkerMen
August 2008 — 978-0-9556259-3-0

InkerMen Press
http://inkermenpress.tripod.com
http://www.myspace.com/inkermenpress

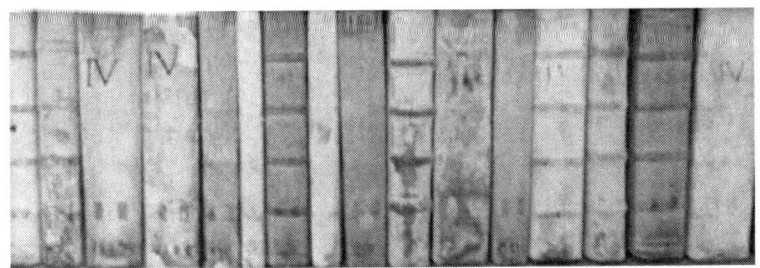

Forthcoming

Maciej Korbowa and Bellatrix
Stanisław Ignacy Witkiewicz
Translated and Introduced by Daniel Gerould
September 2009 – 978-0-9562749-1-5

Works of Illness
Narrative, Picturing and the Social Response to Serious Disease
Alan Radley
October 2009 – 978-0-9562749-0-8

Lightning Source UK Ltd.
Milton Keynes UK
19 January 2010

148809UK00002B/66/P